Steel

Matkas

D1714782

TERRY ROBERTSON

TERRY ROBERTSON

ISBN: 9798849900834

Dedicated to

all Grandmothers

and Great Grandmothers

who shaped this country

during the early

1900's

CONTENTS

ACKNOWLEDGMENTS

This book would not have been possible
without the Steel Matkas in my life
whose direct and indirect influence
shaped me into the person
I am today through DNA
and through the truths
of life that I learned
from them.

CHAPTER ONE

DECEMBER 1906

Maryanna

She regretted her impulsive decision the second she stepped out the door onto the teak deck of the *SS Merion*. The bone-chilling wind whipping across the North Atlantic Ocean pierced through the woven fibers of the lightweight outing jacket as though it were summer gauze. It whipped the waves on the churning waters below sending them crashing into the steel hull creating a spray of water that splashed across the deck. Her intense craving for fresh air had overcome her inhibitions which were quickly reinstated as her petticoat and skirt whipped around her legs. Tendrils of ebony hair escaped from her updo and slapped against her face. Why hadn't she followed the lead of the upper-class ladies in the fine cabins? They never ventured out on deck alone; they always had an escort. They also wore hats and gloves, neither of which she was wearing.

Another thunderous wave hit the starboard side of the ship and she lurched sideways as she struggled to keep her skirts modestly down around her ankles. Frantically clutching them with one hand and her hair with the other, she searched for the next entrance into the safety and calm of the ship's corridor. A wave of saltwater sprayed over her. Behind her she heard leaden footsteps ascending a ladder which went down a hatch to the Zwischendeck. As she turned to see if it was a sailor who could help her, a calloused hand grabbed her left wrist, pulling her arm toward her back. Broken fingernails dug into her skin drawing blood that trickled down her hand and fingers. She gagged at the vile odors on the beefy palm that covered her mouth and nose before she could scream. The slender fingers of her right hand, fighting to release the hold over her face, were like daisy petals attacking an oak tree. A tsunami of fear washed over her constricting her throat, setting her heart to palpitating erratically. A quick thrust of her assailant's knee into hers and she lost her balance. Her legs buckled beneath her as she was dragged back toward the terrifying hatch. Her mind froze as it refused to accept what she knew would happen.

"Bože pomóž me! *God help me!*" she moaned as she struggled fruitlessly to maintain her balance. Suddenly, the hand covering her face jerked violently backward. The fingers dug into her cheek and she tasted blood as her assailant struggled to retain his grip. The second time the hand jerked, the fingers relaxed and slid off her face. Like a rag doll, she was tossed this way and that as her attacker was pummeled, mercilessly. As the viselike grip on her wrist loosened, she wrenched free, stumbling and gasping for air. Oxygen filled her lungs and brain; she steadied herself and looked up. Her burly assailant was pinned firmly to the bulkhead by a tall, slim gentleman who did not seem to be an even match. Turning her head, she saw a passerby scurrying down the deck to summon the ship's officers.

She understood not a word of what the officers said to the gentleman as they approached. As he replied, the familiar words of home caressed her ears. Although she did not understand the officers' language, she certainly comprehended their actions. They handcuffed the assailant and put leg irons on, then turned him over to two sailors who dragged him away with all the care he had used trying to drag her down into the hold.

The officers turned their attention to her. They did not touch her; they gestured for her to follow them. The senior officer strode ahead while the younger one waited for her to follow his commander. He moved into position behind her. The young man moved to her side as they walked the deck.

"Dziękuje. *Thank you,*" she said, tremulously.

His face beamed at the familiar Polish words.

"Your words of gratitude are not necessary. I am honored to be of service to a lady in distress."

No one had ever called her a lady before. She lifted her head and smiled up at him, noting the gravity of his face.

At the medical bay, the senior officer strode into an inner office to confer with the doctor. The young officer held the door open and gestured for her to enter. She inclined her head in a silent thank you. Her wobbly legs were grateful as she sank down on the chair that was nearest to the door. The young man followed her inside. He flustered her as he sat down on the chair next to hers, placing his hat and gloves neatly on his lap.

"Jeszcze raz dziękuje. U mnie w porzadku. *Thank you, again. I am fine,*" she said, desperately wanting to smooth her hair and dress, but not daring to get blood on her second-best dress.

"I will not leave you until I am sure that you are not injured. I will escort you to your cabin and to your traveling companions," he explained in a tone that was gentle, but left no room for debate.

She hesitated, then admitted, "I am traveling alone."

"All the more reason for me to see you safely to your cabin. A lady should not have to venture out without an escort."

Lady. For the second time, he addressed her as he would a woman of the upper class. No one in her tiny village of Osiek Dolnoslakie had ever given her that honor.

Mathilda

She thrust the last few hairpins into the honey blond bun to affix it securely to the back of her head. She slid the top three buttons of her white shirtwaist into the buttonholes that secured the stiffened collar around her neck. She picked up her service badge from the dresser: *Mathilda Lenz, Dolmetscher, SS Merion.* She pinned it on the left side of the shirtwaist and smoothed the black wool skirt with the palms of her hands. She was ready, except for the most important item. She pulled a clean handkerchief from the bureau drawer that was assigned to her and doused it liberally with the Eau de Cologne that sat on the wooden shelf below the mirror. She tucked it into the side pocket of her skirt.

Living on farms and sleeping in barns as a young girl had not prepared her for the first time she had been on the Zwischendeck to interpret for a doctor. Her stomach had never flinched through all the tumult that the North Atlantic Ocean could conjure. But the noxious stench in steerage was so foul and fetid that she thought she would retch. When she spoke of her experience with the other three interpreters who shared her cabin, she had been given a tried-and-true solution. The handkerchief, saturated with the pungent citrusy scent that cut through other smells, was her saving grace. If she felt overwhelmed by the odors of unwashed bodies, festering wounds or vomit, she discretely held the handkerchief to her nose and sniffed as though she were a first-class lady.

She left the cabin and walked the short distance through the narrow corridor to the sick bay. Passing through the anteroom, she saw a young woman holding her left wrist with a trembling right hand. Dried blood stained her fingers and her cheek. Disheveled ebony hair was piled high on her head in an attempt to emulate the first-class ladies. The dark brown eyes below it flickered with distress. Her silver-gray woolen dress had once been fashionable; the charcoal gray outing jacket that she wore over it was far too light a coat for the Atlantic in December. She wore no hat and did not appear to have gloves.

Seated next to her was a young man close in age to the woman. He was tall with thick, wavy dark brown hair. His suit, too, was dated but well maintained. He wore a black canvas duster coat that would rebuff the cold of the promenade deck. Leather gloves peeked out from under the fedora on his lap. He did not touch the woman, but was totally focused on her.

"Guten morgen, Herr Kessler," she greeted the doctor.

"Guten morgen, Fraulein Lenz," he said, without looking up from the patient's chart on which he was writing. "The day has hardly begun and already we are busy. There are two women in Zwischendeck who are in labor. This morning, the woman in the anteroom had just stepped out onto the promenade deck for a bit of fresh air when she was accosted. Fortunately, the gentleman who is with her came to her rescue. It appears that the only language they speak is Polish. Bring the woman in and I will see how well she survived the attack."

"Dzień dobry. *Good morning*," she said, entering the anteroom.

"Jak się nazywasz? *What is your name?*" she asked the woman.

"Maryanna Kompanski," the woman replied, tremulously.

"Dziękuje."

"Jak się nazywasz?" she asked the young man.

"Michał Vinefsky."

She escorted Maryanna into Herr Kessler's office and brought a basin of warm water, soap and washcloths to him. He washed the dried blood from Maryanna's cheek and fingers and applied an ointment to the scratches. She winced when he touched her left wrist. Gingerly, he examined it. It was sprained, not broken. He wrapped it in gauze and bandaged it.

She translated the doctor's instructions. The wrist would heal within two weeks as long as Maryanna refrained from over using it; she should return to the medical bay in one week to have it checked and rewrapped. The jar of ointment would aid the healing of the scratches and prevent infection. Through her, Maryanna thanked the doctor profusely as she left his office.

As she moved from cabinet to shelf helping Herr Kessler gather the supplies necessary for the births of the babies, she saw Michał escorting Maryanna out of the anteroom. He was as close to her as possible without actually touching her.

Maryanna

Still feeling slightly tremulous, she was relieved that Michał insisted on accompanying her to her cabin.

"It is not safe for a beautiful young lady to be walking the decks alone," he said as they traversed the dimly lit corridors.

She smiled at the word 'lady' to which he had added 'beautiful'. She had never thought of herself that way.

"If you will consent, I would like to be your escort to and from the dining room for all meals. Also, if you are so inclined, I would like to walk with you on deck each day that the weather is clement, so that you may enjoy the fresh air in safety."

"You are most kind. I would be grateful for your company," she replied, as they reached her cabin.

"It is not mere kindness," he assured her, "but a desire to see to your safety and well-being."

Even in the dim light, she saw the depth of his concern for her radiating in his eyes. Ripples of warmth began in the very tips of her toes, radiated through her body, quelled the tremors, and heralded the most idyllic week of the voyage and of her life.

Mathilda

The first steps down toward the Zwischendeck and she knew that she would be dabbing her nose frequently with the cologne-doused handkerchief. After a week at sea, the confined quarters reeked of pestilence. She had learned to avert her eyes, looking neither right or left, but straight ahead at the back of the doctor as he strode toward his patient. On her first descent to the crowded third-class deck, she had stopped by a woman sitting distraughtly holding a little boy of three on her lap. The child was in the ravages of consumption; she had seen it many times back home. The doctor had upbraided her sharply for this violation. She was to be the interpreter for the patient he was attending, nothing more.

That first night, sleep had eluded her in the second-class cabin that held four persons in the same space into which at least three times as many were crammed in the deck below. The walls were painted; the bunk beds were made of oak with comfortable mattresses and pillows. Each cabin had an ample washbasin; water was abundant. There was an armoire for clothing. The lower deck, on the other hand, was roughly partitioned with wooden beams. It was divided into two sections: one section for men and the other for married couples and women with children. There were a few cabins for unmarried women but these were never enough. She had heard that the ship could carry 1,700 emigrants. She never doubted the veracity of that number.

She understood the desperation of the thousands who trekked across hundreds of miles to the ports where the ships to the land of opportunity awaited. Piotrkow, where she was born and lived, had become a gathering spot for thousands of emigrants. Villagers from the tiny hamlets all around made their way to Piotrkow where all the ship lines had set up offices in the town square for the sale of passage to America. Once a ticket was purchased, the holder came under the supervision of the ship line. He or she was put on a train whose destination was a port city, Bremen or Hamburg.

Peasants who had never been out of their minuscule villages were astounded to see the valleys, rivers and mountains, the castles and tidy towns of Germany. In the port city, they were housed in cheap hotels to await the ship's departure. Paperwork was filled out and signed, often with an "X" for those who could not read or write. There was a medical exam to be passed, as well as the dreaded delousing and bathing, after which each passenger smelled like hot steam and carbolic acid.

So deep in remembering was she, that she almost bumped into Herr Kessler who had stopped outside one of the birthing cabins. Two men nervously paced back and forth in the minuscule space by the door. They were the fathers - one in his thirties, the other at least ten years younger. Quickly, she appraised their clothes, hair and facial structure to determine their nationalities, and that of their wives. Herr Kessler stepped inside the cabin and she followed. Against each side wall was a cot; on each was a woman in labor. Both were groaning, panting with parched lips desperately in need of water.

Herr Kessler walked over to the older woman who seemed to be in the least distress. She spoke to the woman.

"Mluvite cesky? *Do you speak Czech?*" she asked.

"Ano. *Yes.*" the woman gasped.

"Jak se jmenujes? *What is your name?*"

"Anna."

"Herr Kessler, she is Bohemian. Her name is Anna." He slipped his hands into rubber gloves and examined the woman. "She has had other children. The birth is imminent. I will examine the other woman and then deliver her baby."

She slid behind Herr Kessler to the cot of the other patient who clutched the corners of the sheet that covered her as she writhed in the agony of childbirth. Strands of sweat-soaked black hair had plastered themselves to an oval face framing huge black eyes that had not seen more than sixteen years.

"Du resdt Eydish? *Do you speak Yiddish?*" she asked.

"Yo."

"Vi heistu? *What is your name?*"

"Basha," the woman panted.

Herr Kessler examined Basha. "Tell her that her baby is in a good position in the birth canal. She is small; the birth will take longer. All should go well."

Returning to her cabin hours later, she was exhausted. She had stayed with Herr Kessler through the births of two healthy boys, Medard and Ancel. She had interpreted for the wife of a Kashub man who was delirious with fever. She had soothed the fears of a Russian mother and her seven-year-old son who clung to his mother's skirts in abject terror while Herr Kessler examined the woman for possible consumption. Wearily, she removed her blouse and skirt, which reeked of the odors of the lower deck. She poured water into the wash basin, refreshing her face and thoroughly washing her hands. She slipped into her nightdress and sank down on her bed, closing her eyes as memories of the day surfaced

By midafternoon the winds had dissipated and the languid sun had drawn everyone out onto the decks. On the inadequate deck for the third-class passengers, not an inch of wood could be seen. Men played cards, smoked pipes, chewed tobacco, and told stories from whence they came. Every mother, terrified of rickets, was eager to see her children playing in the sun. The children, released from the prison of the lower decks, ran around tripping over feet and legs. Quickly picking themselves up to run again, they squealed as they reveled in their unexpected freedom.

She had followed Herr Kessler as he gingerly made his way toward a woman who had fainted in the cramped overcrowding. It took skill not to step on hands or feet as they traversed the deck tilting in the rolling swells. As Herr Kessler passed a bottle of smelling salts under the woman's nose, she had heard voices and looked up.

First-class passengers in their afternoon high tea finery were leaning over the railing of the oversized promenade deck. Some were gesturing and . laughing. A few were throwing sweetmeats and coins to the children below who fell on top of each other in their pursuit of one. Their fathers and mothers were oblivious to this enjoyment of the rich at their expense. It bothered them not a whit. She knew they were not envious of those above. In their minds, the ship wasn't much different than Russia or Poland or Slovakia. For centuries they had known their place. Only names changed, not status. The first-class cabin passengers were the lords and ladies; the sailors and officers were the police and army, and the captain was the king or czar.

She sat up in her bed and touched the top of her right hand as she remembered how the Kashub woman had snatched her hand and kissed it. She had looked deeply into the woman's eyes hoping her own eyes would say what her lips could not. "I am no better than you. I, too, come from the land, not the castle. I, too, have worked the fields on farms, raised poultry, worked as a servant girl and a housemaid." But on this ship she slept in a cabin as only a lady would and she was viewed as such by the emigrants.

The energetic, if wheezing, notes of an accordion floated up through the floorboards. As she had done, these men and women in steerage had learned long ago to take one day at a time. The miseries of the long voyage could be endured with merriment and music. Each night as the ship churned its way toward America, when the swells of the ocean allowed, an accordion or harmonica would squeak out Czech polkas, Polish mazurkas and Hungarian czardas. Riotous laughter would float up through the floorboards as some male showoff attempted a wild Russian cossack, squatting and kicking his feet out in rhythm to the music. It required not only great balance and strong legs, but a steadier floor not easily found on a heaving, rolling monster of the sea.

Soon a multitude of voices would be singing a ballad which reminded them of the village tavern or the cottage on the landowner's farm. She knew they were holding hands and swaying to the accordion music, this time aided by the rolling deck.

How simple but heartfelt were these songs and dances when compared to those in the ornate ballroom on the first deck where the fine ladies and their gentlemen danced in formally prescribed motions that had appeared phony and stilted when she first viewed them. The waltz was like a caged animal desperate to escape into an exuberant polka or krakowiak. She wondered, how many of these fine dancers went to bed with light hearts asking for the protection of Father Abraham or one of the saints? She knew that most of those below decks did. No matter how dismal conditions were, their faith that the future would be better never wavered.

She rose up from her bunk and pulled the hairpins out of her abundant tresses letting them fall to her waist. She brushed them until every strand was smooth and shining. She brought the mass forward and braided it for the night. She slipped under the blanket and closed her eyes. As the music of a polka wafted up through the wooden floor, she drifted off dreaming that she was dancing with her lost love, Gottlieb.

Maryanna

True to his word, Michał arrived at her cabin a half hour before the designated time for dinner that evening. As she opened the door, the afternoon spent preparing herself for dinner was amply rewarded. She basked in the delight shining in his eyes as he took in the upswept hair with the tortoise shell combs and the navy silk dress with the Alençon lace collar and cuffs, no longer the height of fashion but fastidiously cleaned and pressed. Her only other adornment was the precious gold cross that had been her mother's and her grandmother's before that and now hung from a slender gold chain around her neck.

He held out his gloved hand in a chivalrous manner as she stepped out the doorway. How dashing he looked in a black suit with a deep grey vest. He walked closely behind her through the narrow corridors and up the stairwells, only stepping in front of her to open compartment doors. In the dining room, he walked her to the table set aside for single women traveling alone. He pulled out her chair and pushed it back slowly. He bowed slightly and smiled; he would come for her at dinner's end. She watched him until he disappeared behind the numerous tables of passengers chatting gaily and enjoying their aperitifs.

With the last morsel of lemon curd tingling her tastebuds, she folded her napkin and placed it on the table. Immediately, she sensed his presence behind her. She put on her gloves and rose as Michał slid the chair out. He guided her deftly through the myriad of tables and through the atrium to a small closet she hadn't seen before. He opened it, freed his coat from its hangar and picked up his hat from the shelf above.

"If it pleases you, I would be most grateful if you would accompany me on a walk on deck. The air is very fresh this evening and the sea is quite calm."

"That would be most pleasant, Michał. It will only take a few minutes to put on my hat and coat and fetch warmer gloves."

The billions of stars glimmering in the dome of the sky that swooped down to meet the waters lapping against the ship's hull, enthralled her only slightly less than the incomprehensible reality that she was walking alongside this wondrous man whom she had met only that morning. Every cell in her body melted into the soft lap of the water and the gentle light of the stars as she felt one with the universe.

As they walked, Michał spoke. "I am twenty-four years old and from a family that was once illustrious in Poland. Five hundred years ago, when invading hordes from the east threatened Warsaw and the regions around it, my family offered the protection of a clan to other families that joined us. The clan acquired a status and influence that was soon noticed by the princes of Poland. My family became part of the nobility until the partitioning by Austria, Prussia and Russia in the late 1700's. During the past one hundred years, the family's extensive estates have been slowly confiscated. There is nothing left but the family crest attesting to its princely history and a small familial house in Warsaw where my father lives."

He inquired about her family. She thrilled to see his rapt attention as she spoke. No one had ever paid that much attention to her back home, except Ignacy. And, of course, Gottlieb. She saw in Michał's eyes the same interest in her that she had seen in Gottlieb's eyes. A look, deep and piercing, hoping to plumb the depths of her being.

"I am also twenty-four. I have an older brother, Ignacy, and four younger sisters and a brother. My father died suddenly when I was eighteen; my youngest sister was five years old. Mother needed help raising my siblings. My sister, Franciszka, is now sixteen and has taken over helping with the youngest ones.

"Ignacy has a wife and children. He traveled to America three years ago and worked hard for better wages than he could ever earn in Poland. He returned home a year ago. He described life in Chicago and how different it was from Osiek Dolnoslakie. I began to dream of all the possibilities in this far-off land. In April, he left again promising me that when he earned enough, he would send the money for ship's passage. While he travels Zwischendeck, he sent money for a private cabin so I would be safe." Her voice trailed off. She trembled with horror as memories of the morning attack assailed her, and with joy as Michał touched her arm to console her.

So lovingly did he speak about his mother, she wished that she could have known this woman who raised the son who was now walking beside her. His mother was also of the nobility, from another family reduced to nothing by the partition. Katarzyna was an educated, genteel woman who insisted that the high status of nobility should not be based on land holdings and estates but on personal conduct. He recounted maxims that his mother had instilled in him:

"Hold your head high, no matter where you are
or what you are doing.
Always make choices based on your conscience
which will never fail you.
Be compassionate to everyone.
Treat women kindly, not just in a chivalrous
manner, but as equals to you.
Labor is honorable. Don't be afraid to get
your hands dirty. Remember that Jesus was a carpenter.
Whatever you have, share it with those around you."

11

Michał explained that as the family estates diminished, several of his cousins had emigrated to America where they felt free to improve their circumstances. Some owned land in an area by a superior lake in a place called Wisconsin. That was his destination.

On the last afternoon of the voyage, she devoted her attention to dressing for dinner. It would be the last time she would be with Michał; she wanted his memory of her to be unforgettable. She brushed the grey dress and jacket and fluffed the limp feathers on the grey hat. With a wrist that was healing, she put her hair up and crowned it with the grey hat firmly secured to her hair with long pearl-tipped hat pins. Michał had suggested a last walk on deck before dinner.

She slid her hands into black gloves when she heard his knock and opened the door. Michał held out his gloved hand. She put her hand in his as she stepped over the threshold. Silently, they made their way through the narrow corridor and up the staircase to the promenade deck. He held the door open as she stepped out onto the deck. The wintry sun did its best to warm them from behind a haze of thin, wispy clouds. Following Michał's lead, she walked silently, observing the barren limbs of strange trees and bushes that crowded the shoreline as the ship steamed up the Delaware River to the port of Philadelphia. They were sailing through American waters. Tomorrow they would walk down the gangplank and onto the hallowed ground of their new country.

As they neared the bow of the ship, Michał's touch guided her to the railing. Each time he touched her, confusing ripples of contentment and excitement coursed through her body.

In his gentlemanly fashion, Michał rarely touched her casually. She was either walking by his side or in front of him. Now she felt his strong arms gently turning her to face him. She looked up and saw an inscrutable intensity in his hazel brown eyes. He took both of her hands in his.

"Maryanna, both of us stepped on board this ship to begin a journey into the unknown, a life we couldn't imagine, in this land about which we know little. I do not believe that I just happened to be in the right place at the right time when you needed help. As we have walked together, my feelings of pleasure in being with you have grown into a deep love for you, into a desire to be by your side for the rest of my life.

"Maryanna, czy wyjdziesz za mnie? *Will you marry me?* Perhaps, in time, you can grow to love me, too."

12

Never in all her secret dreams of falling in love and being asked for her hand in marriage, had she ever imagined that it would occur on a ship on a river in America.

"Michał, tak, wyjdę za ciebie. *Yes, I will marry you.* But I will not grow to love you in time. I already do. The moment you insisted on accompanying me into the sick bay, wondrous feelings began to stir inside me. I have seen what a gentle man you are, yet confident in yourself. Our conversations have shown me that you are upright and your faith is strong. I will always feel safe with you."

The heat of his arms flowed through her as he hugged her briefly and not too close. The fine ladies and their escorts were also strolling the deck and it would have been most unseemly to do otherwise.

"I have a cousin, Jerzy, in Philadelphia," Michał said, his face reflecting pain. "Earlier this year, he and his wife Paulina lost their only child, a little boy named Jozef, in the middle of the night. He was six months old and had a fatal convulsion. I have planned to visit with him and extend my condolences and bring family news to him. He will give us information on the courthouse where we will obtain a marriage license and a church where we will be married in a quiet ceremony. Afterward, we will travel west on the train as husband and wife."

She delighted in his confidence that she would say Yes and in his planning.

"Maryanna, the train from Philadelphia stops in Chicago. We will take time to visit with your brother before traveling on."

"Michał, have you ever lived on the land?"

"My father would take me into the countryside to show me the lands that had been ours, but I have never touched their soil."

"You have lived in Warsaw all your life?"

"Yes."

"Perhaps a growing city like Chicago would suit you better," she suggested, with a timidity that grew when he did not respond. Had she spoken out of turn? She searched his face anxiously, relaxing only when a little smile began to turn upwards the ends of his mustache.

"Maryanna, you are right. I did not think of such a possibility. I chose my cousins in Wisconsin as my sponsors for emigration. I hadn't even considered Jerzy. Chicago is a bustling city that is growing. We will send word to your brother, Ignacy. Perhaps he can help us settle in Chicago."

The sun grew low in the western sky, creating flashes of golden light between the barren branches of the shoreline trees as the ship slowly sailed up the river. She stood at the railing next to Michał, now her betrothed, wondering what lay ahead in the land of endless opportunity.

DECEMBER 1907

Maryanna

"Wesoły Świat Bożego Narodzenia. *Merry Christmas.*" Michał snuck up behind her as she stood at the sink filling the coffeepot with fresh water. He kissed the nape of her neck and patted the sides of her rotund abdomen. She put the pot down on the drainboard and turned toward him, craning her neck upward. Flawlessly choreographed, his lips met hers as he bent to her.

Once parted, she scooped ground coffee from the dented canister and dropped each scoop into the metal basket spreading it evenly around the stem. She placed the basket into the pot, making sure that the stem was nestled in the groove on the pot's bottom. Michał handed the lid to her and she pushed it down on the coffeepot. He struck a match and ignited the gas burner at the back of the stove, adjusted the flame, then carried the heavy coffeepot to the stove, setting it on the burner.

During the time it took for the coffee to percolate, she dumped the potato pierogi into the pot of boiling water on the front burner, filled two small dishes with the peach compote that she had canned during the summer, and set out the loaf of fresh bread and the tub of butter. Christmas Eve was a rogation day, a day of fast and abstinence from meat in preparation for tomorrow, the Feast of Christmas. Michał cut the bread into thick slices. When the pierogi were cooked, he brought each dish to the stove and held it while she scooped the steaming dumplings into them.

They sat down together at the worn wooden table and held hands. Michał said the blessing, thanking the Lord for the food He had provided for them and for the woman who made it so tasty. After a long day at work, he set forth eagerly enjoying every morsel. Satisfied, he leaned back in his chair.

"Maryanna, this is not how I imagined our life together in this land of opportunity. We are cramped in this tiny apartment, always bumping elbows with each other or Ignacy as we move around. There is hardly enough room in the bedroom for the baby's bassinet. I want for us to live in one of those homes that we saw from the train which brought us here from the Union Depot." His face crumpled as he spoke.

"Michał." She reached over and touched his hand. "This is so much harder for you than it is for me. You grew up in a house in Warsaw. Maybe not as big as the ones your family once owned, but certainly bigger than my family's cottage. Nine of us lived there. My parents had the bedroom. Regardless of age, all the children, except the babies, slept in the loft.

"This does not bother me. It is temporary. Your apprenticeship, keeping track of the inventory in the machine shop, is going well. Ignacy tells me that you are highly respected by the men who work with you. You are fortunate to have such a good job. The education that your mother gave you is serving you well. It has kept you out of the blast furnaces and the rolling mills where the work is as hard, dirty and as dangerous as the coal mines back home.

"Michał, wherever I am I will always be happy as long as I am with y-o-u-ohhh!" A pain, such as she had never felt before spread through her abdomen. "I think the baby is coming!"

She was no stranger to childbirth, but she had always been an observer, not the participant. She had helped the midwives when her mother had given birth to the two youngest siblings. She knew what was needed. Yesterday, she had placed the items on top of the dresser in the bedroom.

"Michał," she said, as the pain subsided, "take the pot from the pierogi off the stove and put it on the drainboard. Fill the large pot with water and set it on the burner to boil. It is time to get the połwożna. Give my apologies to Pana Andrzejewska for my poor timing which is taking her away from Christmas Eve celebrations with her family." Another wave of pain assailed her as she stood up.

"Maryanna!" He saw the pain flash across her face. "I can't leave you."

"I will be fine. Franceszka has earned high praise as a midwife from the mothers she has helped. They all encouraged me to use her. Marya Ciesielska, who will be the baby's godmother, spoke to her. She agreed to help birth the baby when my time came, even on Christmas."

He donned his overcoat and hat, grabbed his gloves and raced out the door. As he sped down the three flights of wooden stairs slick with the remnants of last night's snow storm, he noted that the back apartment on the first floor was dark. That usually meant a vacancy; he would speak to the landlord on the day after Christmas. It was a bit larger and there would be fewer stairs for Maryanna to climb with a baby.

The night sky was ablaze with stars that he did not see as he half ran down Buffalo Avenue, turned the corner onto 84th Street and raced down the block to Burley Avenue. He took the stairs two at a time and pounded forcefully on the front door until a boy of about twelve opened it.

"I need to speak to your mother," he said, hurriedly. "My wife is having a baby."

Mrs. Andrzejewski strode down the dark hall, wiping her hands on her apron.

"Pana Andrzejewska, I am so sorry to disturb you on this night of nights. But the baby is coming. My wife is having pain."

"Ah, so you are Michał Vinefsky." A smile spread across her rosy plump cheeks and up to her eyes. "Do not worry, Pan Vinefsky. Babies come when they decide. They pick the time, not us.

"How is your wife doing? This is her first baby, yes?"

"Yes. She did help with the births of younger children in Poland."

"That is good. She will not be as distressed. Go home and wait for me. I will put supper on the table and will come within a half hour. Rest assured that nothing will happen before I get there. First babies take time."

"The pavements are slippery from the snow," he said, with concern for her safety replacing his angst over Maryanna.

"Do not worry; one of my sons will walk with me."

Michał sprinted down the stairs and ran as fast as he could to the apartment. He marveled as he entered the kitchen stomping snow from his boots. While he was gone, Maryanna had removed her housedress and put on her oldest nightgown which she knew would get soiled. She had taken down her hair and brushed it and braided it. She was standing where he always seemed to see her - at the kitchen sink. She was washing the supper dishes. Every few minutes she would grab the edge of the sink with both hands and stand motionless waiting for the contraction to subside. Then she would wash and rinse another pot. She was ready.

True to her word, Pana Andrzejewska arrived within the half hour. She shooed Maryanna into the bed which its occupant had protected with many layers of old newspapers and old towels. The połwoźna bustled around the bedroom and kitchen with the assurance of one who has mastered the task at hand.

Michał paced the tiny kitchen and even tinier parlor. Ignacy, who had been working the 3-to-11 shift at the steel mill, joined him after washing the grime of the mill from his hands and face and changing his clothes. What was taking so long? he fretted. His pocket watch had been retrieved and replaced a hundred times and still no sound from the bedroom, except for an occasional moan and the solid footsteps of Pana Andrzejewska.

At 11:45 p.m., the church bells of St. Michael's cathedral, only five blocks away, chimed the necessity of hurrying to the church for the Mass at midnight to celebrate the birth of Our Lord Jesus Christ. Twelve minutes later, Michał heard a lusty cry and an "Oh!" of wonderment as Maryanna feasted her eyes on the child who had grown inside her. He could wait no longer. He dashed for the bedroom door. As the bells of St. Michael's peeled out in celebration of the wondrous birth of the Virgin Mary's Son, Savior of the world, he beheld his own Mary holding their son in her arms.

JANUARY 1909

Mathilda

She studied her reflection in the mirror hanging precariously over the wooden dressing table laden with the lotions, hairbrushes, hairpins, curlers, combs, soaps, face powders and other beautifying necessities that a young woman must have. The accommodations were similar to those on the *SS Merion,* four female interpreters sharing a cabin.

She adjusted her new service badge. She was now a Dolmetscher on the *SS Bremen,* a steamship of the Norddeutscher Lloyd line, which sailed from Bremen, Germany, to New York. This was her first voyage as an interpreter for the ship line. She spoke five languages and had eagerly embraced the task of learning English while working on the *Merion.* It was a more complicated language than she had anticipated and she was not comfortable when she did not fully comprehend what the captain and crew were saying in English. It was prudent to work on a ship where the captain and crew spoke Deutsch. She was comfortable knowing she would understand all commands and instructions.

Her hours of work would be spent with the ship's doctors who treated the thousands of emigrants sailing to America. There were male interpreters who tended to the medical translation needs of the first-class passengers, as well as all other situations in which translation was necessary. This chauvinistic attitude toward women galled her. She was just as capable of translating accurately in a legal or political matter as in a medical one. Whose brain was really filled with cotton? Hers, or the brain of a male who labeled hers as such in any area outside of tending to the sick?

She took a second glance in the crazed mirror, added a few more pins to the braided bun at the nape of her neck and brushed the powder rag lightly across her cheeks to add a bit more color. Satisfied with the results, she hurried out of the cabin to begin her new assignment.

MARCH 1911

Maryanna

She sat in the wooden rocker nursing Estella, her third child in four fleeting years. Stephan had turned three on Christmas Eve. He was sprawled on her bed napping with Theodora, little Dora, who would be two years old tomorrow, on Estella's Christening Day. Estella was sucking mightily. She looked down at her newest child who had a headful of dark brown hair unlike most babies. Like her father, Estella's hair was thick and wavy and her brown eyes had a touch of hazel in them. Theodora's hair was almost black, and fine like her mother's. She was an imp whose name had been shortened to Dora, because she was just that, adorable.

She switched Estella to her other breast. As the little one nursed, she had precious moments to remember how blessed she was. Life was so good. A horrendous moment on board ship had turned into the biggest delight of her life, Michał. What he was when he had saved her from her assailant was what he was now - an intelligent, kind, physically strong man who loved her tenderly and cherished his children.

She didn't care how many children she had, as long as they were Michał's. When he learned that she was expecting Estella, he bought a house; it was heavily mortgaged, but it was theirs. Until the day they moved, she had to convince herself that they were actually owners of a house by repeating the address over and over: 8345 Marquette Avenue. It was huge - nine hundred square feet. It was a house befitting the mayor of her hometown in Poland. It had been built five years earlier and had an unheard of three bedrooms as well as an indoor bathroom. It had a kitchen with room to move around and an icebox and a stove with four burners. There was a parlor for receiving guests and a back porch for sitting. Loveliest of all, there was land in back of the house, a yard where the children could play and she could grow vegetables and her beloved flowers. There were fruit trees in the yard: two apple trees, a cherry tree, a plum tree and a peach tree. There was a cellar as big as the house above it. It would hold all the vegetables and fruits that she could preserve. Never would this have happened in Osiek Dolnoslakie. There, one didn't decide to buy a house and do it. A couple was lucky if a magnanimous landowner allowed them to live in a tiny cottage.

They had moved in last fall. Ignacy had stayed with them until after the move; he had come back to America in 1909 for a year of work and dallied to help with the move when he learned she was expecting. Afterward, he returned to his wife and children in Mostki, with the promise that he would be back in 1912. She missed her big brother and his humor and easygoing ways; there would always be room in her home for him.

She gazed around the beautiful bedroom in which she was sitting, the sanctuary of her home. She loved the soft grey wallpaper that highlighted rubicund sprays of primroses. The bed, with its heart-shaped walnut wood headboard, was covered with a thick gray-and-white striped pierzyna. She had embroidered pink primroses to match the wallpaper on the hem-stitched pillowcases and had crocheted a pink edging around them. She loved the intricate carving of the walnut wood that framed the mirror above the dresser. It was repeated in the armoire that held their clothes. She sighed deeply. What had she ever done to deserve a man as good as Michał?

Stephan stirred and woke up Dora. Estella, now fully satiated, had fallen asleep on her lap. She settled her into the warm spot in the center of the bed that was vacated by Stephan and Dora. She would fix a quick lunch for her little darlings. She knew Stephan would play with Dora and keep his sister occupied while she made preparations for the Christening tomorrow.

Mathilda

She tucked the scented handkerchief into her skirt pocket with the proficiency of one who has repeated an action a hundred times. Almost, she thought. She had survived over ninety voyages in five years. Had she used the word 'survived'? It was more than survival of the treacheries of the North Atlantic. She had become as used to them as to the rainstorms in Piotrkow. They paled in comparison to the vagaries of life for the emigrants stuffed in the holds of the Zwischendeck.

She had lived her own peasant life of nothing, with nothing to look forward to, in Piotrkow. She understood the desperation of the thousands who were willing to be jammed into unsanitary holds and eat lukewarm soup, black bread, boiled potatoes and herring for two weeks. It had to be suffered to attain their dream - a better life in America and a future for their children. Truth be told, for many it was more food than they had eaten in months.

She had seen scores of young men confidently boasting of a better or easier life than they would have back home. Those who boasted of better fared well, especially the ones who had not a speck of mud to call their own back home. They worked hard and nothing deterred them. Those who boasted of an easier life were scandalized by the hardships of the factories and mills which were the main sources of work for the unskilled peasant.

She had seen countless young women hoping to transform their lives through marriage in America where a dowry was not required. Some were fortunate to be betrothed to men who had gone to prepare the way and were now sending for their beloveds. Some were going into service as maids or nannies, hoping to find a husband among the other servants. Many were going to marry a man they had never met. She disliked the shadchan who brokered marriages between lonely men in America and naive girls without dowries. Once she had reached her intended and married him, many a young woman was disillusioned by the reality that this man did not expect to love and protect her, but to use her to make his life easier and satisfy his urgings as often as he chose.

For five years she had seen the dichotomy. For every voyage sailing to America filled with hundreds of hopeful hearts, there was a voyage back to Europe with disillusioned and heartbroken souls.

There was also the paradox of the classes. She had been privy to the stories of the stewards and male interpreters assigned to serve the occupants of the first-class cabins. These fine ladies and gentlemen frowned on the boisterous merriment of those in third class and blamed it on the accursed vodka and beer. Yet, in the posh saloons on the upper deck, they drank champagne and whiskies with abandon. Was it not the same devil with a different name? They looked down on those in steerage as immoral, lazy, greedy creatures. Yet, they sat for hours playing poker, amassing piles of colored chips. They wondered what the ill-clothed and ill-kempt men knew of civility. Yet, she had seen more sincere gentlemen-like behavior in third class than she had learned occurred in first class. She had heard many stories of supposed gentlemen in their first-class cabins who were but wretched beasts to their wives and peers. They would not hesitate to prosecute a poor man for stealing a railroad ticket, while they stole whole railroads and companies from the rightful owners through chicanery and were then honored as Captains of Industry.

During her crossings, she had made friends with others traveling in second class. Some were people who had a little means and were going to America to establish a business or work in a specific trade. Several had offered her an instant position as a maid or nanny or shopgirl. All she needed to do was to contact them when she was ready to settle in America.

She was used to living a solitary life, relying on no one but herself for twenty years, ever since her father had been killed when she was nine years old. She would be twenty-nine on her next birthday in June. Recently, the memories came flooding into her consciousness of the sweetness of the months with Gottlieb when they were betrothed and in love. The agony she had felt when she learned that he had been killed in battle in a stupid, senseless war had lessened with the years and allowed the return of a longing for such intimacy. It was time to think about a new life.

CHAPTER TWO

APRIL 1911

Maryanna

She sat in the rocker in the bedroom staring at the wall. The pink primroses on the wallpaper that had once delighted her every time she looked at them went unseen. She didn't feel the tug of Estella's eager mouth at her breast. She didn't feel Stephan pulling at her skirt and asking over and over, "Mama, mama, where is Dora?" She felt nothing. Absolutely nothing.

Was it only two weeks ago that the day had begun with sun and the soft, warm breezes of early spring? It was a lovely half block walk from their house to the new St. Mary Magdalene's church where Fr. Kowaleski had baptized Estella. After the baptism was completed, they ascended the stairs from the lower-level church into the vestibule and stepped outside. The soft breezes were now winds whipped up into a gale, scudding grey clouds across a sullen sky and dropping the temperature by twenty degrees. Droplets of icy cold rain fell on their heads and faces. She wrapped Estella firmly in the Christening blanket and held on, tightly. Michał scooped up Dora who was wearing a new spring dress and coat. They hurried home.

All Saturday afternoon, they celebrated Estella's birth into the life of the church, and Dora's second birthday. They feasted on chicken and pierogi, ziemniaki, kapusta, kiszka and kolacky. The men rolled up the rug in the parlor and they danced to the tunes Dora's godfather played on his harmonica. The little imp refused to nap, giggling when her godmother tickled her and screaming with joy when tossed into the air by her godfather.

On Sunday, Michał stayed with the sleeping children while she went to the early Mass with a heart full of gratitude to God for all the blessings bestowed on her ever since the day she met him, the greatest blessing of all. After dinner, he played with Stephan while she sat on the sofa with Estella sleeping on her lap and a curious Dora sitting next to her. Dora was full of questions about her little sister. Why was Estella's skin wrinkly? Why did she make funny faces while she was sleeping? Why didn't she have teeth? Could she eat a piece of Dora's birthday cake without teeth?

On Monday, after Michał left for work, she began the weekly task of washing clothes. She pulled out the heavy galvanized wash tubs and set them in the kitchen. She boiled water on the stove, poured it into one of the tubs, and using the large wooden paddle, stirred the borax powder into the hot water until it dissolved. She poured in cold water to a temperature that suited her. She filled the second tub with cold water. After the clothes were scrubbed with the brush in the first tub and rinsed in the second, she wrung them out by hand and carried them to the back yard. She hung the wet clothing on the clotheslines with the wooden clothespins.

She was grateful that Dora wasn't running around with yesterday's exuberance; instead, she was sitting quietly on the kitchen floor playing with Stephan. In late afternoon, as she was bringing the stiff, but dry, clothes back into the house, she noticed that Dora's face was flushed. She put down the basket of wash and felt Dora's forehead. She was burning with fever! Wash forgotten, she picked her up and carried her into the children's bedroom, gently setting her on her bed. Dora didn't move. She ran into the kitchen and soaked a washcloth in cool water. She placed the cloth on Dora's forehead.

"Michał," she cried out, as she heard him walk into the house after work. "Dora has fever. She is burning up!"

His face mirrored the terror in hers as he burst into the bedroom. It was so commonplace for babies under the age of two to die from many childhood maladies that had no cure. Dora's second birthday proved that she was a survivor. Or did it?

"I will look after Stephan," he said, "while you nurse Dora and take care of the little one."

He went into the kitchen to heat up soup for Stephan and himself. He brought a steaming bowl into the bedroom for her. She thanked him, took a spoonful, then let the soup grow cold sitting on the bedside table as she applied cool, wet cloths to Dora, hoping to break the fever.

For three days she couldn't eat or sleep as she fought a battle for her daughter's life against the fever that raged and waned, only to rage again. When the cough began and the struggle to breathe, she knew Dora had the dreaded pneumonia. The doctor had no cure, only remedies. He prescribed Vicks Croup and Pneumonia Salve. Faithfully, she wet the cloths with water hot enough to open the pores in Dora's chest, but not hot enough to blister the tender skin. Then she gently rubbed the salve into her baby's chest and wrapped her in gauze bands and a towel to keep the vapors in. She prayed that the vapors would loosen the congestion in Dora's tiny lungs.

"Maryanna, Maryanna, you must rest," Michał begged over and over. "You will get sick yourself."

"You are right," she finally admitted, for she had noticed that her supply of milk for Estella was declining when she breastfed her. She could lose two daughters. She would not let that happen. She sent word to Dora's godmother asking her to come and sit with Dora while she rested. She fell into an exhausted sleep the second her head hit the pillow.

She was cradling little Dora in her arms while Michał had his arms wrapped around her shoulders as their daughter gasped her last breath. She felt him tremble as he realized that his adorable Dora was dead. He had been so patient, so understanding. His heart was broken, as was hers. While she doted on Stephan, Dora had entwined herself inextricably in Michał's heart.

The ensuing days had been a blur. There was a little white wooden casket on the oval table in the parlor surrounded by spring flowers. Theodora was resting inside on satin pillows, her angelic face bearing no trace of the disease that had ravaged her. She was wearing the light blue dress she had worn on her second birthday. Neighbors they had just met and those from the apartments on Buffalo Avenue came by to console her, even though they knew there was no consolation. So many had stood where she was standing, by the casket of a son or daughter, some more than once.

She didn't remember how they traveled to and from the cemetery, miles from South Chicago. She did have recurring memories of the tiny grave which had been dug into the fresh spring soil, the lowering of the casket into it and the clods of black earth falling on its pristine whiteness.

Stephan was pulling on her skirt again. "Mama, mama, where is Dora? I want to play with her."

APRIL 1912

Mathilda

"Mathilda, come quickly. You must come on deck at once. I can't believe what we are seeing!" Frieda dashed out of their cabin as quickly as she had dashed in.

She rose from her bunk and pinned her hat firmly on her head. She put on her jacket and hurried along the narrow corridor. As she walked onto the deck, she saw people flocking to the starboard railing. She looked beyond their heads and saw the source of their wonderment. The outline of an iceberg rising out of the frigid waters. She'd sailed through these waters many times; icebergs were nothing new to her. She walked to the railing where there was a gap in the crowd of people. She leaned over and looked down into a frigid hell. Hundreds of bodies were floating in the water among deck chairs and countless pieces of wood.

As her brain tried to process the gruesome sight, she was jostled by a young man standing next to her. In his hands was one of the new handheld Brownie cameras. She had seen such marvels in the hands of a few first-class passengers, but never being held by someone dressed as ordinary as he. She heard him mutter in Czech, "Je červené! *It is red!*" He stared straight ahead; she followed his gaze. Her hand flew up to her mouth in shock. It was red! The iceberg that they were passing had a swath of red paint across its side, ship's paint. She knew with certainty that eight days ago this floe had made contact with a ship. These were the ship's deck chairs and other wreckage bobbing in the chilly waters. And these were some of her precious passengers floating beside them.

The man with the camera raised it and took a photograph of the iceberg. He turned to walk away from the railing.

"Excuse me, sir," she asked, speaking Czech. "Are you Bohemian?"

"I am."

"You have taken a photograph because you think this is the iceberg that was hit by the *Titanic?*"

"I do. I am an amateur photographer. I have been following reports from the survivors of that unspeakable tragedy. A wealthy gentleman I met in the saloon has a cousin who survived the wreck. They have been sending ship-to-shore messages to each other. As morning dawned on the fifteenth, his cousin saw the iceberg from the deck of the *SS Carpathia* whose crew had rescued him and others. He said he would never forget what it looked like. This iceberg matches the description he gave his cousin. And look, you can see where a large swath of the iceberg had been sheered in a collision with an object. I am going to bring the man up here on deck so he can see where his cousin narrowly escaped death."

She looked again at the iceberg and noted the damage to it. She wondered why the *Bremen* wasn't slowing down to retrieve the bodies of the passengers from the ill-fated ship. A ship's officer was walking by; she questioned him. The captain had specific instructions to continue on to New York. Another ship was two hours away. It had sailed from the port of New York with retrieval as its purpose.

She took one more look at the iceberg, but did not look down at the water. It was too horrendous a sight. She turned away from the railing. She would be on duty soon.

Maryanna

She felt the baby kick vigorously in her womb, as if trying to knock Estella off her lap. She really didn't have a lap, just the all too familiar protrusion of her fecund womb. Estella, who had lived to her first birthday last month was every bit the imp that Dora had been. Dora had been playful and an utter delight to watch as she embraced each minute of her short life. Estella was all of that and more, for she was quick of mind and movement.

"Stephan," she called out, as her daughter slid off her lap and scampered away. "Don't let Estella leave the kitchen."

She could rely on Stephan. He was four now and a big help to her with Estella, as the new pregnancy slowed her down. For the first few months after Dora's death, he had asked for her every day. As Estella grew from a helpless infant into a crawling baby who delighted in getting into everything, he embraced her as the new Dora. Without prompting, his four-year-old legs would scamper after her keeping her from the dangers that his four-year-old mind already knew.

Once again, she could admire the primrose wallpaper and contemplate Michał's love for her in those raw months last year. She knew he was hurting, too, yet she felt powerless to help him with his grief. He, however, after working hard all day would take care of Stephan and help her in the kitchen. He sensed when she was receptive to being kissed or hugged; this he did freely at those times. But he never forced himself on her.

Slowly, the ice within her had thawed. Oh, how it hurt when she could feel again! How many tears had fallen into the tubs as she washed clothes, on Estella's head as she nursed, into the chicken soup bubbling on the stove, into her pillow at night! Very patiently, Michał had waited for the evening when she turned toward him, instead of away. He took her in his arms and pressed her to him. A month later, she knew she was pregnant.

She rose from the rocker and went into the kitchen to begin grating potatoes. As she walked, her water broke. It was time to fetch the połwożna, Mrs. Pruzak. It would be an easy birth for the midwife to handle. After three other births, her womb was wide open and this child would sail out.

Three hours later, she was propped up in bed with Stanisław cradled in her arms. Michał sat at the foot of the bed with a squirmy Estella. Stephan sat next to her stroking the black hair of his baby brother.

AUGUST 1912

Maryanna

Little Stash was sleeping contentedly in the wicker pram; its hood was shading him from the blazing August sun. Estella was sitting on the grass in the shade of the apple trees playing with Stephan's wooden blocks, piling them up and then knocking them down with glee. Stephan was at her side pulling the yellow and green peppers from the plants while she picked the ripe tomatoes off the vines. Last summer, she had ignored the garden and they had suffered in the winter for lack of food preserved and stocked in the cellar.

She looked at the bowls of peppers and the basketful of tomatoes. It would be a steaming, busy day. Canning was a hot task in itself. The jars had to be sterilized in a scalding water bath and carefully dried. Anything less and mold would grow in the jars, ruining the contents and making all her hard work for naught.

She brushed a tendril of hair off her face and wiped her brow with the hem of her feed sack apron. She stood up straight and surveyed the rest of the garden. The beans were prolific and the carrots were popping their little orange tops out of the brown, loamy soil. The apple trees were burgeoning with fruit that would be ripe next month. The plum tree was still bearing fruit. The cherry trees had yielded forty jars of canned fruit for winter pies. The peach tree had also done well, due to the hot, humid summer.

"Come, Stephan, help mama carry the peppers into the kitchen." She checked the pram. Stash was still sleeping. She could get the vegetables into the house. Soon hunger would awaken him. She felt the heaviness of her breasts which the little one would be happy to lighten.

Mathilda

The last two weeks had been sheer pleasure. She had sailed on the *SS Prinz Oscar* as a passenger, not as an employee. She had dined lavishly, savoring roast beef and quail, instead of boiled beef and potatoes. She had the luxury of time to sit on a deck chair caressed by the ocean breezes as she remembered the past two months spent with her brothers, Auguste and Ludwig, and their families. Auguste was a first-time father. As she held her niece, maternal instincts she didn't know she had welled up in her with an intensity that was shocking, reinforcing her decision to change the course of her life. She visited with her stepsister, Emilia, who was now a grandmother. Like herself, Emilia had lost her mother when she was a little girl.

She had written to the Szatkowski family from Piotrkow. They were delighted that she had recognized their offer of employment as genuine. A position as clerk in their store in South Chicago was hers. She could board with them. They had no children and would love her companionship.

As she walked down the wooden gangplank and stepped on to the pier in Philadelphia, she reflected that it was exactly four months earlier that she had made her decision after seeing the horrors of the unsinkable *Titanic*. Today, August 20th, 1912, she was stepping foot on American soil, not as a ship line employee, but as an immigrant.

SEPTEMBER 1912

Maryanna

She stood with Michał in the cool shadows of the concrete block cellar surveying the sturdy shelves that he had put up for her along one wall. Jars of canned fruits and vegetables were lined up like so many soldiers at attention. Indeed, they were the army that would keep hunger at bay during the coming winter. There were quarts of red and green tomatoes, kapusta (it had been a bonanza year for cabbages), Polish dill pickles, banana peppers, numerous jars of cherries, pears and peaches, twenty quarts of sliced apples for pies and thirty quarts of applesauce for the table.

Bags of onions and potatoes hung from the rafters. Herbs were strung together and hung up to dry. Michał had placed an order at the general store on Buffalo Avenue for sacks of flour, rice, sugar and salt. When the provisions came in, he hired a horse and cart to fetch them from the store. She set the pots used for sterilizing the canning jars on the shelf. She breathed a deep sigh of satisfaction. Her family would be well fed during the frigid months that would soon be upon them.

Michał pulled the string that operated the single light bulb. She walked outside into the late September sunshine while he shut the cellar door. Together, they climbed the cement steps up to the back yard where Stash was sleeping in the pram. Estella was squealing with delight throwing a ball with Stephan. He put his arm around her waist. She felt the soothing brush of his mustache as he kissed her cheek while the aureate autumn sun poured down its benediction.

Mathilda

After breathing the fresh air of the ocean for six years, she was unprepared for the unwavering haze from the steel mill which was three blocks from the Szatkowski's General Store. There was no escaping it. On board ship, after enduring the foul air of the lower decks, she could walk up on the promenade deck and fill her lungs with unpolluted ocean air. Here, the red-orange dust from the mill hung in the air as long as the mill was in operation which was every hour of every day of every week of every month. Blast furnaces could not be turned on and off at will, she learned. It took days to bring one up to the proper heat to melt the ores that created the steel.

Whenever she wasn't waiting on customers, she spent every minute dusting the tables where sundry items were enticingly on display. As soon as she wiped a surface clean, the grimy, reddish film would coat it again. It was a losing battle.

There was one breath of air that did refresh her; it came in the form of a very proper gentleman who frequented the store. He intrigued her. His clothing was that of a laborer in the mills, but his manner was more polished. And a man, any man, was a rarity in a general store, unless he owned it. If a woman was shopping for a suitor, a general store was not the place to look, even though it did carry items that men used, like shaving mugs and soap and razors. Married women did the shopping for their husbands. And single men coaxed their landladies to pick up whatever they needed.

She noticed that Helena Szatkowski seemed to know what items he would buy and began collecting them as soon as she saw him enter the store. He was about forty years old with dark brown hair, always well combed, and a mustache to match. He was of medium height and build. She sensed there was power in his muscles camouflaged by his workman's jacket. She noticed that he spoke fluent Polish with Helena and a little less fluent Czech with Mrs. Janota who lived down the street and happened to be in the store the first time she saw him. The second time, she noticed him glancing in her direction as he waited at the counter for Helena to complete his order. She turned away and busied herself with stocking cans of corn on the shelf.

"Dzień dobry, Panu, *Good day, sir,*" she greeted him, the third time she saw him. Helena had gone to her home a few blocks away on South Park Drive. She had been left alone in the store.

"Dzień dobry, Pana, *Good day, madam.*" He smiled broadly as he handed her the list of items he needed, enough for a family. It was odd that he did the shopping and not his wife. Perhaps, his wife was ailing. He had brought two sturdy sacks with him for the potatoes, apples and canned items. She tore a brown paper bag from the string and filled it with the tomatoes and fresh bread. He hoisted the bags from the counter.

"Dziękuje, Pana. *Thank you, madam,*" he said, flashing a huge smile that turned up the ends of his mustache.

"Proszę. *You are welcome,"* she responded.

"Helena," she asked when her employer returned a few minutes later, "who is that gentleman who comes in every week for groceries? I never see his wife. Is she ill?"

"Good gracious, no, Mathilda," Helena chuckled. "Franciszek is a widower. He's been coming to the store ever since we opened it two years ago. He's a boarder with Mrs. Homer, on Marquette Avenue, to be exact. It's about a mile from here. The area is mostly small farms and prairie. It is starting to build up. But there aren't any stores. He helps his landlady by picking up her groceries on his way home from work.

"Mrs. Janota told me that he had married a widow with two children in Czechoslovakia. They had a daughter; his wife died from diabetes when the little girl was four years old. She said that he came to America nine years ago. When Anieska was fifteen, he sent for her and her stepbrother. Last month Anieska married a young man, Mike. They met while taking English classes at Sullivan School. Frank, everyone calls him that, also went to Sullivan School when he first came to South Chicago. He speaks English quite well, but isn't comfortable with it.

"Mathilda, all the young widows around here look longingly at Frank. They know he is upright and would treat them and their children well. He has shown no interest in any of them."

A gleam came into Helena's eyes. "You, with your dark blond hair and blue eyes, might have caught his eye. I saw him looking in your direction last week. He would be a good husband. If he shows any interest in you, I hope that you will reciprocate."

Her face flushed as Helena spoke about Frank. The wounds in her heart, once so raw and deep, were healed. Her heart was now craving the closeness of a relationship. Even if it wasn't the tumultuous love that she had felt for Gottlieb, it would be better than the abject loneliness she had endured for so many years.

She was at the counter the next time Frank came into the store. Helena murmured something about a task she had to do in the back room and scurried away. Frank's face creased into a smile of pleasure when he saw her standing there. He greeted her and handed his list to her. The nape of her neck grew warm as she felt him watching her dart about the store. Her cheeks flushed. He was waiting for her at the end of the counter and took the heavy basket from her. He carried it to the register and packing area. As she tallied up his order, he watched her with smiling eyes. When the bill was paid and the groceries packed, he did not pick up the sacks.

"Jak się nazywasz? Jestem Franciszek Kravczyk. Wszyscy nazywaja mnie Frank. *What is your name? I am Franciszek Kravczyk. Everyone calls me Frank.*"

"Jestem Mathilda Lenz. *I am Mathilda Lenz.*"

"Ah, you are German, yet you speak Polish so well."

"My parents were German. I grew up in Piotrkow."

"Mathilda," he said gently, savoring the name. "Mathilda, on Sunday, if you would consent, I would like to walk with you out toward the prairie. The breezes of autumn have cooled the air which is fresher on the prairie than it is so close to the steel mill."

"You are most gracious to ask. I would like that."

"It will be a most lovely afternoon. I will call for you at two o'clock."

She was sure that he already knew, but she explained to him that she was boarding with the Szatkowski's.

He nodded his understanding, picked up the parcels and slowly walked toward the door. He turned and bowed slightly toward her.

She was standing befuddled as Helena came bustling out of the back room. No doubt Helena had heard everything and purposely stayed out of sight. She was right. Helena was bubbling.

"I knew it, Mathilda," she chortled, excitedly. "When Henry and I found out that you were coming to South Chicago, I told Henry that if ever there was a match for Frank, it would be you."

"Helena, Frank only asked if I would like to walk with him on Sunday. Nothing more."

"Mathilda, it is a walk into your future. I know it."

NOVEMBER 1912

Maryanna

Michał had finished the kielbasa and potatoes and was leaning back in his chair, lighting up a cigar. She refilled his coffee cup and added the dollop of milk that he liked.

"Michał, it is time to take in boarders again. I don't like seeing you work so hard, all those extra hours. Ignacy wrote to me that he is not coming back to work in the mill. There is so much unrest and dissension in Europe that it is palpable. He said that he can feel in his bones that a massive war will break out. He is worried that if he comes back here to work and war does break out, he will not be able to get back home. If war does breaks out he wants to be home with Stanisława and their children. He has four now: Katarzyna is almost twelve; Adama is nine, Felix is four. The little one, born in September, is Zygmunt. Ignacy knows many single young men in Mostki who are eager to come here. We can use the extra bedroom as lodging for a boarder or two."

"Are you sure you want to do this again, Maryanna?"

"Yes. You were by my side and helped me live after losing Dora, even though your heart was broken, too. If you agree, after the holy days of Christmas, I will write to Ignacy. Two men can easily share the bedroom. They will be working most of the time. There will only be a little extra wash. Two more mouths to feed are nothing. The cellar is well stocked. The extra income will help."

Mathilda

She sat in her chemise as Helena worked her dark honey tresses into a coil low on the back of her head. She wasn't much at keeping up with fashion, but Helena was. Although Helena was only ten years older than she, the woman had become a mother hen ever since her arrival in Chicago. Helena had fussed and clucked over her every step of the way. In the beginning, she had difficulty adjusting to the idea of being the object of someone's sincere concern. It had always been the other way around. She was exceedingly grateful to Helena for pampering her.

She wasn't sure who was more excited about her marriage to Frank. It had to be Helena who was running around like a chicken without a head, a phenomenon which she had personally witnessed working on a farm. For herself, it was the interminable longing to be with him for the rest of her life.

How quickly a Sunday afternoon walk in September had blossomed into a full-blown love for each other. That Sunday, enormous emotions stirred within her; emotions that had lain dormant ever since Gottlieb died. While her outward appearance spoke of the woman she was at age thirty, inside she was eighteen again and reeling from the tides coursing within her. She knew that Frank felt the same. Each time they walked, he pressed his hand a little more firmly into hers; he walked a little closer. During those Sunday afternoon walks, the streets of America were truly paved with gold for her. Not only the streets, but the sun, the leaves falling in autumn splendor, the air, the sky.

They shared their history with each other. Frank confirmed that he was a widower; his only daughter, Agnieska, had married Mike in August. She spoke of the untimely deaths of her parents, of her years of servanthood and caring for her brothers, of her years as an interpreter on the steam ships. He had lost his first love and she spoke of hers that had never come to fruition.

On their fourth walk, they strolled up South Park Avenue to 79th Street and Rainbow Beach. Frank had taken her to the beach on their first walk. She had been enthralled with Lake Michigan, a lake so big that you could not see the opposite shore.

The day was sunny, but rife with the chill of October. A west wind was at their backs as they sat on the narrow breakwater just north of the steel mill. They sat silently, holding hands and watching the waves crash onto the stone steps below them. A few sea gulls soared, dove and soared again.

"Mathilda," Frank spoke her name softly, as he took both of her hands in his. "We are not ignorant youngsters just starting out in life. Both of us have experienced joy and tragedy. We have worked hard and survived. Next month, I will be forty years old. Not a strong or a young man. But I feel there is still life within me. I want to share that life with you. Could you love me and share life with me as my wife?"

"Frank, you must already sense that I have love for you. I can think of no greater joy than being your wife."

Frank released her hands, drawing her toward him and kissing her cheek. The soft brush of his mustache tingled on her skin hours later as they sat on the wall planning their future together. Months earlier, she had felt the stirrings deep inside her, in her womb longing to be filled with child. What had been a dream then was now a possibility.

"Mathilda, there is one matter of great importance to me. I am Catholic and my faith is a core part of who I am. I am a widower, so I can marry again within the church. It is my desire."

"Frank, my dear parents were Lutheran. Through the years of working for families and on ships, it has not been possible for me to attend church services. But I do believe in God, a good God Who has guided me through life and Who has brought us together. Whatever it takes to become a Catholic, I will be happy to do."

And so had begun the thrice weekly sessions with Fr. Kowicki at St. Mary Magdalene parish. It was a new solid brick structure on Saginaw Avenue in a developing neighborhood burgeoning with Polish Catholic children. From the vestibule, steps led down to the church on the first level. The upper two levels housed the school and the convent for the Felician sisters who taught the children.

Every Tuesday, Wednesday, and Thursday, for three weeks, Frank stopped at the store after his shift ended at three o'clock. Helena shooed her out the door and they walked a goodly mile down 83rd Street past Russell Square Park, St. Michael the Archangel cathedral, Sullivan School and then on to the boarding house on Marquette Avenue where Frank lived. The further west they walked, the fewer were the homes.

Mrs. Homer, Frank's landlady, happily included Mathilda at her supper table. She noticed that Mrs. Homer, who wasn't much older than Frank, fussed over him like Helena did over her. After supper, they walked the two blocks down Marquette Avenue to the rectory for her catechism lessons. Afterward, Frank would escort her back to her home.

"So, what name have you chosen?" asked Fr. Kowicki at the conclusion of the last lesson.

"Name?"

"Yes, the saint's name you will take when you are baptized."

"I did not know that I needed to choose a name."

"Sophia," Frank said. "Your name should be Sophia - Sophie."

"An excellent choice," said the priest. "It is a name honored for centuries in the church. It means wisdom."

And so, yesterday she was baptized and was now Sophie. It felt like a kiss whenever Frank said her name; his lips puckered up as he pronounced the "So-."

A hairpin jab punctured her reverie. She saw Helena's ruddy face in the mirror beaming as she surveyed her handiwork.

"Now for your bridal dress, Mathilda, I mean Sophie. Oh dear, I don't think I'll ever get used to your new name," Helena chirped, excitedly.

As she and Frank were planning the wedding, she had decided on wearing her Sunday best dress and hat for the ceremony. After all, it would be a small ceremony with only a few people present, most of whom she had known for only a few months. Helena would have none of that. She took her to the bridal shop on Commercial Avenue and helped her select a dress and veil and all the accessories, oohing at this and tsk-tsking at that. Emphatically, Helena stated that the wedding finery was a bridal gift from her and Henry.

Helena slipped the dress over her head; her fingers never faltering as she fastened the long row of pearl buttons down the back of the dress. She bade Sophie sit down while she fastened the veil to her hair.

Sophie stood up and turned toward the full-length mirror to see herself in all her nuptial splendor. She did not recognize the woman staring back at her. The bridal gown was exquisite. White taffeta formed a strapless underbodice and underskirt. Snow white tulle striped with delicate lace formed the bodice, the high neckband, and the full Edwardian sleeves which were gathered into a slim sleeve along the forearm. The deeply tucked waistband and bretelles, trimmed in lace, were fashioned of tulle as was the full skirt which was lavishly adorned with lace florets. Soft tulle edged in lace formed her veil crowned with artificial flowers.

She felt surreal dressed in so much finery as she stepped out under a cool, sunny sky of a Tuesday morning in November. Henry helped her up onto the cowhide leather seat of his gleaming black buggy; Helena climbed in beside her. As the horse clopped along, she delighted in being driven to church, instead of walking.

"Here comes the bride!" chanted Mrs. Homer's daughter, as the buggy pulled up to the church. She and her mother were standing with Frank, his daughter, Agnieska, Mike and his sister and niece, awaiting her arrival. Mike's niece had been the flower girl at his wedding to Agnieska in August and was happy to reprise the role. The arrival of the bride was their cue to enter the church and they trooped in with several other neighbors.

She felt like a queen as Henry helped her out of the buggy with Helena behind her making sure her gown and veil didn't snag or get hung up as she stepped down. As soon as she was firmly on the ground, Helena flitted around her adjusting her gown and veil while Henry tethered the horse. Then, he walked to her side and crooked his arm. She put her hand on his forearm and walked with him into the church, up the aisle to the altar where Frank was waiting. As Henry put her hand into Frank's, its warmth radiated into her

36

hand and through every cell of her being. She didn't recite the vows of matrimony; she said each word with full knowledge that she would be united to Frank for as long as she lived.

As Henry drove them to the photographer's studio on Commercial Avenue for the portraits, she was aware of nothing but the closeness of Frank now sitting next to her in the buggy. He held her hand in his as Helena sat upfront next to Henry, chatting away. She never heard a word Helena said.

Merriment was in abundance as was the Polish food on which the guests feasted. She marveled at the quantities of pierogi, kapusta, roasted chicken, kielbasa, kolacky that appeared effortlessly from Helena's kitchen and just as effortlessly were reduced to crumbs. As the afternoon sun began to wane, she and Frank thanked their guests profusely and took leave of the merrymakers, eager to begin their new life together.

That night she learned that Frank did, indeed, have much life in his forty-year-old body. She reveled in the intensity of sensations that she had never felt before.

CHAPTER THREE

MARCH 1914

Sophie

An overabundance of pillows cushioned her back while in her arms she cradled the most amazing sight she had seen in her thirty-one years of life: a little girl, with her father's deep brown eyes and wisps of his dark brown hair framing her tiny face. Mrs. Jarecki was straightening up the bedroom. She felt refreshed by the sponge bath that the połwożna had given. As the little one began to whimper and squirm, Mrs. Jarecki taught her how to suckle her daughter at her breast. She was a mother!

"Matka Sophie," Frank announced, as he entered the bedroom and sat down next to her on the bed. He slid his arm around her shoulders as he beheld the miracle of his newest daughter, Julianna Sophie. It was a moment of sheer bliss.

Maryanna

She dumped the chicken pieces into the boiling water to cook, then began cutting up the celery, carrots and onions for the soup. Spring sunlight flooded the wooden table in the kitchen where she worked methodically. She had sent her sister Stella with three-year-old Estella to buy the Polish rye bread that Michał loved. She wasn't much of a baker. Michałowski's bakery did a much better job than she ever could. Stephan was at school. Sitting in the center of the kitchen, Stash was happily banging pots and pans together. He would be two years old next month. While Stephan was more reserved, Stash was carefree, happy with everything. She kept chopping vegetables for the huge pot of soup that would be their mainstay for the next few days.

Michał had agreed to her desire to have boarders in the house. To her chagrin, however, they did not turn out to be men working long hours at the mill. Instead, they were her younger sisters.

Stella arrived last summer. Ignacy apologized profusely to her in his letter a year ago. He had been talking to their younger brother, Stanisław, about America and Michał's willingness to have boarders. Stanisław did not readily embrace the possibility; he was apprenticed to a farmer and was happy working in the fields.

Stella overheard the conversation and immediately jumped on Ignacy. Why couldn't she go? There were no prospects for her in Osiek Dolnoslakie. Look at how well Maryanna had done in America. Would her dear brother deny her the same opportunity? Ignacy was an easy pushover when it came to his baby sisters, Stella and Teodora. He was fifteen when Stella was born, almost old enough to be her father.

In the six years since she had seen her, Stella had blossomed from a gawky fourteen-year-old girl into a woman of twenty. She was shorter than Maryanna but similar in features with the same ebony hair and dark eyes. She smiled readily and easily. She was an older version of Stash; she was happy and content with the simple joys of life.

Stella found employment as a hatmaker at Dom Mody, a dress and millinery shop on Commercial Avenue. She insisted on paying board to her older sister. Estella had gravitated toward her aunt, as if Stella was a magnet. When Estella wasn't napping and her aunt was home, the two of them would be holed up in Stella's bedroom, singing and laughing.

She would never forget that evening in early December when they were sitting in the parlor, relaxing after a day of hard work. The knocker on the front door sounded. Michał opened the door.

"Dobry wieczór! *Good evening!*" she heard a young voice giggle. She hurried to the door.

"Teodora!" she exclaimed as she embraced her sixteen-year-old baby sister. "Michał, this is my youngest sister, Teodora, and..." She had no idea who the jittery young man was.

"Oh! Maryanna, this is Michael, my husband. At least that's what we put on the ship's manifest. We were able to have a space to ourselves that way," Teo giggled again.

"Come in! I didn't know you were coming! Did you write to us and the letter was lost?" she asked, noting the roundness of her sister's stomach as she entered the house into the lighted parlor where Stella jumped up from the side chair and ran to hug her sister with exuberance.

"We didn't have time," Michael said, as he tossed two ratty bags into the tiny hall.

"How did you get here?" Michał asked.

"Ignacy helped us get tickets for the ship and train. We left port on November 22nd," Teo bubbled. "We came into New York three days ago, on December 2nd. Before we left home, Ignacy gave us money for the train and told us how to find you. He said that you would help us."

"When are you due?" she asked.

"Three months, or so."

"We extend our welcome to you," Michał said, reservedly. "I will help Michael with a job at Carnegie Steel. You are welcome to stay with us until you have your baby."

"Teodora, you and Michael can have my room. I will happily sleep on this sofa until you have the baby. Oh, I am so excited to see you!" Stella embraced her sister, her partner-in-crime back home, a second time.

"Come," she said, to her sister and Michael. "You must be hungry. Let me prepare a meal. Meanwhile, warm yourselves with a hot cup of coffee."

"Coffee!" Teodora exclaimed. "We haven't been able to get coffee back home in two years. How wonderful!" She and Michael plopped themselves on the sofa.

Three weeks later, on New Year's Eve, Teodora and Michael were legally married. Eager to embrace the ways of their new homeland, her youngest sister called her husband 'Mike' and he called her 'Teo'. Teo's baby was due any day now.

The chicken was boiled. She removed the pieces from the water with a slotted spoon and put them on a plate to cool so she could pull the meat off the bones. She allowed the water in the pot to cool before skimming the fat from it. Then, she added the vegetables to the pot, carrots first together with bay leaves and salt. When the carrots were half cooked, she added the celery and onions. She deboned the chicken and cut it into pieces, adding it to the pot. She lowered the heat and let the pot simmer to reduce the broth to a rich, golden consistency.

She was handing a peeled raw carrot to Stash to munch on, when she heard a sharp cry from the bedroom where Teo had been napping.

"Maryanna!" Teo was screaming. "Come quickly. Oh my God, the pain! I think the baby is coming!"

Teo's shouting startled Stash and he began to cry. Maryanna bent down to soothe him. As if on cue, Stella and Estella walked into the kitchen. Her sister had a basket full of fresh rye and white breads. Her daughter had a tiny basket which she held carefully so as not to break the crullers inside.

"Your timing is perfect," she said to Stella, as Teo let out another loud cry which frightened Estella. "We need the połwożna. Mrs. Pruzak lives on the next block at 8342 Saginaw. Go to her house and tell her that Teo's labor has begun. It is her first baby. Take Estella and Stash with you, so I can prepare the bedroom for the birth."

She set a large pot on the stove and poured water into it, setting it on a low heat. She gathered towels of various sizes, sheets, baby blankets and nappies. She filled a bowl with cool water and set it on the table next to Teo's bed. All the while she spoke softly but firmly to Teo. Teo's pains were coming regularly, but she knew from her own experience that the birth would not happen for hours.

She greeted a hungry Michał at the door when he arrived home from work. She set out a soup bowl, filled it with the hot chicken soup, taking care to give him the largest pieces of chicken together with the vegetables and broth. She cut several generous slices of the fresh rye bread and set it on the table with the tub of butter. She filled a large mug with steaming coffee and added a touch of milk. She put several of the crullers on a plate by the cup. All was ready by the time he had finished washing his hands.

When Mrs. Pruzak arrived, she tended to a terrified Teo with the experience of her many years. She, herself, had borne nineteen children, of which fifteen had survived. Her huge family was legend in the neighborhood.

All evening, Michał and Stella looked after Stephan, Estella and Stash. It allowed her to sit by her baby sister's bedside, wiping her sweaty brow with cool cloths, soothing her and letting Teo dig her nails into her arms as each contraction reached its climax. Her little sister was so ignorant of the aftermath of lovemaking. As the eldest daughter, not only did she have her own experiences of childbirth, but she had seen her mother go through labor with Stanisław and Teo. While being the baby of the family had its pleasures, the position blinded one to the realities of life.

Shortly after midnight, in the wee hours of March 14, Teo gave birth to a daughter; she also chose the name, Estelle. She took her niece from Mrs. Pruzak and washed her, gently but thoroughly. The little one had brown hair much lighter than her own children's and gray eyes. She rubbed lotion on the little body, diapered her, and wrapped her in blankets while the midwife tended to the afterbirth and assessed that all was well with Teo.

She placed the newborn into the arms of her mother. When the room was straightened, she called Mike to come in and meet his daughter. He worked the late shift and arrived home shortly before the baby was born. As he entered the room, she exited and closed the door on the new family.

JULY 1915

Sophie

The latest battles in Europe were temporarily forgotten as the gossips in the neighborhood buzzed with the salacious news in the *Dzienik Chicagoski,* the Polish daily newspaper. The lifeless body of a newborn baby had been found in the maid's quarters at the South Shore Country Club on 71st Street and the lakefront. Questioning of the employees by the police confirmed that the mother was a young, unmarried, Polish woman named Jozefa. The young woman stated that her sister was not able to bear children. Her sister's husband became obsessed with dying childless. He had paid for her passage from Europe. With her sister's consent, she had entered into an agreement to bear a child for him and her sister. When the child was stillborn, she did not know what to do. The brother-in-law confirmed her story. The death of the child was ruled as accidental, but both were sentenced to three months in the Bridewell for concealing a death.

She ran her hands down the long apron stretched over her ever-expanding waistline. Her baby was due in four months; she had begun to feel it kick. Never could she imagine Frank doing such a thing. He did not need to bolster his ego and prove he was a man. She tried to fathom the workings of the man's mind; she failed. Why was it that important for the man to raise a child that came from him when there were so many orphans who needed homes? How could his wife be so complicit in such a doing? Was she coerced? Or, had she entered into his obsession to such a degree that she was willing to do anything, even sacrifice her own sister, to his dementedness?

That evening she saw Frank shake his head as he read the official article in the newspaper.

"Sophie, this man is the brother of my coworker, Piotr Bilinski. Piotr is hurt, angry and embarrassed to think that his flesh and blood would engage in such immoral behavior. He had no idea that that was the reason his brother had sent for his sister-in-law. He has only seen Jozefa a few times since she arrived in South Chicago.

"Piotr says that she is a gentle, trusting soul. She, too, had come through Ellis Island as he did and they shared their stories of the process. Piotr was horrified to learn that she had been detained at Ellis Island because she had insufficient funds to travel to Chicago. He shook his head as he said to me, 'How could my brother be so callous as to allow her to travel cheaply in steerage with all its discomforts and not even provide her with enough money to travel safely to Chicago? And for what purpose?'"

SEPTEMBER 1915

Maryanna

Yesterday, Stella had happily traipsed up to the attic and brought the boxes down. It was time to transfer their contents to a drawer in the dresser. One box held the baby blankets. She picked up the one on top. It had been a gift from her landlady on Buffalo Avenue. She closed her eyes and there was Stephan, snug in the ecru wool. Born five minutes before midnight on Christmas Eve, Michał said that giving him a healthy son was the best gift she could ever present to him.

This baby was due any day now. It was three years since Stash was born and she was happy to feel life inside her. Truth be told, she loved being pregnant. She never experienced many of the side effects which plagued most women. Michał said she blossomed when she was with child.

Teo was expecting her second child in December. They both hoped the cousins would be boys who would grow up together, more as twin brothers, than cousins. As she stretched to put the baby blankets into the drawer, she felt the first mild contraction. After four babies, she knew this one would come quickly. She called to seven-year-old Stephan who was reading to Estella and Stash, and bade him run and tell Mrs. Pruzak that the baby was coming. She pulled the pierzyna off the bed, so it wouldn't get stained, and set it on the rocker in the corner. She pulled out the towels and turned the gas on under the huge pot of water on the stove. Yesterday, Michał had filled it for her and set it on the stove.

Michał, the younger, arrived with a lusty cry that his father heard in the kitchen. She smiled, tired but happy. Then, as she watched helplessly, his skin turned sallow. It was the fatal anemia, Mrs. Pruzak explained, with a mixture of knowledge and sorrow. The lusty cry sank slowly into a whimper until he breathed his last. Four hours after his birth, she sat stone-faced cradling the body of her lifeless son.

NOVEMBER 1915

Sophie

The little one nestled contentedly in her arms as she sat in the oversized rocker nursing her. Albina was definitely her daughter with wisps of honey blond hair and eyes like the color of the sky on a sunny winter's day. She was overjoyed. Her newborn was strong and healthy with robust arms and legs that confirmed all the activity she had felt in her womb for the last three months.

Little Julia sat next to her watching her baby sister nurse. She would be two years old in March. She had been weaned in September to ensure an adequate supply of milk for this little one who seemed insatiable. While Julia was a quiet child, she was sure that Albina would be the exact opposite.

APRIL 1916

Maryanna

"Maryanna, I could use that," Teo said, as she sat in the rocker in her sister's bedroom, absentmindedly bouncing John on her knee. "You aren't thinking of sending that to Stanley, are you?"

"Yes, I am, Teo." She didn't look up at Teo. If she did, she would see John and all the emotions she had dealt with in the past six months would come raging back. She didn't want her mind to begin the unsolvable debate. Why did Teo's John live? Why did her little Michał die at birth? She took the large beige blanket, wrapped it in soft paper and put it in the box for Josephine's baby.

"Teo, I will give you the items that are suitable for a boy, but all clothing and anything else that can be used for a girl, I am sending to Stanisław and Josephine. They do not have access to stores down in southern Illinois as we do up here."

"I don't understand why Stanley didn't stay up here," Teo pouted. "It was so nice to see him again."

"I miss him, too, Teo. When I left home almost ten years ago, he was only twelve. When he arrived last summer, I was delighted to see the man he has become and proud to call him my brother. He was happy being a farmer back home and I don't think he would have come to America if the war hadn't changed his life.

"Stanisław loves working outside in the fields in the sun and the fresh air. He felt stifled in the mill, even though the wages are good. That's why he went downstate to LaSalle."

Teo interrupted her. "I wonder what Josephine is like?" she asked, twirling a strand of John's brown hair in her fingers. "She's younger than I am! Too young to be having babies."

"You should know. You were only sixteen when you showed up at my door with Mike, and Estelle on the way."

"We were in love, Maryanna, so in love!"

"Do you think that Stanisław and Josephine don't love each other? You grew up with him, Teo. You know him better than I do. I remember him as a boy who loved the outdoors and wanted to bring home every hurt creature that he found and nurse it. Mama had to put a stop to that. The house was

45

too small for all of us. If Stanisław had his way, we would have been sharing our beds, not only with each other, but with dogs and cats, birds and pigs. What was he like as he grew into manhood?"

"Not much different," Teo mused. "He was always embracing one cause or another, listening to the rabble rousers who roamed the villages spouting their ideas. The only time he seemed truly happy was when he was apprenticed to that farmer. The farmer was a good man. I think Stanley looked upon him as a replacement for our dad. I think that's why it hit him so hard when the farm was confiscated and he could no longer work with the man."

"Right now, he needs all the help we can give, Teo. We have a niece. A niece that he named Theodora after you." And after my beloved Dora, she thought, silently.

She closed the box now filled to the brim with the necessities every baby needed. Michał would take it to the Post Office on Commercial Avenue later in the day.

"Come, Teo," she said, walking out of the bedroom and into the kitchen. "Let's have a cup of coffee and a piece of the streusel coffeecake that Stella bought at the bakery this morning."

DECEMBER 1916

Sophie

Frank stomped his feet on the mat by the door as he entered the apartment and took off his coat, hat, gloves and overshoes. A few flakes of snow on his mustache were as cool on her cheek as his lips were warm on hers. He kissed the top of Julia's head as she sat on the floor. He lifted Albina, putting the little one on his lap as he sat down next to her on the worn plum-colored sofa. She thrilled to see the tenderness in his eyes as he gazed at his newest daughter, Irena, in the glow of the candlelight.

She slid her hand from under her sleeping newborn and clasped his. Could there ever be a more perfect Christmas? Two days ago, she brought forth Irena, as strong and healthy as Albina. Yesterday, Frank surprised her with a little Christmas tree which he placed on the round oak table by the windows in the parlor. The table was covered with a round linen cloth that her mother had embroidered when she was expecting her brother, Auguste. This treasured link to her mother was the only possession that she had carried with her through all the years of servanthood and working on ships. It had taken on an ivory sheen over the years; now it shone in the light of the candles that Frank had put on the tree.

"Sophie," Frank said. "I forgot to tell you. I saw Piotr at work yesterday. Jozefa gave birth to a healthy boy on the twentieth. They named him Władysław. Piotr is so happy."

The good news was an unexpected Christmas present which gave her happiness. Piotr was a good man. While his brother and sister-in-law left the city as soon as he was released from the Bridewell, Piotr focused his concern on the abandoned Jozefa. Frank had told her how Piotr vigorously defended Jozefa against any salacious remarks made by his coworkers. This past January, he had married her, putting an end to all the ribaldry made at her expense. She was now his wife; he was her protector. She, in turn, had given Piotr a son.

She settled back, cuddling against Frank. Never could she have imagined a Christmas such as this. Perfect contentment, sitting in the glow of the candles with a loving husband at her side and three beautiful, healthy daughters surrounding her. She felt a kindred spirit to the Mother and Child that Christmas celebrates.

APRIL 1917

Sophie

For the second time in less than two months, she stood in the parlor staring at a small white casket in which her daughter was resting. On the round table next to it was a profusion of candles and flowers from friends and neighbors.

Her mind flashed back to Christmas morning and the tree that had stood on the table, an evergreen, symbolizing everlasting life. Her daughters, so healthy that day, were now as lifeless as the dried needles that had fallen from the tree in January. Little Irena had never lived to see even three full months of life. She was stricken by the diphtheria in February. Every maternal instinct within her had raged powerlessly as she had watched her baby slowly die, struggling to breathe as the disease ravaged her tiny lungs and suffocated her. She thought that her heart had been bled dry as she ached to hold Irena in her arms again.

She had been wrong. Fresh waves of grief assailed her as she gazed at the little cherub face of sixteen-month-old Albina whose body was resting peacefully after the same struggle. Albina had giggled and laughed and run all over the apartment eager to explore every new thing, clapping tiny hands which now lay lifeless on her chest. If she could only feel those hands patting her cheeks once more!

Through the holiest days of Christian faith, she had done everything she could to help her child live. In the end, she was as helpless as the Holy Mother had been on that first Good Friday as She watched her Jesus die. She wondered why it was called good. What is good about watching the love of your heart slowly die? Through Holy Saturday and Easter Sunday, she had watched Albina weaken in her fight with an infection that was stronger than she. Yesterday, on Easter Monday morning, Albina had taken her last breath as she lay limp in her mother's arms.

She felt Julia tugging at her skirt. She bent down and lifted her up in her arms. She watched as her oldest daughter, now her only daughter, stared solemnly at the peaceful face of her little sister. What was going through her child's mind? How could a three-year-old comprehend death when her thirty-five-year-old mother couldn't? Why were these little ones given to her for such a short time only to be cruelly snatched away?

She felt Frank's arm around her. There was a tremor in his muscles. She knew without looking that tears bathed his eyes. She was comforted. She had Frank. The Holy Mother had no spouse to put his arm around her; her Joseph had been long gone.

NOVEMBER 1918

Maryanna

"Michał, I want to go," she said, as she stood in front of the mirror over the dresser, pinning up her snow-white hair. Her hair had turned white when she was twenty-seven years old. People said it was because of the loss of Dora. That was poppycock.

"I want to go before the ground hardens and the snow makes it impossible to travel." In these last three years, it was the one thing that she missed about the villages back home. The graveyards were always next to the churches or a short walk to the edge of town. Here the cemetery was miles away amidst farmland. She would never understand why.

She leaned into him as he came behind her, kissing the nape of her neck. She wanted - she needed - to visit her babies. In truth, he wanted to visit them, too. They never spoke much about it amidst the constant work of everyday life.

"Whatever you want, Maryanna. If Sunday is a good day, we can take the children out on the trolley. It will be good for them to breathe the fresh air of farmland."

Sunday lived up to its name with cloudless skies and an unusually gentle breeze. She, Michał and the children, dressed in their Sunday best, walked to the trolley stop on 93rd Street. The trolley took them to Michigan City Road in Calumet City. From there it was a short walk down a gravel road to Holy Cross cemetery. She had packed a small wicker basket with a canteen of water and treats for the children. They would be hungry in the middle of the afternoon.

As she stood at the gravesites, the pain of seven years clutched at her heart. She stared at the dates on the tombstones: April 1911, September 1915, February 1917, February 1918. Seven years had passed since she lost Dora. Three years ago, little Michał lived exactly four hours. A year and a half later, Elzbieta, lived less than one day. This past February, she had lost Władysław; he was stillborn. She would never know these children, flesh of her flesh and Michał's. What would each of them have been like? How would they have looked? Acted? Sounded? What would have repelled them? Delighted them?

A squeal erupted behind her. Six-year-old Stash was chasing Estella through the empty field across from the cemetery. While she had lost much, she had much for which to be grateful; those two imps and Stephan who was standing next to her, his dark eyes inhaling everything they saw. She called out to Estella and Stash. These were the children who had survived. When they ran to her side, she opened the basket and handed each one a biscuit and the canteen of water which they shared. Life went on.

"I'm ready to go," she said to Michał. They embraced each other, then turned and made the sign of the cross as they gazed on the multitude of tiny graves that dotted the Guardian Angels section of the cemetery.

Sophie

She clutched the little one to her breast, greedily. The dark blond hair and blue eyes were so much like her own. Just like Albina, Victoria had her mother's looks and a healthy glow in her cheeks. But she knew what could happen. Painful memories of Albina and Irena in their little white caskets assailed her.

She had empathized with the women on shipboard who had lost babies and children, with the women in the neighborhood who had stillbirths and experienced the deaths of their children from pneumonia, diphtheria, diarrheas, and croup. Not until she became one of them did she understand the depth of grief that the loss of the fruit of the womb could evoke. Now there was an epidemic of influenza that was sweeping the country and the world. It was called the Spanish flu. Thousands of people around the world were dying every day; no age was immune. The old and the young were the most vulnerable.

Desperately, she began to pray in silence. "Please, dear God, do not take this little one from me. Please!"

As though she could read her thoughts, Mrs. Jarecki, the połwożna who had assisted her during the births of all of her daughters, sat down on the bed next to her.

"Sophie, Sophie," she said, tenderly. "Your grief is still so fresh. It is less than two years since you lost your darling daughters. I helped you bring those little babies into this world. I rejoiced with you when they were born and grieved with you when you lost them. But only you know how profound is the grief in your heart.

"Of the six children that I bore, only two survived. Each time, I thought I could never feel such pain and live. Each time, I did feel such pain, and lived. Those four babies of mine are the reason I became a połwożna. Not only to experience the joys of a mother giving birth, but also to grieve with her when she lost a child. To let her know that she is not alone, that her grief is real, that another child will never replace the one lost, that in time our hearts do heal and we can feel joy again.

"Sophie, our men, most of them in this community, work in the steel mills taking raw ores and transforming them with much labor and sweat into the steel that is making possible the tall buildings they call skyscrapers. The men's strength is in their bodies. These are strong, tough men. They are men of steel.

"But we are strong, too. Perhaps, even stronger. For nine months we nourish the little one growing in our wombs. Then we labor and sweat to give birth. Our strength is not only in our bodies but also in our hearts and minds. When we lose a child, we have to take the rawness of grief and use it to build the lives of our living children so that one day they can stand tall and strong. We are the steel matkas."

OCTOBER 1919

Maryanna

She rejoiced with all her heart as she heard the spirited cry of the little daughter to whom she had just given birth. None of her other children had been so strident in their demand to be noticed. She laughed inwardly. This little one was saying, "Look, I'm here and I'm staying." She had given Michał another child, a daughter who was hale and hardy and ready to take on this new world. Sabina Sylvia would do well.

CHAPTER FOUR

OCTOBER 1920

Sophie

"Sophie! Sophie! Przyjdź szybko! *(Come quickly!)*" She heard timid Mrs. Mezydło shouting as loudly as she could. She dropped the wooden spoon on the table and ran out onto the rear porch. There was a large hole in the porch railing where a board should have been. Julia was standing by the hole holding her doll and crying. Victoria was nowhere to be seen. She flew down the two flights of stairs. She couldn't see beyond Mrs. Mezydło's ample figure at the bottom of the stairs. She could hear her murmuring, "Zdrowaś Marya, łaski pełna *Hail Mary, full of grace,*" as her rosary beads slipped through the fingers of her left hand. She dodged around her neighbor. Vicki was sitting in the grass. Her lips were bloody and there were cuts and bruises on her legs. As she lunged forward to examine her daughter's limbs, Vicki stood up. "Mama, mama," she called in a bewildered tone, raising her arms to be held. She scooped up her baby daughter and hugged her tightly.

"Vicki," she said, looking into her big blue eyes, "what were you doing?"

"I was sitting down, Mama."

"Were you leaning against the railing?"

"Just my back, mama."

She hugged her daughter again, as thoughts of what could have happened tumbled through her brain.

"Sophie, Sophie!" Mrs. Mezydło stammered. Tears were streaming down her face. "Matka Boża, *Mother of God,* I was sitting on the steps praying the

52

rosary when I saw her fall right in front of me! I thought she was dead. But she sat up!"

As her neighbor was voicing her terror, Frank walked into the yard and Vicki slid down out of her arms and ran to greet her papa. Frank gaped at his daughter's bleeding lips.

"Sophie, what happened?"

"Vicki is all right, Frank. A strut on the porch railing came loose and Vicki fell. She is okay. See, she is walking and running. It just happened. I will tend to the cuts. She will be fine."

Frank wasn't satisfied. He scooped Vicki up into his arms. "I'm taking her to Dr. Lubin," he said. "She could have internal injuries." He strode across the yard.

"Julia," she called. "Come down and sit with Mrs. Mezydło. Papa and I are taking Vicki to the doctor around the corner. We will be back soon." She had to race to keep up with Frank who was moving quickly down Exchange Avenue toward 87th Street and Commercial Avenue.

Dr. Lubin confirmed that Vicki was fine - and very lucky.

OCTOBER 1921

Maryanna

"Michał, Sabina's second birthday is Sunday. Let's celebrate with a big dinner and an afternoon of dancing." She was kneeling behind him on the bed kneading the soreness out of his shoulder muscles. He worked so hard to provide for her and his children and never complained. She kissed the nape of his neck as her fingers plied his taut muscles.

"A good idea," he replied, instantly. She knew he was smiling. As dignified as he was, a good mazurka or polka released his inhibitions. He was light on his feet. In his younger days he had danced the Russian cossack, squatting near the floor and kicking out one foot or the other to the frenetic rhythm of an accordion.

Her mind was already in full gear calculating how many people and children there would be. Her sister Stella had married Ludwig four years ago and now had three-year-old Vince; Teo would bring Estelle, John and her four-year-old Theodora. Their cousin, Josie, who had immigrated to South Chicago about three months before Teo, would bring Chester and Virginia. Josie's brother, Theodor, was only 18 years old when he emigrated the year Stephan was a baby. He had married Valeria eight years ago; they had no children and kept to themselves. It would be good to see them, if they accepted her invitation.

Teodor and Josie's dad, Jan, was her mother's brother. He had been her happy uncle back home in Poland. How she had looked forward to visits with Uncle Jan when she was a child! He was always singing songs and telling funny stories. Josie took after her dad. She and Teo had much in common; they were always looking for gay times. She wondered if Josie had anything else in common with her husband, Joseph, except their name. They were such opposites. Josie moved swiftly and laughed a lot, perhaps too much; Joseph was solemn and brooding. She wondered what her cousin had seen in Joseph. Perhaps, the marriage had been arranged back home? Josie never said and she would never ask.

The neighbors would come marching down the street with their specialty dishes. She could count on pierogi, babke, gołabki, crowding out her roasted chicken with kielbasa and kapusta. She would order a birthday cake from Michałowski's Gold Cup bakery.

The only item missing from the celebration would be the beer. This prohibition law was stupid. It had put the tavern owners out of business in the neighborhood. Those women who had shouted long and strong for the law had nothing better to do with their time. They knew nothing of a man's need to have a drink after a long, suffocating day in a steel mill; it relaxed them before going home to their wives and children.

She was a realist. She knew there were men who didn't know when to stop; their wives and children suffered because of it. Still, it didn't seem fair to punish everyone for the shortcomings of a minority.

Michał had never been one to frequent the taverns, but he did like his beer. There were several bottles of wine in the cellar; they would have to do. Michal would ask Andrzej to bring his accordion; the men would roll up the rug in the parlor. It would be a grand time.

Sophie

She and Frank sat side-by-side on the swing he had just hung on the underside of the big porch that spanned the front of the house. Autumn refused to believe it was October and embraced summer's warmth and its greenery. Faint touches of gold and orange tinged the still-green leaves. Seven-year-old Julia was sitting on a hassock in the parlor upstairs cross-stitching a child's sampler. Three-year-old Vicki and her friend, Tillie, were splashing in the pond across the street and feeding the goldfish. Their daughters were safe. She took Frank's hand, tenderly stroking the ever present callouses, the reward for all his hard work. How fortunate she was. She, who had once slept in barns, was living in a house with so many comforts, all thanks to this upright man who had chosen her to share life with him.

Last year she had witnessed a side of him that she had never seen before. He had always been calm and somewhat easygoing. After the porch railing gave way and Vicki fell into the yard, he had become like one possessed. He nailed pieces of wood to the railing. He installed a gate at the top of the steps leading to the apartment. No more apartments, he insisted; he would buy a house with a yard where his daughters could play safely.

Through all of last year he worked as many hours as he could at the rail yard saving for a down payment. He roamed the prairies looking for the right house. He found it at 8216 Manistee, one block from Mrs. Homer, his former landlady.

The house had been built around the turn of the century as a farmhouse. The upper floor consisted of a large kitchen, a parlor, and two bedrooms. Wide porches spanned the front and back of the house. Frank hired a plumber to install indoor plumbing. Part of the kitchen on the upper floor became a bathroom with a toilet, sink, and clawfoot bathtub.

One large area on ground level near the back entrance was outfitted with a double tub stand with a wringer in the middle. No longer would she have to wring out the soapy clothes by hand. He had electricity and gas lines installed. New windows were installed with storms and screens that could be changed with the seasons. The remainder of the ground level became the work kitchen with a deep porcelain sink, a ceramic gas stove and room for work tables and a dining table with chairs. There were storage shelves for food stuffs and pots and pans and, wonder of wonders, an icebox to keep milk and butter from going rancid.

East of the house, the streets on Burnham, Muskegon, and Exchange were paved and dense with housing. On Manistee and west, the roads were still gravel. There were a few houses scattered along Marquette, Saginaw and Colfax Avenues. Beyond that all was prairie. Contractors were considering building a row of brick bungalows across the street where the girls were playing in the pond.

"What more could we want out of life than what we have now." She leaned in to him as their feet slowly set the swing moving back and forth in a rhythm of contentment.

APRIL 1923

Sophie

"Frank, it's perfect. Exactly as it should be." Every evening for the past two weeks, he had worked on building a chicken coop for her. She had described to him what the poultry coops had looked like on the farms where she had worked as a young girl. He built it according to her description and erected a wire fence to surround it and give the chickens a place to run and eat.

On Saturday, Frank went to hire a horse and wagon. She fixed thick ham sandwiches on Polish rye bread and wrapped them in butcher paper. She filled a glass container with hot German potato salad. She put both into a hamper together with a small jar of Polish dill pickles. She added canteens of milk for the girls and coffee for herself and Frank. On top, she carefully placed a covered plate containing one of her twelve-egg pound cakes.

Vicki was running around outside, jumping up and down in anticipation of riding in a wagon with a real horse. Julia was sitting quietly on the rocker watching her fix the picnic basket. When Frank arrived, she helped her mother carry the basket and several old pierzynas to the wagon. Frank settled the girls inside the wagon on the pierzynas and sternly warned Vicki not to stand up while the wagon was moving. They traveled south for an hour past houses that grew further and further apart until the gravel road was bordered only by fields tilled and ready for planting. They saw a grove of shade trees, oaks and maples whose light green leaves had furled out last week and were dazzling in the sunshine.

Frank stopped the wagon. The girls threw the pierzynas over the sides, then clambered down and opened them up on the grass. She took the hamper from the wagon. They ate leisurely, savoring the delicious results of her cooking and baking. Vicki grew restless and ran off to explore beyond the trees; reluctantly, Julia followed.

She always marveled at how two sisters couldn't be more different. Vicki was curious about everything. Julia was content with what was in front of her. She knew Julia resented looking after Vicki and especially running after her. Julia wanted a sister who would sit quietly next to her and do as she was told. That wasn't Vicki. She wondered if either sister would have had a kindred spirit in Albina or Irena. She would never know. Julia would have to deal with it. She had given birth to them, but she was not the one who had decided their birth order.

The meal finished, she gathered up the leftovers and put them in the hamper. Frank settled the girls in the back of the wagon. Twenty minutes later, they were pulling into the poultry farm. She was aware that the farmer grew uncomfortable when Frank stood by her smiling while she did all the negotiating. In the farmer's world, men always did the bargaining, whether or not they knew what they were doing, while the wives stood silent. Today, he had a new experience, selling to a woman who definitely knew poultry.

On the journey back home, Julia and Vicki shared the back of the wagon with crates of chicks, ducklings and goslings. The poultry would grow up together and the geese would be great protectors of the chickens. Vicki picked up a young chick from a crate and stroked its soft feathers. She offered one to Julia who declined. She, herself, was happy and stroked Frank's hand as he held the reins. Now she could augment their income selling eggs, chickens, ducks, and in the fall, perhaps, a few turkeys that she would fatten up. She would also use the downy goose feathers to make the coveted pierzynas and sell those. The stripped chicken feathers could also be used for pillows. While they were not as soft and the sharper quills tended to poke through the ticking, they were far better than straw pillows.

Julia was nine years old, the age she had been when she started working on a farm outside Piotrkow. Julia could help clean the poultry and deliver it as well as the eggs. Vicki, at five years of age, was old enough to learn how to feed the chickens. She had been careful to make sure there was at least one cockerel among the chicks. Now all she needed was a big healthy tom cat to keep mice and other predators out of the coop. There were plenty of young feral cats in the area; she would keep her eye out for the one she knew would be easy to train for the job.

MAY 1924

Maryanna

"Josie, you can't do this," she said. "Joseph is a good man. For over ten years, he has worked hard to provide for you and your children."

How did she miss the signs? Was she that trusting or that dense? True, she had wondered what her cousin Josie had seen in Joseph. They were such opposites. Foolishly, she had thought that Josie was dropping by more often so Chester and Virginia could play with Stash and Sally. She had noticed that Josie did focus her attention on Walter, their boarder. She never thought anything of it. Walter and Joseph were best friends.

Walter had left Poland when he was twenty years old; he had a wife and child back home to support. He worked in Michał's area and was in need of a place to board. Michał offered to have him live with them, at least temporarily. The temporary had turned into years. In 1918, she had grieved with him when his wife and child died in Poland, both victims of the Spanish influenza. He no longer had anyone waiting for him back home. He and Josie's husband became best friends. They did everything together. They fished. They played cards. They even filled out their war registration cards and applications for naturalization together. They were inseparable. It was another classic case of opposites attracting. Joseph was in his thirties, quiet and moody; Walter was in his twenties, outgoing, laughing often, easy to be with, just like Josie.

"It's too late, Maryanna," Josie said, as she heartily bit off a piece of plum coffeecake and took a mouthful of hot coffee liberally laced with milk and sugar. She had cut her long hair into the fashionable bob of the 1920's and her skirt hem had risen considerably. She sat comfortably across from her cousin who was more than ten years older than Josie.

"Josie, what are you thinking?" Maryanna asked.

"I'm thinking that I can no longer live this dreary life. Joseph does not have the drive that Michał does. We have been here for more than ten years and the dream of a better life with Joseph is just that, a dream. We are still living in a cramped apartment on Buffalo Avenue with a boarder, trying to make ends meet. Joseph is content with it; I am not. He goes to work, comes home for supper, spends time with Walter and considers it a good life. He has no desire to change it.

"That's not me. When we came to America, it was to have a better life, a house to call our own and no worries about where the next meal was coming from. That will never happen.

"Look at you, Maryanna. You have a spacious house with indoor plumbing and all the conveniences. And you, yourself, said that Michał is eying the brick bungalows that they will be building on Essex Avenue.

"I want what you have! And so does Walter. You know his story. Losing his wife and child hurt him deeply, but he has still remained optimistic and open. You've seen how much he loves your children and plays with them. He is the same with mine. He is hopeful that he can have a child of his own again - with me. We are kindred souls, not opposites.

"Walter is leaving for Detroit at the end of this week. He knows that he can find work in the Ford auto plant. It's a cleaner environment, not filthy like the steel mills. He has saved his money and will buy a house for us. When the divorce is final next week, the children and I will go to Detroit and we will marry there."

"Josie, what did your brother Theodor say?"

"Theodor and Valeria are a good match. They love each other; they like the same things. They have no children so they are free to do as they like. Teo envies them.

"Maryanna, your youngest sister is also at the breaking point. She has more reason than I do. At least Joseph has always been faithful to me. She, too, wants a home that is hers; not rented. Mike doesn't care where he hangs his hat or under whose bed he puts his shoes. He's all for a good time today; tomorrow will take care of itself." Josie finished the last of the coffeecake on her plate and drained her coffee cup.

"Walter will talk with Michał this evening after supper. Please let him know that I am so grateful for all the hospitality that you and he have shown to me and to the children these past few years."

"Josie, you are family. Our door will always be open to you and to your children. It will be hard to tell the children you are leaving, especially Stash and Sally. With eight years difference between Estella and Sally, there isn't the closeness of sisters. Sally has come to look upon your Virginia as her sister. They are very close. This will be a huge loss for Sally."

Josie said nothing. She rose and carried her plate and coffee cup to the sink, setting them on the drainboard. She smoothed her dress and walked to the back porch.

As Josie called to her children, Sally threw her arms around Virginia and shouted, "I love you, Ginny. See you next week." Tonight, she would have the unenviable task of telling Sally the sad news and watching her little heart break.

MAY 1925

Maryanna

Why was she always the last to hear? Did she appear that formidable to her sisters that they hesitated to let her know what was happening in their lives? Stella and Teo were close in age and grew up playing together while she, ten years older, had been more mother than sister to them. She had no choice after their dad died.

Michał decided to buy one of the newly built brick houses on Essex Avenue. They had moved in April. It was a brick bungalow with a basement rather than a cellar. There were two entrances to the basement; a cement set of steps outside and a spiral staircase inside. No longer would she have to deal with inclement weather in the winter to fetch jars of food that were stored in the cellar.

The house had an open parlor with an archway dividing it from a dining room. There was a built-in mahogany cabinet in the dining room with deep drawers and shelves protected by beveled glass doors. She was unpacking the wooden crates filled with the better dishes and putting them on the shelves, when Estella returned with Stash and Sally. They had walked to their Aunt Teo's to visit with their cousins.

"Mama," Estella asked, "why did cousin John say his papa is gone? I asked when he was coming back and John shrugged his shoulders. Why would he say that?"

"Did he die and go to heaven?" Sally asked.

"No, Sally," she said quickly. Her daughters' questions dumbfounded her. After the children were in bed, she fixed a cup of coffee for Michał, who was sitting in the parlor reading the *Dzienik Chicagoski.*

"Michał, have you seen Teo's Mike?"

He looked up from the newspaper. "What do you mean?"

She repeated her daughters' questions. "Sally thinks her Uncle Mike died. Estella is perplexed; she doesn't know what to think."

"I have not heard anything. Since my promotion to foreman, I'm not in close contact with Mike; he works in the rolling mill with Theodor. I'll see if I can talk with Mike tomorrow."

She tossed and turned all night thinking about her baby sister and wondering what was going on. By the time she rose at 6 a.m., she had a plan. She bustled around the kitchen fixing a hearty breakfast of eggs and ham and fried potatoes, fresh bread and butter, and strong coffee for Michał and for seventeen-year-old Stephan, who was now apprenticed to his godfather, Vally, a painter and hanger of wallpaper. She made a lighter breakfast of oatmeal and cinnamon toast for Estella, Stash and Sally. She filled Michał's lunch box to the brim; she knew he was always sharing with some fellow who couldn't make ends meet. He left at 6:30, giving her the never-failing kiss on her cheek, usually as she was dishing up breakfast for the younger children. She fixed a lunch box for Stephan and lunch bags for the schoolchildren. By eight o'clock the three were on their way to work or school. Hurriedly, she washed and dried the dishes and put them on the shelf. She let the pots and pans sit on the drainboard to air dry.

She put on the navy dress that she had worn on Sunday. She pinned up her white hair and set the navy straw hat firmly on top, affixing it with two long pearl-tipped hat pins. It was a cool morning and she put on the long black wool coat that Michał had given her for Christmas two years ago. She wrapped up four of the little cherry pastries from the bakery and put them in a brown paper bag. Cherry was Teo's favorite. She grabbed her purse and set out. She had never walked alone from Essex to Exchange before. She wasn't sure exactly how many blocks she had to walk. She would count them. It would distract her. She reached the corner of Essex and 84th Street and turned east. Kingston. Colfax. Saginaw. Marquette. Manistee. Burnham. Muskegon, Escanaba. Exchange. Nine blocks.

She turned right on Exchange and headed for 8445. She climbed the stairs and rang the bell.

"Good morning." Teo's smile faded when she saw her.

"Good morning, Teo," she said, as she stood on the porch holding the bag of pastries. "May I come in?"

"Of course, Maryanna. Please forgive the mess. I haven't had time to straighten up this morning." Teo, who was still in her housecoat, ran her fingers through her short, uncombed hair as she held the door open while her sister entered the house.

Her dark eyes took in everything in one swift glance. Teo wasn't exaggerating when she apologized for the mess. If anything, it also wouldn't be exaggerating to say that is would take much more than straightening up to get her house in shape. With all the older brothers and sisters fawning over her, baby Teo had never learned to pick up after herself. She always knew that an older sibling would do it for her and laugh at her sloppy ways.

Even the parlor, kept clean in every household for receiving guests, was littered with papers and clothes that needed washing. Teo invited her into the kitchen, hurriedly grabbing plates and spoons off the table and wiping it down with a cloth that had seen better days. She watched silently as Teo found two mismatched but clean cups on the shelf and set them on the table, filling them with steaming coffee. She saw Teo's eyes light up when she unwrapped the cherry pastries. Once they had taken a bite or two from the pastries, she cut to the chase.

"Teo, what is going on with you and Mike? Yesterday, Estella said John told her that his father was gone. Sally wanted to know if he had died like Martin Koloszewski and was in heaven."

"He's in heaven, all right," Teo said, angrily. "His own idea of heaven. Which is to leave me and the children in one hell of a mess. He took off, Maryanna. Just like that, he said he had had it with South Chicago and was going to Ohio or Pennsylvania. I have no idea where he is."

"When did this happen?" Her heart reached out to her little sister whose angry words concealed a terrifying fear of what would happen to her and her children.

"Two weeks ago, I needed money for food and Mike said he didn't have any. He had just been paid and I asked him what happened to his wages. He swore and said he was sick and tired of working in that hell hole of a steel mill. It was no better than working in the coal mines back in Poland. There was nothing to show for it but dirt. He wanted to be his own man, not tied down to a sniveling wife and a bunch of kids.

"Maryanna, we had quite a spat. And what was I supposed to do, I asked him? He said that it was up to me to figure that one out. He'd had it. We've had these spats before. I thought it was just another one. But when I came home from your new house the next day, he was gone. He had packed his better clothes and left a note on this very table. Only a note. No money. Nothing. I didn't know what to do. I took the children over to Stella's. She was fixing supper for Vince and included my children.

"Fortunately, Ludwig was working the three-to-eleven shift. She packed up food for us to take home. As much as she can, without raising his suspicions, she has been helping me keep food on the table. But what am I going to do about the rent?

"Maryanna, what am I going to do? I don't know how to do anything. I can't earn enough to pay the rent and keep food on the table." Teo finished her monologue as though she were running a race and sat back, exhausted.

"Teo, why did you not come to me at once? Michał is not as hardhearted as Ludwig. He would not begrudge you in your need. Were you that afraid of *me*? Of what I might say? We may not always see things in the same way. There are many years between us. You are my flesh and blood.

"Teo, we will help you, willingly. You aren't pregnant, are you?"

"Thank God, no! That louse has left me alone for quite a while, which was fine with me."

"I will talk to Michał about your immediate expenses. You will need to work to support yourself and the children. We have enough food for all of us. The garden last summer was very bountiful."

"Thank you, dearest sister, thank you. I will do as you say." Teo jumped up from her chair and bounded over to give her older sister a hug; now, she would not have to worry for a few days.

She knew exactly what was going through Teo's mind as she hugged her back. Teo was the grasshopper living for today. She, Maryanna, was the ant, industriously keeping her household prepared for the future. Stephan had told her about Aesop's fable after he had read it in school.

Sophie

"Julia, these chickens need to be taken to Rabbi Horowitz on Phillips Avenue for koshering. He is expecting you at four o'clock." She watched as Julia reluctantly put the two crates in the wooden wagon and left the yard taking the shortcut through the alley behind the house. She knew that Julia disliked taking fowl to the Rabbi, but it had to be done. Her own ability to speak Yiddish had made her a favorite in the expansive Jewish community north of 82nd Street. Her poultry business had expanded rapidly in two years. She sat down outside the chicken coop and began stripping feathers.

DECEMBER 1925

Maryanna

She sat at one end of the kitchen table opposite the large window watching as the rays of winter sun created a halo around Estella as she rolled out dough for kolacky. From some ancestor, her daughter had inherited a love of baking, which she herself, disliked. Give her flowers and she nurtured them into beauty. Give her flours and the result was a disaster. Estella had known what to do just by watching her mother's pathetic attempts.

"Criminy, it is *cold* out there," Sally shouted, as she stomped the snow off her boots before charging into the kitchen ahead of Stephan. She ran to the table to stick her finger into the povidła filling for the kolacky.

"Keep your wayward fingers out of that bowl," Estella threatened halfheartedly, waving the wooden spoon menacingly at Sally who laughed, then ran off with the parcel that was in her hand.

Stephan was watching Sally's enthusiasm with a smile on his face. On Christmas Eve, he would be eighteen years old, a man. She appraised him with her dark brown eyes that were a mirror of his. His hair was as black as hers had once been. It was thick and wavy like his father's, a feature she had always found attractive. He had his father's olive complexion and build. He was swift on his feet and moved easily; he was strong without an excess of muscle.

Stephan was an enigma. His manner was easygoing, but it was a thin veneer hiding his true self. Not like fourteen-year-old Stash, who had the same temperament minus the seething desires hidden beneath it. Stephan wanted more. He was constantly reading books on history, politics, business. She failed to see what good history did. That was the past. Now was now. Live today. When she mentioned her thoughts to him, he said that history taught one how to live today. She had no idea what he was talking about.

He had apprenticed with his godfather, Vally, learning how to paint houses, plaster walls and hang wallpaper. He had wallpapered the living and dining rooms and the bedrooms in the new house. She was proud of his work and never failed to tell visitors that her son had done the wallpapering.

Stephan was eleven when Sally was born; as she grew from baby into toddler, he spent a lot of time with her, taking her for walks, reading to her, taking her to the park by the stadium and pushing her on the swings. She had never asked him to do those things for his baby sister; he just did.

Once he graduated school and began his apprenticeship, it seemed like she rarely saw him at home. She knew he lived there because his clothes showed up in her wash basket and his bed was rumpled every morning. His casual ways were a magnet and he was always off with a group of guys going fishing and wherever else young men went. When the perch were running in Lake Michigan, he would be off to the seawall at Calumet Park. She could always count on a bountiful catch for the Friday fish fry.

"I left the tree in the backyard, Ma," he said, taking off his coat and hat. "Stash and I will set it up in the parlor for you."

"Looking good," he said to Estella, eyeing the kolacky.

"Keep your mitts off," she said briskly, while simultaneously handing one to him. "These are for company."

"Aren't I company?"

"As little as we see of you, you could be."

"I'm a busy guy," he said, snatching another pastry.

"How come Stephan can have dessert before supper and I can't?" Sally whined, prancing back into the kitchen.

"Because I'm the big brother," he said, as he strode toward the bedroom he shared with Stash.

Sophie

The only times in her life that she set foot in a schoolroom were those days when she met with the sisters who taught her daughters at St. Mary Magdalene grammar school. She never sat in one of those contortionist desks and she wasn't about to start. She was delighted, however, that today, three days before Christmas, Frank had received his naturalization papers. He had encouraged her to take the classes at Sullivan School with him. She had no inclination to do so. She obeyed all the laws of which she was aware and felt deep gratitude to America for the freedoms which she enjoyed. But, ironically, even though she spoke five languages fluently, she struggled with English and was not comfortable when speaking it. Her sentences came out in a stew of words.

Frank was now a citizen of the United States. His achievement needed to be celebrated. She would go to Mokry's and select a fine beef roast and cook it with the celery, carrots and onions that he loved. She would make a thick gravy from the juices and whip up a pot of mashed potatoes. Best of all, she would bake the twelve-egg pound cake that was his favorite dessert. In the pantry, she had jars of peaches that she canned during the summer. She would whip up heavy cream and serve the cake with peaches and cream. It would be a real treat to have a summer dessert in December.

JUNE 1928

Sophie

She sat on the porch swing hemming a pierzyna while waiting for Julia to return from school. She watched as her daughter walked slowly down the sidewalk looking neither to the right nor to the left. Julia had celebrated her fourteenth birthday in March and was taller than her mother. With her dark brown hair and eyes and slim build, she looked like her stepsister, Agnieska. Even her personality was more like Agnieska's. That puzzled her. The physical characteristics came from Frank. But the personality that made Agnieska and Julia feel like the world owed them a living and better hop to it, that was not Frank, who was even-keeled and optimistic. There was one major difference between Julia and Agnieska. While their dark eyes never missed a thing, Julia rarely expressed an opinion. Agnieska, on the other hand, never hesitated to say what she thought, especially to her stepmother. From which ancient relative of Frank's had Agnieska and Julia inherited the negative temperament?

"Julia," she said as her daughter unlatched the trellis gate and walked into the front yard. "Mrs. Cohen came by today for her stewing chickens and eggs. She has neighbors who need a babysitter. I told her that you would be interested. Vicki is old enough to deliver the poultry and eggs. Mrs. Cohen is expecting you at her house this afternoon at five o'clock. She will take you to meet the Berman's. They have one son, Shelley. He is three years old."

She cherished the smile that broke out on Julia's face as she realized that she would no longer have to work with the poultry. Julia smiled rarely. That was another trait so like Agnieska. She sighed as Julia walked into the house without saying a word; at least she had smiled. She would take what Julia was able to give. She went back to hemming the pierzyna.

Maryanna

"Maryanna, school will be out next week." Teo chattered, rapidly. "I need to get away. Let me take Sally to Michigan to play with Ginny while I visit with Josie. Ginny misses her cousin; she thinks of Sally as her little sister. They haven't seen each other since Walter and Josie visited two years ago. I promise I will take good care of her and return her safely to you." Her spiel completed, Teo bit off a mouthful of cake and took a huge gulp of coffee.

She sat with her youngest sister at the kitchen table drinking coffee and eating slices of the cherry streusel cake that Teo had picked up at the bakery on her way over. It seemed that she was always sitting at a kitchen table drinking coffee and eating cake at life's most traumatic moments.

"How is Josie doing, Teo?"

"She's happy, Maryanna. She has her own house. Walter loves her children as if they were his own. Chester and Virginia are happy, too. It is a huge relief for them not to have to tiptoe around because they didn't know what mood their father might be in."

"What about you, Teo? Why do you need to get away?"

She took a long look at her baby sister. She herself had ignored the rising hemlines and kept her long hair in a bun at the back of her head. Years ago, Teo had embraced the new look with enthusiasm. She sat across from her in a floral chemise with silk stockings. Her hair was marceled and her cheeks and lips were rosy with powder and rouge. This was the fashion of the Roaring Twenties, as she had heard the decade called.

Teo had survived the last three years. She had found a position in one of the dress stores on Commercial Avenue. She didn't have the ability to wait on customers and be a shop clerk, and her inventory skills were lacking, but she had a knack for arranging the clothing in ways that were attractive to customers and generated sales. It didn't pay much, but enough to cover the rent and utilities. The store owners often gave her items that were returned or couldn't be sold because of a minor imperfection. Most likely she was wearing one of those dresses.

There had been an added bonus. After her Estella had graduated from St. Mary Magdalene elementary school two years ago, Teo had talked to the owners about hiring her niece. Estella had a good head for figures and she was now a valued shop clerk and cashier. Aunt and niece worked together at the dress shop.

"Teo, I can't give my permission without Michał's approval. You know that he did not approve of Josie's betrayal of Joseph. I know that you would take good care of Sally. I'm not sure, though, that he will be willing to let her accompany you, but I will ask him." She took one last sip of coffee, now tepid, knowing full well that he would not.

SEPTEMBER 1929

Maryanna

"I haven't seen Teo since early last month," she said to Stella who had stopped by for a basket of the prolific tomatoes. She had finished picking the tomatoes and was sitting on a metal chair watching the monarch butterflies flitting among the diervilla. Between tending to her vegetable garden, preserving its bounty and the preparations for Estella's wedding in October, she had little time to pay attention to anything else.

"Come sit," she said, patting the chair next to hers.

"Don't you know?" Stella plopped down on the empty chair.

"What am I supposed to know? Is she all right? Are the children well? Is something wrong?"

"Teo and the children are in Detroit."

"Are they visiting Josie again? How can they still be there when school is already in session?"

"Maryanna, didn't you know that Teo met someone when she visited Josie last year?"

"Stella, she never said anything to me about it. Nor did you!"

"Walter introduced Teo to his friend, Jack. Before prohibition, Jack was a bartender. He took Teo to speakeasies in Detroit so she could dance."

"It's going to be a hot one today, Stella. Would you like a glass of lemonade?"

"That would hit the spot, Maryanna. It was a long, warm walk."

She carried the extra basket of tomatoes with her into the kitchen as she went to fetch the lemonade. Her baby sister still wanted to play. The maxim was true that everyone grows older, but not everyone matures.

"So, what is going on, Stella?" She handed her sister one of the glasses of lemonade.

"Jack was born in Chicago. He knows his way around the city. He works at the Ford plant in Detroit and has a car. During the past year, he has driven down periodically to spend time with Teo.

"In early August, he came down to Chicago and told Teo to pack up whatever belongings she wanted of hers and the children. They drove back to Detroit and were married on the fifteenth of August by a justice of the peace. John and young Theodora have started school there."

"Teo is married! Why has she not told me of this? Why have you not said anything?"

Stella squirmed, uneasily, and took several gulps of the lemonade. She deflected Maryanna's question.

"Estelle is not happy with the move. She loved working as a waitress at the Tea for Two restaurant on Commercial Avenue. She had to quit her job and leave her friends. She wrote to me saying she wants to come back to South Chicago. If she did, where would she live?"

"Did Estelle mention anything about how things are in Detroit?"

"No. Well, the lemonade hit the spot, Maryanna. Thank you for the tomatoes. It's a bit of a walk, so I'll be starting back." Stella jumped up, kissed her sister, picked up the basket and hurriedly left the yard.

The suddenness of the departure confirmed her suspicions: Stella knew more than she wanted to admit. The fact that she had never mentioned anything to her older sister about Teo's involvement with this guy, Jack, was proof. The closeness that Stella and Teo had as little girls back home resumed in South Chicago as married women. Stella worked as a milliner and was into fashion like Teo. They both embraced the short skirts and bobbed hair that she abhorred. Stella wasn't as flamboyant as Teo; her husband, Ludwig, would have none of that. As difficult as he could be, it surprised her that Stella got away with as much as she did.

She was blessed. She never had to go 'behind her husband's back' as her sisters sometimes did; she and Michał truly were one in heart and mind.

Sophie

She heard the first rumblings of financial turmoil from her Jewish customers. They were talking about things called stocks and bonds. Their husbands worked on Michigan Avenue or LaSalle Street in Chicago's Loop. She still had no idea what that meant either - Loop. She knew loops in sewing, knitting and crocheting, in rope, in walking in circles. What kind of loop did Chicago have? She had never been there. The closest she ever came to downtown Chicago was Maxwell Street, the bazaar to top all bazaars. Where else could such a bazaar exist but in a crazy city that had a Loop?

She loved Maxwell Street. One could find anything in the shops or tents or down the endless rows of open-air tables that were crammed into every inch of space up and down the street. The price quoted was never the price paid. Only a fool wouldn't haggle. She loved haggling.

She would walk down Maxwell Street slowly. She might see a dress that caught her eye for Julia or Vicki. She would pick up the dress and look at the price tag, then put it back down on the table.

"You'll never find as beautiful a dress for that price," the merchant would say.

"It is pretty, but so is the price."

"It's a bargain at $2.00. Look at the fine fabric."

"Too fine for my pocketbook."

"That dress is worth more than the price that is on it. Look at the detailed sewing. You are an astute woman. You see it."

"The workmanship is good, but the price is not for me," she'd say, while turning to walk away.

"Wait," the merchant would call out, then drop his voice as she came closer. "Don't tell anyone. I will sell it for $1.75."

"It is still too much. I have to have money to feed my poor children. I can only afford one dollar."

"One dollar?" he would mutter while striking his forehead with the palm of his hand. "One dollar? And how can I feed *my* children, if I sell it to you for one dollar?"

"Thank you for your time."

"Wait," he would say again, putting his finger on his lips. "I shouldn't do this, but I can tell that you are a woman who appreciates fine things and this dress will have a good home with you. I will sell it to you for $1.50."

"$1.00."

"How can I stay in business with a price like that? $1.50."

"$1.00."

"You drive a hard bargain. I will sell it to you for $1.25."

"Agreed."

He would wrap the dress in tissue paper and tape it. She'd smile as he handed the parcel to her. Both were satisfied. As she walked away, she would hear him saying to the next customer, "You will never find as beautiful a dress for that price."

Loops. Stocks. Bonds. The words made no sense to her. It was that crazy English language which gave her so much trouble. What made sense was working with one's hands, caring for one's family. That is what mattered. As long as she and Frank did that, all would be fine. She picked up the egg basket and headed to the chicken coop. She needed twelve eggs to make her famous pound and sponge cakes; the yokes for the pound cake and the whites for the sponge cake.

CHAPTER FIVE

OCTOBER 1929

Sophie

She had never seen her stepdaughter so agitated. Agnieska's face rarely showed any emotion. If it did, it was only the slightest glimmer of what she might be feeling. She was sitting on the wooden bench by the chicken coop stripping feathers for pierzynas on a summery October afternoon when the trellis gate slammed, startling her and sending the hens to squawking and wandering around, aimlessly. Agnieska came striding down the sidewalk at an unusually fast pace.

"Good day, Agnieska."

"Not much good about today. I didn't like what I've been hearing about that Wall Street in New York, so I decided to close out my account at the Union State Bank on Commercial Avenue. I missed the streetcar, so I walked all the way to 92nd Street and the bank refused to let me have all my money! Mr. Brockman said that we had nothing to worry about. Our money was safe in the bank. However, he only had so much cash on hand. To be fair to everyone, he would only allow a person to withdraw half of the money in their account. How can our money be safe if he doesn't have all of it to give back?

"Sophie, if you and dad have any money in that bank, he'd better get it out of there, immediately." Agnieska plopped down on the other side of the bench, tucking her black coat under her legs away from the errant chicken feathers that were floating around the yard. Her purse was on her lap and she held it so firmly with both hands that one would think a horde of robbers was just around the corner.

"Agnieska, we've never had the kind of money that you do. Your life is different from ours. You have no children. You always have boarders renting upstairs. And prohibition has been a boon for you."

"You could do the same thing, Sophie. The money you make with your poultry and eggs is truly chickenfeed compared to what you could be earning if you did what I do. You wouldn't have to work so hard."

"What you and Mike do is your business, Agnieska. Frank and I are quite content with our life. There is enough to provide for Julia and Vicki. That's the most important thing."

"My father has always been so righteous. What benefit is there to living here, if you don't take advantage of all the opportunities?" Her stepdaughter stretched her legs out in front of her. "Back home, there were no such opportunities."

"Agnieska, you would not be here if it were not for your father. How many opportunities did he pass up so that he could save enough to send for you and your brother?" Her normal rhythm of stripping the chicken feathers had quickened.

Her stepdaughter was beginning to annoy her, again. There was no love lost between the two. She always tried to be sensitive in her relations with Agnieska, respecting her as Frank's first daughter. She knew full well that her stepdaughter resented her intrusion into her father's life. She was the one who usurped the time and attention that Frank's firstborn felt should be hers in its entirety.

Agnieska glowered at her comment. She stood up abruptly. "I'd better get this home," she said, tucking her purse under her left arm and holding it in place with her right hand. She walked toward the alley gate to take the shortcut to her house two blocks west on Colfax.

"Agnieska, give greetings to Mike from me and Frank," she said, without interrupting her work. Her stepdaughter was one person who didn't need feathers to stuff her pierzynas; she could do it with dollar bills.

Maryanna

Where had eighteen years gone? She was sitting on the bride's side of St. Mary Magdalene church. Huge bouquets of golden chrysanthemums and canna lilies graced each side of the main altar enhancing the six-foot tall gold candelabra and the bee's wax candles that they embraced. The priest was wearing the long chasuble used at a High Mass. He turned from the altar to face the groom and bride. The bride was her Estella vowing to be faithful and true to Tomasz. So much was changing, it was dizzying trying to keep up.

When she and Michał were married, she wore her best dress, the silvery grey one that she had worn aboard ship, and he wore his suit. There were only five people in the church in Philadelphia: the priest, Michał, his cousin Jerzy and his wife Paulina, who were their witnesses, and herself. They were married in the morning. Paulina fixed a bountiful dinner at noon. By evening, they were on the train bound for Chicago.

Today, her daughter was wearing bridal clothing that only the upper class wore back home in Poland. She looked at the yards of tulle that cascaded from an ivory beaded lace headband that Estella wore around her forehead. The yards of tulle in the veil won't make up for the yards of fabric that she thought should be in the dress to cover Estella's legs. Instead, the ivory lace dress with pearls and beads shimmering in the candlelight was short, the fashionable flapper style. She frowned; she was sure that her younger sisters, Stella and Teo, had a hand in it, convincing Estella that she should wear what she wanted instead of a long dress that was more modest.

Stella was sitting in the pew behind her with Ludwig and Vince. Teo wasn't there; she was in Detroit with this Jack whatever-his-name-was.

As if he knew what she was thinking, she felt Michał patting her hand. Her heart still fluttered at his touch. After all these years, he was still her dashing savior, even though time was making inroads into his hairline and flecks of gray were invading it. It was so much easier for him to adjust to the changing times. Not that he approved of the craziness of the Roaring Twenties. He would always be upright in his thoughts and actions. But he could accept change much better than she.

"Maryanna," he had said when she balked at Estella's choice of wedding dress, "she wants to fit in. She wants to be American, not a foreigner. She loves fashion and goes downtown to all the fancy stores to see what other women are wearing. She only wants to dress like those women. She doesn't want to act like some of them do."

Michal would stand up for Estella. She knew that he would never forget his beloved Dora, but once he had accepted the shock of her death, he had lavished on Estella all that she knew he would have given Dora. There were these doctors in Europe who were studying why fathers seemed to favor their daughters and were hard on their sons and why mothers seemed to dote on their sons and demand much from their daughters. Stephan had read about these studies and found them intriguing.

She looked to the right at Stephan standing next to Tomasz. He was handsome at twenty-two years of age, even more so in his wedding tuxedo. Did she really favor him above Estella? She didn't think so. After all, was it not her duty as a mother to teach Estella all she needed to know to be an upright, industrious wife and mother?

She felt a jolt against her left arm. At ten, Sally, sitting next to her, was mesmerized by her sister's finery. No doubt she was daydreaming about her own wedding day. Being seventeen and bored by it all, Stash had nudged Sally. He constantly teased her in the way only a big brother can. Sally was not one to sit back and do nothing. If she didn't like what was going on, she fought back.

The organist began pumping out the recessional. She watched Estella and Tomasz rise from the kneelers. The priest raised his hand in the last blessing. The newly married couple turned to walk down the aisle toward the life they would share together.

The attendees scrambled out of the pews using the side aisles to hurry out of the church ahead of the bridal couple. As the newlyweds exited the church, friends and relatives showered the bride and groom with rice and barley, a sign that they would never go hungry during their married life. Tomasz had a car and the bridal party piled in. They had an appointment at the photographer's studio on Commercial Avenue for formal portraits of the wedding party.

Everyone else joined her and Michał in the one-block walk down Marquette Avenue from 84th Street to 83rd. They walked past the house that held so many happy and tragic memories for her, to the new Marquette Gardens banquet hall where Michał had arranged a wedding reception. When they lived down the street, White Eagle Grove had a clearing that people used for celebrations when the weather was clement.

Joe Wieczorek, who owned the tavern next to the grove had purchased the land two years ago. Prohibition had closed his tavern so he sought other ways to earn a living. At one end of the grove, he had built a large banquet hall. It was a one-story building with a huge kitchen along the back fully equipped for baking and cooking large quantities of food. There were two banquet rooms; a small one for up to one hundred people and a large one for bigger celebrations. On the right side of this room there was an area with a slightly raised platform for musicians and singers. Surrounding it was a dance floor with ample room for the lively krakowiaks and polkas. The remainder of the room held a multitude of long tables and chairs. The ceiling had multiple chandeliers which could flood the room with light or be dimmed so that it was like dining or dancing by candlelight.

Vince and Sally were given the job of lookouts to alert them when Tomasz's car pulled up. She and Michał stationed themselves at the entrance with the traditional bread and salt. As Estella and Tomasz walked into the reception, they were given the bread and salt. The loaf of bread was a symbol of everyone's hope that the couple would never be in need; the tiny container of salt was a reminder that there would be difficulties in their life and they must learn to cope with them together. Ideally, any problem would be as small as the salt cellar.

The afternoon and evening became a kaleidoscope of feasting on an abundance of Polish food, straining to be heard over the enthusiasm of the orchestra, and wearing one's self out dancing exuberant polkas.

As the hours of merriment wore on, it was time for the Oczepiny. She stood on the edge of the dance floor as Sally, all of Estella's friends and Tomasz's sisters gathered in a circle around Estella who was sitting on a chair in the middle. With great ceremony, the maid of honor, unpinned the veil and removed the headband that Estella wore; her days as a maiden were over. She stood up and a white frilly apron was tied around her waist; she was now a married woman ready to embrace the duties of a wife.

The onlookers parted the circle to allow Tomasz to enter it. The chair was removed; he and Estella danced together while everyone stood watching. As the music ended, the circle parted again allowing the couple to walk through. They left the reception to begin life together.

With a grateful heart, she watched as Estella became the first of her children to leave her in happiness. Dora would have been twenty years old and no doubt married as well. Perhaps she and Michał would already be grandparents. Had all her children lived, she would now be mothering three teenage sons. What if they were like Stash? Innocently enjoying all that came his way, never thinking of the consequences? Could she have survived two more like him? She could.

Stephan was the one she worried about. He was so quiet, always thinking. He was two years older than Estella. To her knowledge, he had shown no interest in any young girl. He seemed to prefer his male friends with whom he spent time when he wasn't working or reading. It was unrealistic to worry about his age. Tomasz was twenty-nine, a full ten years older than his bride. She and Michał were both twenty-four when they married. She did remember that before she left Osiek Dolnoslakie, she had overheard a few people calling her a spinster and an old maid.

Leaving Stephan and Stash to stay with the revelers who would dance and sing until the wee hours of the morning, she left the reception with Michał and Sally to walk the four short blocks to Essex Avenue. She embraced the crisp chill of a mid-autumn evening and prayed that her daughter's new life would be filled with as many blessings as there were stars in the heavenly vault.

SEPTEMBER 1931

Sophie

"Tell me what happened, Frank," she said, as he slumped down in the chair by the huge maple dining table in the downstairs kitchen. Frank was not a slumper. His posture conveyed the result of the interview. The Great Depression, as everyone was calling it, had entrapped them last year. Frank was laid off from his job with the B&O railroad. As the pace of steel production slowed, so did the need for railroad cars to bring in the ores and dispatch the newly made steel. When work at the steel mills picked up again, he would be called back. Meanwhile, they had no income except what she earned from the poultry business.

She poured two steaming mugs of coffee, set one before him and sat down across from him with the other cup. The sunlight streaming through the window behind her highlighted Frank's face. He was fifty-nine years old. There were a few lines in his forehead and a furrow between his eyebrows which were as dark as was his mustache. He still had a full head of hair which he parted on the left side and combed neatly. There were hints of grey in it, especially at the temples. His face was ruddy from years spent outdoors repairing the railroad cars. He had retained his slender build altered only by a slight increase in muscle flaccidity that came with age. He was still a handsome man.

"What happened, Frank?"

"I did not want to go to the charity office. It is my responsibility to take care of my family. But I thought that maybe I could receive some temporary assistance until I am working again and then I would pay it back. The office is on Commercial Avenue near 88th Street. It's a block from our old apartment, Sophie.

"When the man learned that I had a house, even though it is mortgaged, he said that he could do nothing for me. If I sold the house and used up all the money, then I could come back. If I did that, you and the girls would have no place to live. You would be on the streets. How helpful would that be?

"The man said that if I told him I was renting the house, he would help me. He paused waiting for me to speak. Sophie, you know I cannot lie. I thanked him, picked up my hat and left.

"I do not want something for nothing. I would pay back what I was given once I was working again." His head drooped again.

"Frank, don't worry," she said, reaching across the table to pat his hand. "We will get through this. As long as I have the chickens and the eggs, there will be food. And we have the fruit trees and the vegetable garden. The most important thing is that we can pay the mortgage every month and the property taxes.

"We can..."

Vicki came dashing in the door and thumped her schoolbooks on the end of the table.

"Mom! Dad!"

"Vicki, your father and I are having a conversation."

Vicki's smile did a vanishing act as she picked up her books and started for the staircase to the second floor.

"Vicki," Frank asked, "what are you so excited about?" There was no question that Vicki was his favorite. He loved Julia and treated her well, but her standoffish ways were hurtful to him. She knew that Julia loved her father in her own way, but she was not given to outbursts of affection. Vicki, on the other hand, could hug the breath right out of you.

Vicki paused and looked at her. She knew she should not have interrupted adults who were speaking.

"It's okay, Vicki, what has happened that you are so excited?"

"Today, Monsignor Mielczarek came into our class and said to Sister Constance that he needed two girls with good penmanship to do work in the rectory. Sister chose Wanda and me to help write in the parish books. Three times a week we will walk over to the rectory after school and write in the books."

"Vicki, that is a fine honor. No wonder you are excited. Your dad and I know that you will do an excellent job. We are proud that you were chosen by the monsignor."

Once again, Vicki thumped her books on the table so she could hug her parents with abandon. Then she dashed upstairs to change out of her school uniform.

Frank was smiling as she fetched the coffeepot from the stove and refilled their cups. She took a long sip before continuing their happily interrupted conversation.

"Julia is looking for a full-time job. Shelly Berman is in school now, so she isn't doing much babysitting. Agnieska has her spending so much time at her house washing and drying the beer bottles. If she paid her for it, it would help, but she feels that Julia should help her because they are sisters. Agnieska says family helps family without any strings attached."

"I do not understand how she can disobey the law and live with herself," Frank said, with great disappointment in his voice. His firstborn daughter had been in the business of making liquor in her house for the past four years. Her illegal business grew larger every year and she demanded that Julia help her.

"Frank, you are such a good man, and everything you have told me about your first wife, Barbara, Agnieska's mother, has always been to her credit. Your stepson Frank and stepdaughter Sophie are good souls, as well. It puzzles me when Agnieska's behavior is the exact opposite."

"What will be hard," Frank said, changing the sensitive subject of his first daughter, "is telling Vicki that she will have to go to Cole School next

September, because we won't be able to afford the tuition at St. Mary Magdalene. Look how happy she is," he said, burying his face in his hands.

She reached across the table and took both his hands in hers. She smiled tenderly at him. "Frank, this is just a little salt in our lives; we can turn it into sugar."

Maryanna

Was she a caterpillar living in a cocoon? Her family seemed protected from the suffering and struggling of her neighbors brought on by the depression. She did not want for money to buy the necessities for her family or even a few items that weren't.

As a foreman at Illinois Steel Company, South Works, Michal's job was not affected by the depression. Stephan was now working as a weigh master at Republic Steel in Hegewisch and his job was not in jeopardy. Neither was that of Estella's husband, Tomasz, who was a pipe fitter at South Works. Stanley was working as a book binder in a field that appeared not to suffer greatly from the depression.

Illinois Steel was the largest employer in South Chicago. As the demand for steel lessened, thousands upon thousands of unskilled laborers were laid off. It created a domino effect in the community. Every other business and industry suffered: the railroads, the utilities, the stores in the shopping district on Commercial Avenue, the local grocery stores, and the collection plates in the churches.

She knew that Michal and other members of the Holy Name Society at St. Mary Magdalene had formed the Church Committee to respond to the needs of parishioners. Each week when they met, the Monsignor gave them the names of more families in need. The unusually hot summers curtailed the bumper crops of vegetables, but she managed to can as much as she could and give jars of food to the committee.

Estella was much more gifted than she. Her hours at the dress shop had been cut drastically as sales declined and the owners struggled to keep the shop open. Estella used the extra time to sew layette outfits for the women who were expecting babies, especially the new mothers who didn't have a chest of hand-me-downs from older siblings. She made the outfits from white cotton and pink and blue scraps of fabric that she received from the woman who did the alterations at the dress shop. Whenever she visited, Estella had been bringing the outfits so she could see them. Each outfit was better than the one that preceded it.

Today, they were sitting on the sofa in the living room, when Estella brought out the latest outfit from her sewing bag. It was neither pink nor blue, but all white with edges trimmed in delicate white lace with a cap to match.

"Estella, you have outdone yourself with this lovely outfit. Someone's baby will be so lucky to be dressed in it."

"Yes, he or she will. Not someone's baby. Your grandbaby, Ma."

"Estella!" She was dumbfounded, thrilled and a wee bit frightened all at the same time. Her daughter had suffered from rheumatic fever as a child and the effects were long lasting.

"Are you feeling well? Will it be okay?"

"I'm fine, Ma. Doctor Lewis gave me a good going over. Everything is okay. As long as I follow his directions, there should be no complications. The baby will be born at South Chicago Hospital, not at home like we were. That way, if there is any problem, there will be other doctors to help."

"That is good, Estella. How different things are done today than when I had Stephan and you. The new procedures. The new medicines. When are you due?"

"In March, Ma." Estella smiled and patted her nonexistent stomach.

APRIL 1932

Maryanna

Seven months later, she and Michał were sitting on the same burgundy sofa anxiously awaiting the arrival of Estella and their first grandchild. Earlier in the day, Tomasz had driven his in-laws to the wake at Dalewski's funeral home on South Shore Drive and then drove them back home. Her cousin, Theodor, had lost his wife, Valeria, on the 8th of the month. For many years, they had been childless. Six years ago, there was great rejoicing when a daughter, Loretta, was born followed by little Pearl, two years later. Now, there were two little girls who had no mother. Her heart ached for them and for her cousin. Valeria's death stirred up a nagging fear in her. Estella had rheumatic fever as a young girl; if she died too soon, what would happen to the grandson she would be meeting in a few minutes?

"They're here!" Sally shouted from her perch by the front windows. Minutes later, as Estella placed little Tomasz in her arms, everything else was forgotten except the miracle she was holding.

"Estella, Tomasz," Michał said, glancing at his son-in-law, "have the christening here. There's plenty of room for both our families. There is great need for us to celebrate even though times are rough. New life must be celebrated."

"I agree," she said, as Estella picked up her newborn son from arms that were reluctant to give him up. Her daughter sat down across from them on one of the wing chairs and was feeding a hungry Tomasz. Sally was flitting around the chair desperately hoping her sister would let her hold the new baby after the bottle was empty. This baby had ousted her from the position of youngest member of the family; the least her sister could do was let her hold the usurper.

It was the second Sunday in April. It was a full sun day with gentle whispers of warm weather in the wind. That morning she had opened the windows half way to air out a house rife with the odors of cooked cabbage, kielbasa, cigars and cigarettes.

Stephan and Stash dragged chairs from the dining room and joined the group.

"Are we having a party?" Stash asked, eagerness in his voice.

"I can get beer from Mike's wife," Stephan said. "Let me know how much we need."

Mike was one of his best fishing buddies. Mike raised pigeons, a hobby of which he wanted no part. When it came to fishing, however, Mike was there with his boarder, Victor, and Sylvester and Johnnie. Mike had a car, so they didn't have to lug fishing gear, or worse, a hamper full of perch on the streetcar. When Mike picked up Stephan, he always dropped off a few bottles of beer.

"Would she be able to make enough for a big celebration?" Michał asked.

If he had one fault, she thought, it was his love of beer. Not downing one stein after another, but the enjoyment of a cold beer in the evening after a hard day's work. Prohibition had been hard on him in that respect, until Stephan learned that Mike's wife was brewing beer.

Sophie

Vicki burst into the kitchen as she was cracking eggs and separating the yolks from the whites to make Frank's favorite pound cake and a sponge cake. Each cake required a dozen eggs: the pound cake used a dozen yolks and the sponge cake needed a dozen egg whites. It was an audacious treat at a time when food was scarce. She could have sold the eggs and paid a utility bill. But, after months of chicken soup, tomato rice soup, potato pancakes, borsch, French toast and oatmeal, they all needed a treat to bolster them as the depression dragged on, endlessly.

"Mom!"

"What is it, Vicki?"

"Monsignor Mielczarek came into the office this afternoon as Wanda and I were writing in the parish ledgers. He said that he was planning on using us as his secretaries for one more year beginning in September when we are in eighth grade. I told Monsignor I would not be returning to St. Mary Magdalene school because Dad was out of work and was turned down for charity and couldn't afford the tuition. He looked surprised.

"Monsignor said, 'Vicki, you are coming back to school and will receive your diploma. You work hard for your diploma and I will help you get it. I will see you on the second floor in September.'"

"Mom, he also said that when I come to work in the rectory on Monday, he will have something for me. What do you suppose he meant?"

"Vicki, I have no idea." She was as much at a loss to figure it out as was her daughter. Frank had taken a walk to visit his daughter, Agnieska. When he returned, Vicki relayed her conversation to him with the same excitement. He, too, was not sure what the Monsignor meant. They would have to wait until Monday to find out.

They saw Vicki running down the street as fast as she could on Monday afternoon. She was grinning from ear to ear. The trellis gate banged behind her as she hurried down the sidewalk and into the house. She ran to her dad and put an envelope in his hand.

"Monsignor Mielczarek brought this to me and said that I was to give it to you as soon as I arrived home."

She stopped stirring the pot of soup and watched as Frank took the envelope addressed to him. Slowly, he opened it. Inside was a note from the Monsignor informing him that he had met with the Church Committee. An arrangement had been made with the Hunding Dairy to deliver two quarts of milk to the house every other day. Also, the committee would send an envelope to Frank each week with four dollars inside for food. This would continue until Frank was called back to work.

The note also said that Vicki's tuition for eighth grade was being paid. She would report to class on the first day of school in September and she would continue to work in the parish office each week after school.

The first four dollars were inside the envelope. Praise be to God! She crossed herself. Tonight, she would pray an extra rosary in thanksgiving for God's goodness.

SEPTEMBER 1932

Sophie

"Julia," she called out as she saw her daughter traipsing down the stairs heading toward the back door. "Where are you going?"

"To Agnieska's," Julia replied, as she opened the door, stepped out, and quickly closed it.

From the kitchen window, she watched her daughter walk briskly through the back yard and down the alley toward 82nd Street. She was wearing her new navy dress with a white scalloped collar and navy pumps. Her hair was brushed until it glistened. She had caught a glimpse of rouge, powder and lipstick on her face. A navy hat with a small feather sat jauntily on her head. Julia never dressed up when she was going to wash beer bottles for Agnieska. She never walked so eagerly toward a task she hated.

Julia had turned eighteen in March. Her looks were so much like Agnieska's, with sable hair, a long straight nose, a mouth that rarely smiled and Frank's deep brown eyes. She was slender with long fingers like her dad's.

She sighed and punched down the bread dough on the table, kneading it and folding it again. Whereas Vicki was an open book, Julia was the book that only a key could unlock.

Each morning, before she left for her job at the Hyde Park Laundry, Julia would grab a cup of coffee and a biscuit, consuming them silently while standing at the kitchen sink. She was home for supper, but said little at the table. In the evening, she would go to Lottie's or Bernice's homes with her embroidery bag. She wondered if Julia's friends talked while their needles created lovely designs on pillowcases, tablecloths, doilies and dresser runners. In Polish tradition, she was embroidering linens for her trousseau.

After receiving her first paycheck from the laundry, Julia had given her dad a small amount of money for room and board. She wasn't able to give him more because she needed a place to store her linens. She was using the money to make a down payment on a cedar chest that she was buying at Bay Furniture.

She sighed again. It was a huge expense at a time when every dollar was needed for food and utilities. She divided the dough and put each half into a bread pan, covering them with a teacloth and leaving them on the table so the dough could rise. Even though she had measured, mixed and kneaded one batch of dough, she knew that one loaf would be a little denser than the other. They would not be identical, just like daughters.

Maryanna

"Hi, Ma," Stephan greeted her as he dropped his metal lunch box on the kitchen table. "When's supper?"

"Didn't Ma give you enough for lunch, Mr. Lawyer, or did you fill your lunchbox with books," Stash teased, as he sat drinking a cup of coffee and blowing smoke rings with his cigarette.

"Food for the mind, Stash. Books are food for the mind. You should try reading one." He grabbed a paczki from the plate on the table, bit off half of the prune-filled pastry, taking the remains with him.

As she browned the chunks of beef in the pot, she could hear the faucet in the bathroom going full volume. Both sons had their father's penchant for cleanliness, a trait for which she was grateful. When her family sat down to supper, the only aromas she wanted to inhale were those of the soups, meats and bread on the table.

"I'll be ready for supper in five minutes," Sally shouted, as she dashed in the door, running toward the bedroom she shared with her cousin, Estelle. Sally had missed sharing the room with her big sister, Estella, even though Estella was eight years older. Laughter was always echoing from behind closed doors.

Cousin Estelle was only five years older than Sally, but their personalities were opposites. Quiet Estelle was a foil for Sally who was always bouncing around with exuberance. Sally knew that in that quietness her cousin harbored a deep love for her.

Shortly after Estella had married Tomasz, Michał agreed to let her niece board with them. Teo, her mother, had dragged Estelle and the two younger children to Detroit when she married Jack whatever-his-name-was. Estelle was miserable in Detroit. She had no friends and she had to leave a job she loved. Fortunately, her employer loved her as much as she loved the job. She was rehired when she returned to South Chicago.

As Stephan sat down at the table, she noticed that he was wearing a white shirt and necktie.

"Hey, did you forget how to read a calendar?" Stash teased. "It's not Sunday."

"You're all gussied up," Sally chimed in. "Are you going to a funeral? Did one of your fishy friends fall into the lake because he was no match for a perch? Or was it a smelt?"

"Funny," Stephan muttered.

"If it isn't a fish, then it's a girl!" Sally chortled. "You fell, not into the lake, but hook, line and sinker for a girl."

"Sally!" she reprimanded her daughter.

"It's okay, Ma," Stephan said, as he rose from the table. "She's just having a little fun. I'm going over to Mike's house," he said, as he kissed her on the top of her white head. He grabbed his coat and was out the door and down the steps.

When had he ever dressed like that to go to Mike's house?

CHAPTER SIX

DECEMBER 1932

Sophie

Christmas was three weeks away. She was planning what needed to be done before the day arrived. It would be a holy day different from those of years past. The Great Depression was not easing up; trying to make ends meet grew harder and harder. In October, she bought a turkey from Mokry's meat market and put it in the pen with the chickens to fatten up. By Thanksgiving, she had a huge bird that provided many meals. She had roasted the bird in the downstairs oven. She boiled the turkey neck and the giblets and cut them into tiny pieces for the gobs of stuffing made from the stale bread that she had saved. She had whipped up a potful of mashed potatoes and made her special recipe coleslaw.

There were two or three hens in the coop that would make good roaster chickens for Christmas. She would cook side dishes and bake the traditional holiday desserts, including the flaky, melt-in-your-mouth ammonia cookies that were Julia's favorite.

As she thought of Julia, she saw her descending the stairs and heading straight toward her.

"Mom, while I've been helping Agnieska, I met someone at her house. His name is Steve. He's a friend of Mike's and Victor, their boarder. We've been taking long walks together to Rainbow Park and to the Gayety Theater and Soda Shop. Mom, I would like you and dad to meet Steve and his parents. Could we have them for dinner on Sunday?"

Ah, the hints that Agnieska had been dropping were true. Her step-daughter had been gloating that she knew something about Julia that her mother didn't. She had chosen to ignore the hints. Now all of them came back like so many daggers into her heart.

"Julia, this is the first I am hearing about a suitor. Why have you never mentioned him before?"

Julia shrugged her shoulders.

"Why has he never come by the house?"

"Mom, it was easier to meet him at Agnieska's."

"Did you think we would not approve?"

"Mom, I have not met Steve's parents, either. We thought it would be a good idea if everyone met at dinner."

"Julia, you know that I enjoy having guests. I would be happy to have this young man and his parents for dinner. I will talk to your father when he returns from the barber shop."

"Thank you, Mom." Julia's eyes sparkled. She gave her a rare smile and headed back upstairs.

She would have to savor what she was given from Julia. A smile was better than nothing. If that were Vicki, she'd have been smothering her with hugs until she was in danger of suffocating.

Maryanna

"Julia is the stepsister of Mike's wife," Stephan said as she and Michał walked with him down 83rd Street to this girl's house. The weather had cooperated for this important dinner engagement. A full sun bleached by winter cast warm rays on a breezeless day.

"Agnieska's mother died when she was about four years old. Her father came to America to support her. He sent for her when she was fifteen. She married Mike when she was eighteen, and a few months later, her father married again. His name is Frank; Julia's mother is Sophie. Their last name is Kravczyk."

When they reached Marquette, she looked compulsively to the right for a glimpse of the first house they had owned. The house where four of her children had lived and four had died before they had a chance to live. The house where she and Michał had woven the strands of joy and sorrow into an unbreakable cord of marital love for each other. At Manistee Avenue, they turned to the left and crossed the street. The Kravczyk house was a half block north of 83rd Street..

Stephan opened the gate in the trellis; she and Michał stepped through. They climbed the stairs to the door and the parlor where she knew the girl's parents were waiting, as anxious as she.

"Dzien dobry. Jestem Frank. *Good day, I am Frank,*" Julia's father bade them welcome as he opened the door and held it open while they entered the house.

"Dzien dobry. Jestem Michał. To jest moja żona, Maryanna i mój syn, Stephan. *Good day. I am Michał. This is my wife, Maryanna, and my son, Stephan,*" Michał replied. She stepped from the entrance hall into a small parlor that definitely met her standards of cleanliness and neatness. The brown jacquard horsehair sofa and armchairs were brushed and tidy. The tables were highly polished and covered with embroidered cloths. Standing next to the table by the window was the mother and her two daughters. The younger girl, about fourteen, was her mother's child; they shared honey blond hair - the mother's liberally streaked with grey - the same light blue eyes and ruddy facial features. The older one favored her father in looks with brown hair that was almost black, dark brown eyes and a tall, skinny figure.

"Dzien dobry," she said to the mother. "Jestem Maryanna. To jest mój syn, Stephan. *Good day. I am Maryanna. This is my son, Stephan.*" She patted his arm as he stood beside her.

"Mile widziany. Jestem Sophie. To sæ moje córki, Julia i Vicki. *Welcome. I am Sophie. These are my daughters, Julia and Vicki,*" Sophie greeted her. "Vicki will take your coats and hats."

Stephan turned to help her with her coat. He gave it to Vicki, who smiled at him as he quickly slipped out of his coat and gave it to her with his hat and gloves. Her arms piled high, she took the coats into the adjacent bedroom and laid them on the bed.

Michał had been standing in the little entry hall with Frank. As he stepped into the parlor, she thought she saw a look of puzzlement flicker on Sophie's face.

Sophie

"Michał, to jest moja żona, Sophie. *Michał, this is my wife, Sophie,"* Frank said. "Sophie, to jest Michał. *Sophie, this is Michał."*

Michał smiled broadly and bowed slightly toward her as he was introduced. There was something about him. She dismissed the thought as quickly as it had surfaced. She had met thousands of people over the years; so many of them looked like someone else. At the moment, there were more important matters to occupy her mind, like making sure that dinner was ready to be served.

"Welcome to our home," she replied. " Please, sit down and make yourself comfortable. Nasz dom jest twoim domem. *Our home is your home."* She excused herself and walked into the kitchen, beckoning Vicki to follow.

The table gleamed with the good dishes that Frank had given her one Christmas years ago. Crimson red roses entwined in an ivy garland bordered each ivory plate. They rested on a spotless white tablecloth flanked by napkins embellished with embroidered flowers, a tribute to Julia's dexterity with a needle.

Vicki spooned the mashed potatoes from the pot into a huge tureen. She poured the smooth-as-silk gravy into a bowl while her mother arranged the pieces of roasted chicken on a platter. The homemade bread and butter were already on the table. Vicki pulled the dish of coleslaw and the pitcher of milk for coffee from the icebox. The 12-egg pound cake and the sponge cake were sitting on the sideboard.

While she set about her tasks in the kitchen, her ears were tuned in to the conversation in the parlor. Frank and Michał were sharing information amicably. She heard a shout of recognition as both men confirmed that each thought the other looked familiar and realized that they were part of the large St. Mary Magdalene Society of Men and participated in the huge outdoor Eucharistic processions each summer.

When the table was ready, she hugged Vicki to thank her for all her help. She gave Vicki the dinner plate that had been prepared for her while they were setting up the serving dishes. As was the custom, she was too young to be part of conversation at table with adults. Vicki happily hugged her back. She ran down the stairs eager to eat dinner and play with Skulk, the current henhouse cat.

She stood in the parlor doorway, a signal for Frank to invite their guests to table. Both men sat at either end of the table while she sat on one side with

Julia and Maryanna and Steve sat across from them. If it weren't for Frank and Michał, the conversation during the meal would have been awkward. As they ate and talked, she realized that both men seemed to be cut from the same cloth. They were devoted to their families and to their wives, she noted, as she saw Michał turn toward Maryanna to make sure that she was comfortable. As he did so, a startling image from long ago flashed across her mind. Impulsively, she began to interrogate her guests. Frank looked at her, quizzically.

"Maryanna, when did you emigrate to America?"

"In 1906."

"And you, Michał?"

"I also emigrated in 1906. We met on board ship."

"Did you sail on the *SS Merion?*"

"Yes! How would you know?" Both Michał and Maryanna gazed at her in bewilderment.

"Maryanna, did you ever need medical assistance during the voyage?" she asked Steve's mother, breathlessly.

Steve and Julia stared at her with perplexed expressions.

"I did," Maryanna stammered, quietly.

"Maryanna, Michał, I was your interpreter in the medical bay after the...the accident on board ship."

"Ma, I didn't know you had an accident on board ship!"

"It was nothing, Stephan. Your father came to my rescue. I had sprained my wrist while walking on deck one morning and he escorted me to the sick bay. That's how we met."

She would not add any details to what Maryanna chose to divulge to her son. It was her business and Michał's.

All around the table there were exclamations of disbelief and amazement. She felt Frank's hand on hers, squeezing it tightly. She saw Michał do the same to Maryanna.

She rose to clear the table and Julia rose with her. Together they put the leftovers away and served coffee and dessert. The stilted conversation that had permeated the earlier part of the meal had disappeared in a puff of realization that events of twenty-five years ago had planted seeds that were now bearing fruit.

Each family was eager to hear about the journey that the others had made from Poland to America to the present day. She was pleased to see that Steve was soaking up every word. He was a handsome man, similar in looks and physique to his father, but more relaxed in manner.

As Michał related his family history, she understood the origin of his chivalrous ways, enhanced by the Victorian era in which he grew up. Living in Warsaw, and with his family pedigree, he would have been aware of what was going on elsewhere in the world. Even in Piotrkow, the families for which she worked were in tune with what was occurring on the rest of the continent, the politics, the wars, the economic ups and downs, the marriages and deaths of kings and queens. It was only in the villages, such as the one from which Maryanna had come, that current events were unknown or deemed unimportant.

There was also personality. Steve was lapping up all the information that his parents and she and Frank were sharing. He was asking questions about her years as an interpreter on ship lines. Julia sat quietly with her hands in her lap.

The coffeepot drained, generous portions of each cake demolished, and conversation exhausted, Maryanna moved to rise from her chair. Steve jumped up and slid the chair out from under her. She offered the rest of the cakes to Maryanna who eagerly accepted; her two younger children, Stash and Sally, would enjoy them. Julia went into the bedroom to fetch the outerwear while she boxed up the cakes. Cordial farewells were shared in the parlor. The limpid sun cast long shadows as Steve and his parents walked through the trellis gate.

Julia was in the kitchen stacking the dishes in the sink. Vicki bounded up the stairs bringing her plate. She had washed it in the sink downstairs, but it belonged with the good dishes upstairs. She looked around the kitchen.

"Mom, where are the cakes?" Disappointment filled her face as she learned they had been given to the guests. In these hard times, it was the rare occasion when her mother could afford to use a dozen eggs for cakes. While she had been playing with Skulk downstairs, she had been dreaming of a big slab of sponge cake topped with peaches canned last summer and a dollop of whipped cream.

Sloughing off her disappointment, she commented, "Well, it seems that dinner wasn't going too well in the beginning. I only heard dad and Mr... Mr. what's his last name?"

"Vinefsky," Julia said. "Their last name is Vinefsky."

"Okay," Vicki continued. "I only heard the voices of Dad and Mr.

Vinefsky. Then something must have happened because I could hear everyone talking all at once and shouting and laughing."

"Vicki," she told her daughter, "I met Mr. and Mrs. Vinefsky on board ship when I was an interpreter on the *SS Merion*. There was an accident on deck and Mrs. Vinefsky sprained her wrist. Mr. Vinefsky happened to be nearby and he escorted her to the medical bay. I was on duty that morning and interpreted for them and for the doctor. That was how they met each other and I came to know of them."

"Wow," said Vicki, her fourteen-year-old eyes as round as the saucers she was drying. "What a romantic story!"

You don't know the half of it, she thought, as she folded the tablecloth and put it and the napkins in the wash basket while Julia and Vicki finished the dishes.

JANUARY 1933

Sophie

"Frank, what are we going to do? Julia is so stubborn. She insists on being married this June."

Steve had come to the house the evening before. He and Julia sat in the parlor upstairs. After an hour or so, they came downstairs to where she and Frank were sitting in their rocking chairs. Julia had a huge smile on her face and her eyes sparkled like the black star sapphire ring that Mrs. Cohen sometimes wore when she came to order poultry. She and Steve stood before her and Frank.

"I have asked Julia to marry me," Steve said, "and she has accepted. I hope you do not have any objections to our intentions."

She remained quiet, letting Frank respond. She knew that he was hurt. This was not the tradition. It was customary for a suitor to ask the father for his daughter's hand in marriage and receive his blessing before ever proposing to his intended.

Frank rubbed his hands together. "I wish I could give Julia the same kind of wedding I gave Agnieska. Without a steady paycheck coming in, that is impossible. I have been hearing that the steel mills will be recalling some of their workers. Steel will be needed for some of the projects that President Roosevelt is proposing. The railroad will be hauling ores. Many of the cars will need repair after sitting idle for years. If Julia and Steve will wait until I'm called back, we could have a wedding at Marquette Gardens."

"Frank, recalling workers is the best news I've heard in a long time. It's been worrisome wondering how much longer we could hold on. Thank God, we've always managed to scrape enough money together to pay our mortgage. We have a roof over our heads."

They were resting downstairs in the sitting area that Frank had created. Being home all day, he had noticed that his young daughters spent most of their time upstairs sitting in their bedroom or at the kitchen table. There was no longer any need for the big open space downstairs where they had played as little girls. He had many friends with time on their hands and experience in various trades. He persuaded them to help him make some changes in his house; in return, he would help them with their projects that required more hard work than money. A friend who was a plumber came across bathroom fixtures that could be had for next to nothing. A contractor whose home building halted when the depression hit had no place to store them and was eager to get them off his hands. The end result was a full bathroom on the ground floor and a bedroom with a closet.

Now they sat in a cozy area opposite the bedroom, each one comfortable in their rocker with a round table between them and a braided rug that she had made to keep the dampness of the floor from their feet.

"Looks like you added to the house just in time," she said, as she sewed on buttons that had fallen off one of his shirts.

"It's getting harder for both of us to climb those stairs many times a day," he said, not mentioning how much more difficult it was for her than for him. Arthritis was affecting her limbs, though she brushed it off. "Now that we have a third bedroom, if Julia and Steve need a place to live, they can have the bedroom upstairs and we can live down here. We spend most of our time down here, anyway. Maryanna and Michał don't have room with two children and her niece in their house. We only have Vicki."

"Maryanna and Michał are good people. He's like you, Frank. I hope that his son takes after him."

Maryanna

"Ma, Dad, I have something to tell you. Yesterday, I asked Julia to marry me. She accepted. Her parents do not object."

She wasn't surprised at Stephan's announcement. She was surprised at her innermost reaction. She did not want to let him go. He was her first-born, the one she had always counted on and who always came through for her. He was her helper from the time he was a toddler playing with Dora, to when he was growing into manhood, yet happily took Sally under his wing. One minute he was her son slathering butter on his bread; the next minute, he was husband-to-be to a girl who seemed nice enough but, in her opinion, was too skinny to be very healthy.

"You're getting married? There's going to be a wedding? Will it be at Marquette Gardens? When? Will it be like Estella's? Can I be a bridesmaid?" Sally's mouth was running a mile a minute.

"Sally, enough. It will be up to her parents to make decisions for the wedding. Julia's father is not working in these hard times. And it is up to her to decide who will be bridesmaids. Her sister, Vicki, will probably be her maid of honor."

"But, Ma."

"Sally, listen to your mother. Your time will come. You will be asked to be a bridesmaid so many times you will grow tired of it."

"Never!" she smiled.

JUNE 1933

Sophie

She stared at the black contraption sitting on the small round table in the parlor. She had never felt the need of it but there it was, another way for her stepdaughter to lord it over her.

It all started two weeks before Vicki graduated; she began looking for work. With the depression still holding them in its vicelike grip, more ways to save had to be taken. Frank could no longer afford the luxury of a daily newspaper. Vicki would go to her friend Tillie's house. Tillie's brother, Ed, would give Vicki the Help Wanted ads. One day she found an ad from a woman who needed help with household duties; a telephone number was listed. Vicki went to Rush Pharmacy across the street from the church to use the pay telephone. She called the woman and arranged to meet her at her apartment building.

Mrs. Hyman's husband had a business and often entertained for his brother, Martie, who worked for Flo Ziegfeld on Broadway. Martie brought famous performers and showgirls for dinner. Mrs. Hyman needed someone to help her set up the dining table with the best linens, crystal and china, to help serve the guests, and to clean up afterward. She asked Vicki for her telephone number so that she could call her when she was needed. Vicki gave Tillie's number to Mrs. Hyman.

"Mom, Dad, we have to have a telephone! The days and times I work will vary. We need a telephone so that Mrs. Hyman can call me when she needs me."

"Vicki, slow down," Frank said, admonishing her, while smiling at her exuberance. "It is good for you to find work in these hard times. But you know we can't afford a telephone."

"I will pay for the telephone when I start working," she said.

"But it needs to be installed. We don't have money for that."

Vicki's face looked desolate, then brightened immediately. "I'll ask Aunt Agnieska."

She opened her mouth to tell Vicki she didn't think that was a good idea, when Frank said, "I'm sure my daughter will be happy to help." She closed her mouth and clenched her teeth. Agnieska was careful never to say anything in front of her father, but she never let her stepmother forget that they would lack nothing if they had joined her in her bootlegging business.

Br-ring! Br-ring! She jumped as the sound emanated from the oak ringer box on the wall behind the table. Vicki came running out of the bedroom and picked up the long tube hanging from the clip. "Hello? Hello?"

She glanced around the parlor to be sure that everything was as pristine as could be, then walked into the kitchen where the large table had been set, just as it had been on that Sunday in December when she had met Steve and his parents.

She walked into the bedroom that she had shared with Frank these many years. Mike had helped Frank move their bedroom set downstairs. Julia and

Steve had purchased a set of their own at Bush Furniture. Its walnut wood gleamed against the pale pink wall paper with the grey stripes. She had made a pierzyna for the bed and new goose down pillows which Julia had covered in elaborately embroidered pillowcases edged in crocheted lace. An embroidered runner that matched the pillowcases protected the dresser top. Julia did beautiful needlework.

She opened the closet door. Julia's white satin wedding gown hung from a padded hangar. White satin pumps stood side-by-side in perfect symmetry on the floor next to the huge box with the lace cap and veil. In four days, her daughter would be standing where she had stood with Frank over twenty years ago, in front of the altar at St. Mary Magdalene's. Julia and Steve would make the same promises that she and Frank had made. A silent prayer flitted up from her heart asking for abundant blessings on them. Her fingers brushed the ruffled pink dress that Vicki would wear as bridesmaid.

She closed the door and started for the stairs. She and Frank would have liked to have a big reception for their daughter at Marquette Gardens. It didn't seem to matter to Julia and Steve. They were content to have a small gathering at home. She hurried down the stairs as fast as her arthritis would allow. She had cakes to bake, meats and side dishes to prepare.

Maryanna

How distinct was the wedding of a son from that of a daughter! Even the ceremony was viewed from a different vantage point in the church. When Estella married Tomasz, she had been sitting on the left side of the center aisle, the bride's side. Today, she was on the right side, the groom's side. There had been no preparations for her to make. All she had to do was to dress up and show up.

She felt a rivulet of sweat trickling down from her hair coiled into a tight bun at the nape of her neck. The navy silk dress and jacket felt plastered to her skin. It was only ten o'clock in the morning and already the heat was stifling.

Julia looked cool as a cucumber in her white satin floor-length gown with sleeves that puffed to the elbow, then fit tightly to the wrist. Her dark hair was set in waves that peeked out from the fitted lace cap to which was attached a nine-foot tulle veil edged with deep scallops of lace. Her heart swelled as she turned her gaze to Stephan. He stood tall, shoulders back military-style, cutting a dashing figure in a black tuxedo and starched high-collared white shirt. If he was sweltering, he didn't show it. She felt Michal's hand on hers as Stephan pledged to take Julia, and Julia pledged to take him "to have and to hold from this day forward, for better, or worse, for richer, for poorer, in sickness and in health," until death parted them. She had just gained a daughter-in-law.

Sophie

"Let me help you," she heard as she reached into the oven to pull out the pans of roasted chicken. As she straightened up to put a pan on top of the stove, she saw Agnieska tying an apron around her waist and reaching for one of the serving platters and the tongs. Dumbfounded, she stood watching her stepdaughter piling pieces of chicken on a platter. Of all people, Agnieska, helping her! This was a first. Julia's wedding day will be a day to remember for more reasons than Julia will ever know.

As the bridal party arrived from the Urbanowicz Photography Studio on Commercial Avenue, she pulled the cold bowls of potato salad and coleslaw from the icebox, as well as pitchers of icy lemonade and tea. Heaping mounds of homemade biscuits were on the table with crocks of butter and dishes of Polish pickles and those Spanish olives everybody was raving about.

She glanced out the kitchen window. Her new in-laws were sitting in the shade of the apple trees talking with Frank, Mike and Victor. Their youngest son, Stash, was checking the chicken coop with Sally. She wondered why Steve did not ask his brother to be best man. Instead, he chose Johnnie Redmerski. She didn't know much about Johnny. He lived exactly one block over on Marquette with his parents and sisters. He was a close friend of Steve.

Julia's selection of Estelle Wolski as her maid of honor wasn't too surprising. Vicki was too young for the honor. Julia had hit it off with Estelle the first time they met at the Vinefsky home. She recognized Estelle as a waitress at the Tea for Two restaurant on Commercial Avenue. Estelle was Steve's cousin and was born four days after Julia. She was a lovely young woman with a gracious personality that set her blue eyes to twinkling.

A flash of motion distracted her thoughts. Sally was running pell mell toward Vicki. Sally was a year older than Vicki and had finished her first year at Bowen High School. She hoped that Sally wouldn't put crazy ideas of going to high school into Vicki's head. What good could come of it?

She was happy that her girls had eight years of schooling with the good Felician sisters. She appreciated the high standards that they set for their pupils and expected of them. In a world she never could have imagined while milking cows in Poland, her daughters were living in houses with indoor plumbing instead of outhouses, artificial lights instead of candles and kerosene lamps, automobiles instead of horses and buggies or carts, radios that need only a turn of a knob to hear the latest news or listen to music, telephones that let you talk to someone without going to their house, and those aeroplanes which some crazy men flew across the Atlantic Ocean in hours instead of the weeks she had spent on every crossing. It was incredible!

"Sophie," Agnieska called out, as she tromped down the stairs, "everything is set for dinner upstairs."

Both women untied their aprons, hung them on the hooks by the sink, and went out together to greet the happy couple.

APRIL 1934

Maryanna

Less than a year later, she was sitting again on the groom's side of the church, without the suffocating heat that had melted her last June. In fact, she had donned her lightweight navy woolen spring coat for the short walk to the church. The altar was resplendent with an abundance of lilies that adorned it since Easter Sunday less than three weeks ago. Unconsciously, she nodded her approval as she noticed the robust health of the plants; someone else in the parish also loved flowers and babied them, too.

Her attention shifted to movement beyond Michał. Julia was slowly moving into the bench, the child within her leading the way. Pregnancy was good for her daughter-in-law; it brought color to her cheeks and flesh to her bones. Stephan smiled at her and winked as he followed his wife. He had been so proud the day he had told his father that soon he would be joining him in responding to that honored name. He would be a good father.

Frank, Sophie, and Vicki were sitting in the bench behind her. Sophie leaned forward and patted her shoulder. Every Sunday, she and Michal were invited to a dinner that Sophie prepared. She had shared with Sophie that Stash loved the girl across the street, since she was fifteen. There hadn't been anyone else for either of them. Stash had waited patiently until Esther was eighteen.

She glanced across the aisle. Lottie was sitting alone in the first pew, staring, unseeingly, at the main altar. What should have been an occasion of joy for her neighbor who lived across the street and her daughter was a source of immense discord and pain. Her husband was not sitting next to Lottie. Not because he was in the vestibule eager to escort his daughter down the aisle, but because he refused to give his blessing to this marriage, even threatening Esther with dire consequences if she wed Stash. How dare he mar the joy of his daughter?

Strains of music from the organ wafted from the choir loft. She turned in the pew to see Sally doing her best to walk sedately down the aisle and restrain her enthusiasm at being a bridesmaid. She wore the pale pink silk dress with short puffy sleeves with ease and was comfortable with the lace gloves that covered her arms above the elbows. Her youngest was a child no more. The bounce of the wide brim on the matching straw hat and the slight jiggle of the huge bouquet of pink roses were the only indications of the excitement which Sally strove to contain.

Esther was lovely in a simple, white, long-sleeved silk gown that was enveloped by a magnificent veil edged with a deep band of exquisite lace. Turning toward the altar, she saw Stash watching his bride with unabashed love.

Estella was at the house overseeing the preparations for the reception that would follow. Esther's father refused to have one in his home. It would be a small event; Esther's many brothers and sisters were not allowed to participate. They would be peeking through the lace curtains on the front windows to see how beautiful their sister was in her bridal finery and wondering what festivities were going on in the house across the street. Even in the peaceful atmosphere of the church, the tension was palpable.

MAY 1934

Sophie

"Sophie, I can't afford to replace the carpet, if you wear it out pacing back and forth like that."

"Why is it necessary to have babies in a hospital? Hospitals are for sick people. What's wrong with the połwożna? They've been birthing babies for centuries."

"The current thinking, Sophie, is that fewer babies with problems at birth will die, if they are born in hospitals where measures can be taken to save their lives. Maryanna might not have lost three babies, if that had been the case fifteen years ago."

"Too much is changing too quickly. Hospitals are so far away from home," she muttered. It wasn't that she thought having the baby in a hospital was frivolous. It wasn't that all hospitals were so far away. What was really rankling her was that, because of the distance, Julia would be driven home from the hospital by the only relative who had a car, Mike. And, of course, Agnieska would go with him and Steve, which meant that her stepdaughter would see little Sylvia before she did. It wasn't fair.

Vicki opened the front door, shouting, "They're here! Mike just pulled up in front of the house." She slammed the door and went flying down the front steps and sidewalk.

Through the lace curtains, she could see Julia bracing herself with her right hand as she slowly emerged from the back seat of Mike's Plymouth holding tightly the little blanketed bundle in her left arm. Steve jumped out of the other side with Julia's valise. Vicki was hovering around Julia trying to get a look at her niece.

Frank rose from the sofa and took her arm. "Come, Busia," he said, teasingly. "Time to meet your granddaughter." He guided her into the little hall and out the door onto the wide front porch. She watched as Julia slowly made her way up the steps with Vicki and Steve following close behind and Mike and Agnieska bringing up the rear.

Julia was smiling broadly. She lifted the edge of the blanket covering the little one's face. "Meet your wnuczka *(granddaughter),*" she said, radiant with pride. Tufts of light brown hair framed the face of the cherub who was fast asleep. Steve held the door open as Julia and she and Frank trooped into the house. Julia went straight for her bedroom where the white bassinet stood in one corner of the room.

She had soft sheets on the mattress and a blanket tucked in at the foot. She had stocked the dresser drawers with vests and diapers, caps and booties, baby sweaters, long nightgowns, kimonos and blankets that she had sewn or crocheted. A tray stood on top of the dresser, in the corner next to the bassinet, with lotions, wash cloths, soft towels, diaper pins. A large protective cloth with a rubber backing, for changing the baby, was folded neatly at the foot of the double bed.

Vicki followed, eager to see her niece and observe how her sister cared for the baby. She could hear Sylvia whimper as she was awakened so Julia could change her diaper. She heard Vicki oohing and aahing at every tiny sound Sylvia made. She felt her heart expand with love for this first grandchild of hers who, as powerless as she seemed, was forging a bond between two disparate sisters. Frank sensed her impatience as they sat on the horsehair sofa in the parlor. He patted her hand.

At last, Julia was leaning toward her. She reached up as the little bundle was placed in her arms; she pressed Sylvia to her heart. Frank put her arm around her shoulders and reached over to touch the babe's head. How gnarled his hands looked next to the silky-smooth skin of their granddaughter. This child was the reward for all the years of hard work that had wreaked havoc on his hands and hers. All that they stood for and struggled for and believed would now live in future generations. She looked into Frank's eyes and saw in them the same love that had won her heart over twenty years ago.

MAY 1935

Sophie

She put the finishing touches on the 12-egg cakes. The sponge cake would be served with fresh strawberries from the garden and the heavy cream that Vicki was whipping up in the steel bowl. She was frosting the pound cake in a pink-tinted buttercream. On the sideboard in the upstairs kitchen was a large pink candle to be put on the cake for Sylvia to blow out. The shot glass, silver dollar, and the rosary were waiting beside the candle to determine Sylvia's personality; they would be placed on the tray of her high chair. The shot glass represented sociability; the coin, prosperity and ambition; the rosary, religious awareness. What would Sylvia choose? Julia had reached for the rosary; Vicki, for the silver dollar.

The past year had flown by with so many changes. Best of all, Frank had been called back to work at the B&O. The people next door moved and Steve rented the apartment from the landlady whose daughter and son-in-law lived on the second floor. She missed sidestepping around the kitchen as Sylvia crawled around, but, truth be told, the upstairs had been crowded with the crib in the parlor, once Sylvia outgrew the bassinet.

"I'll take the cakes and cream upstairs," Vicki said, "and put them in the icebox."

She knew Vicki missed playing with Sylvia every evening after she came home from work at the laundry. For the past few months, she had been the sole occupant of the second floor and began a campaign to get her and Frank to move back upstairs. She had mixed feelings about that. The stairs were not as easy to negotiate. She needed to be on the first floor in the big kitchen and out in the yard where the chicken coop was. Vicki promised she would be their feet. The upstairs bedroom was warmer than the one downstairs; it was nearest to the coal stove. There was damp ground below the wooden floor on the first level. She had been quite persuasive and they had moved their bedroom set upstairs.

She dumped the bowls, spoons and other utensils into the sink and turned on the hot water. Within a few minutes, she had the contents of the sink washed, rinsed and on the drainboard to air dry. She took the soapy dish cloth and washed down the top of the table. She untied her apron and hung it on the hook. Time to go upstairs, rework her braided hair, and change her dress.

In the mirror over the dresser, she could see the crucifix on the wall behind her bed. Her heart filled with gratitude for all the blessings she had been given this past year. The knocker sounded on the front door. She heard Frank open the door and Mike's voice as he entered with Agnieska. Steve's family would be arriving soon.

Maryanna

"Ma, what am I going to do? Felix is killing Esther. He's her dad; she loves him. But he won't have anything to do with her as long as we are married. He won't see her, talk to her. And he won't allow her to see her family, her mother, kid sisters and brothers. He's tried to do the same thing to Sigmund and his wife Louise because they were in the bridal party. But Sigmund stood up to him and he won't back down; I think Felix is afraid of his eldest son. He knows he can't browbeat him.

"So, he's taking it out on Esther's mother because she was at the wedding, even though he forbade her to go. It's tearing Esther apart. It's tearing the family apart. Her father is determined to get our marriage annulled." Stash was slumped in the chair across from her at the kitchen table. She had poured him a cup of hot coffee; it sat untouched.

"Stash," she said, keeping her tone of voice even while her insides were raging against Felix. How dare he do this? What kind of idiotic reason was the fact that he was a teetotaler and Stash and his father weren't? And because of that, his daughter couldn't possibly have a good marriage? It was utter nonsense.

"Stash, I am devastated for you. I know you love Esther and would do anything for her because you love her. Your father knows it, too. He has gone over to see Felix and, in his gentle way, he has tried to reason with him. He has asked Felix to give you and Esther time to prove that both of you will forge a good marriage. Felix wouldn't listen to a word your father said. He just about threw him out of the house, calling him a drunkard, shouting he could never believe the word of a drunk." She pressed her lips together in silence. She couldn't share the vitriolic statements that Felix had made against Stash.

Her bereft son lifted his head and took a sip of the now tepid coffee. She picked up the cup and dumped its contents into the sink, refilling it from the coffeepot percolating on the stove. Stash took a sip of the hot beverage to clear the emotion blocking his throat.

"At first, her mother would call her when Felix was out of the house. One day, little Felix blurted out that he, too, wanted to talk to his sister like mommy did. His father went into a rage and tore the phone off the wall. He won't allow any letters between Esther and her family. No one else is allowed to touch the mailbox. When he's home, he waits for the mailman. He has even demanded that Joe at Rush Pharmacy tell him if Esther's mom comes in to use the telephone. He's turned the house across the street into a prison.

"Louise is wondering what kind of family she married into only three weeks before us. Felix is accusing her and Sigmund of violating his demands. He's right; they are the only members of the family that we see because they don't live with him.

"What am I going to do, Ma? I love Esther. I want to spend the rest of my life with her. She feels the same. But not seeing her big family is killing her. She can't eat; she's losing weight. She hasn't seen her mom or little Felix or baby Lizzy since Christmas when her dad was working and we sneaked over. She was like a second mom to Lizzy ever since she was born. That's really when Esther and I started spending time together. She'd be taking Lizzy out in the pram for a walk; I'd join her when she turned the corner. As she grew older, we'd take Lizzy down the street to Eckersall Park and push her on the baby swings. We'd tease each other and laugh about looking like a married couple.

"Ma, every minute we spent together increased my love for Esther. The happiness that we looked forward to as husband and wife has been sabotaged by her father. Not only will he not allow her to see her mother, he sends her nasty letters alluding to what could happen to her mother if she doesn't leave me and come home. He twists the knife in her heart by relating all the cute things that Lizzy is doing. Ironically, he's bringing me down to his level, guardian of the mailbox to try and circumvent his letters that would cause Esther pain. I work; I can't be there every time the mailman arrives.

"Ma, I told Esther I'd do anything for her because I love her. I meant it. Do I have to give her up so she can see her family? I don't want to, but if it's the only way to give her family back to her..." his voice trailed off as he buried his face in his hands.

CHAPTER SEVEN

AUGUST 1936

Maryanna

Here she was, playing musical church pews again. Two years ago, it was right side for Stash and Esther. Today, it is left side for her niece, Estelle, marrying Leon Josefowicz. She slid into the pew and sat down. What a bittersweet moment! One half of her heart was thrilled because Estelle was marrying a good man. The other half was brimming with sorrow for Stash who was sitting next to her, stoically alone.

Stash had agreed to sacrifice a life with Esther so that she could have her family back in her life. The divorce had become final earlier in the year. Stash had moved back home. She knew it killed him every time he looked across the street and saw the house where Esther had lived. If there was any balm, it was that Esther refused to live under her father's roof. She was living with her brother Sigmund and Louise in their apartment on Baltimore Avenue. She would visit at home with her mother and family when her father was working.

This was the fourth time divorce had reared its ugly head in her family; it was the only time that it was not the desire of her relative. Twelve years ago, it had been her cousin Josie, leaving Joseph behind and running off with Walter to Detroit. They never had children of their own, but he had been a good father to Virginia and Chester. She wondered what happened to Joseph; he had left South Chicago and no one seemed to know where he went. It still irked her that she had been so naive and had no idea what was going on between Josie and Walter who had been her boarder!

She looked up at the back of her sister Teo's head. Seven years ago, she had gone to Detroit with her three children and this Jack whatever-was-his-last-name. It had been traumatic for Estelle who was no longer a child. Today, her sister was sitting in the first pew with another husband, Glenn. Jack hadn't lasted more than a year or two when Teo was restless again. She couldn't get a straight answer out of Teo as to where and when she met Glenn. Stella told her he had several sons and daughters and had left his wife shortly after the youngest was born. Teo had married him within the last year and was now living with him in St. Louis.

Teo was looking good, she admitted to herself. At forty years of age, she still had her dark, curly hair framing full cheeks and dancing eyes. She was stylishly dressed as mother of the bride in a mauve chiffon dress with short, ruffled sleeves and long gloves. A wide-brimmed hat with primroses and feathers sat jauntily on her curls. No wonder she caught many a man's eye.

Her niece, young Theodora, sat next to her mother. At eighteen, she was a beauty, inheriting her mother's dark hair and flashing eyes. She sat regally in a pale blue chiffon frock with long sleeves that buttoned at the wrist. A small blue cloche hat covered her tresses.

She felt Stash jostle her a bit as he moved over to make room for Steve and Julia. She patted his hand, reassuringly. Estelle had been Julia's maid of honor. She wanted Julia to be part of her wedding as matron of honor. Julia's rotund abdomen precluded that. She would be welcoming Stephan's second child - her third grandchild - in three months.

The first strains of the bridal march broke her reverie. She stood up to watch Estelle walking up the aisle on the arm of her uncle, Michał. Only God knew where her own father, Mike, was.

NOVEMBER 1936

Sophie

"Mom! Dad! I'm so excited! Julia asked me to be Julianne's godmother." Vicki burst into the kitchen talking nonstop while she pulled off her coat and scarf and hat.

"How is Julia?" She was cutting potatoes, carrots, onions and beef into chunks for a hot, satisfying stew. Now that Frank was working steadily, she could satisfy his craving for meats other than the chickens and ducks she raised.

"Mom, Julia is looking well and happy. Wow, being in a maternity ward is like being a rich person on vacation. Julia doesn't have to lift a finger. The nurses take care of everything. We had a really nice visit. I gave her the cookies that you made. She was happy to receive them and asked me to give you her thanks.

"After our visit, a nurse took me to see Julianne in the nursery. It's amazing! It is one large room with one wall that is all windows facing the corridor. Only the nurses are allowed into the nursery. They take the babies from the bassinets and bring them over to the windows. Each bassinet has a pink or blue ribbon tied to it.

"Julianne is the cutest thing! She has black curly hair and dark eyes like Dad. She's a tiny thing. You're going to love her, Mom! Well, of course you're going to love her. She's your new granddaughter." She stopped to catch her breath.

Frank looked up from the newspaper which he could once again afford. "What's this?" he asked, distractedly.

"Dad, Julia asked me to be her godmother. What do I have to do to be a godmother?"

"Vicki, don't worry about it. Just answer the questions the priest will ask you. They are not difficult questions. You will be asked if you are willing to help the parents raise the child in our faith. Who is going to be her godfather?"

"Steve's brother, Stash," Vicki replied. In a flash her exuberant face melted into sadness. "Dad, how could that man do that to him and Esther? What kind of father is he? Even I could see how much they love each other."

"Vicki, Esther's father is not well in his head. No loving father would do that."

"Dad, if I had a father like that, I wouldn't let him win. If I fall in love with someone and marry him, I will stay married! And I would see my mother whenever I pleased."

"Your personality and spirit are different than Esther's. And you don't have any younger brothers and sisters that you love and would miss. It is hard to leave those you love.

"It was hard for me to leave Agnieska. She was only nine years old when I came to America. I heard that we could have a better life here; that's what I wanted for her. It has been good. Even through this Great Depression, our lives have been much better than they would have been in Poland.

"Vicki," he said, mischievously, with a huge smile that turned up the ends of his mustache, "if you were in Esther's shoes, we'd see a performance greater than Sarah Bernhardt ever gave."

"Dad!" Vicki bear hugged him, delighted with his comment.

ക്ക്ക്

"I'm so nervous," Vicki complained, the Sunday morning of the christening.

"Vicki, relax. Answer the questions truthfully. You will be fine," Frank said, as he sat on the old rocker bouncing Sylvia on his knee. "More, dziadza (grandpa), more," Sylvia pleaded, as the twinge in his knee slowed him down.

Vicki slipped into her winter coat and hat and donned her boots for the two-block trek to the church with her brother-in-law and sister and little Julianne.

"Vicki, Steve and Julia stepped out the door." She had been standing by the kitchen window watching the house next door. Julia had the little one well bundled against the weather in a heavy woolen blanket. Vicki would meet them by the gate.

She set about making gravy for the potatoes she had whipped into mounds of creamy white goodness. Frank was keeping Sylvia out from underfoot. She loved watching Sylvia run about, but not when she was carrying platters and bowls of food from stove or icebox to the table. She couldn't sidestep as easily as she did when her girls were little.

She heard the knocker clack on the front door. That would be Steve's parents arriving a bit early. They had probably walked as far as the church with Stash. She turned the flames off under the gravy and moved it off the burner to sit on the warm stove. She took off her apron and smoothed her dress before joining her guests.

As she entered the parlor, she saw Michał grabbing Sylvia and swinging her around high in the air. She heard the little one squealing, "Dizzy, dziadza, dizzy."

"How is Stash?" she asked Maryanna, solicitously. She was worried that

109

asking him to be Julianne's godfather would be for the worse, conjuring up thoughts of what might have been for him and Esther.

"He's getting better. If that cur, Felix, had any brains, he would see how much Stash loves Esther. All that good-for-nothing can see is that he won."

"Now, now, Maryanna, get hold of yourself. I do agree with you, wholeheartedly. Stash has made the ultimate sacrifice of love, willing to forego his happy life for her sake. It takes a strong man to do so. You have raised a son of which any mother would be proud."

The christening party piled into the parlor, stomping the snow from their boots. Vicki was carrying Julianne and headed straight for her parents' bedroom where she laid her on the new pierzyna. Julia followed with the bag of diapers and a change of clothes. Frank paced impatiently waiting for Julia to change her. Then, he scooped up his granddaughter and sat down in the rocker to wait for the bottle of milk to warm up on the stove.

While Julianne downed her bottle, Vicki brought up from downstairs the platters of meat and helped her set all the serving bowls on the table. Somewhere in the commotion, Agnieska and Mike arrived. Julia settled a sleeping Julianne in the center of the bed and joined everyone at table. Frank prayed the Grace before Meals. She watched with a satisfied smile as ten famished people demolished in an hour what it had taken days to prepare.

MAY 1937

Maryanna

Was there something in the water back home in the 1890's that gave her cousins and younger siblings crazy ideas as adults? She pulled the letter out of her apron pocket and read it again.

> *Dear Maryanna,*
>   *I don't know how to tell you this sad news. My hand is shaking and tears are blurring the ink. Stanley has disappeared. Two months ago, I came home from the public aid office and he was gone. He left a note on the table together with one dollar*

*and two dimes. He said that it was all that he had and to use
it for the children.*

*No one in town has seen him since. For months, he's
been talking crazy. He's convinced that this depression is the
work of the devil and that if he can get enough people to pray,
it will end. He started standing on street corners shouting to
people to stop and pray. I begged him to stop this crazy
behavior; it was hurting our children when their friends made
fun of him. He wouldn't listen and even turned on me.
Our pastor tried speaking to him, but it was as if Stanley
was possessed. Nothing would stop him.*

*Now, I don't know what to do. We have not had
the money to pay the mortgage for over a year. Before that, we
would pay what we could and the bank was understanding.
But the bank cannot wait any longer and we must leave the
house at the end of the month.*

*Maryanna, I have nowhere to go; I don't know what
to do. I still have the middle boy and the twins. Please help,
Maryanna.*

God bless you and Michał for anything you can do.

Josephine

She waited patiently until Stash and Sally left the dinner table and Michał
had settled back in his chair relishing a third cup of coffee and a cigar. Then
she pulled the letter out of her apron pocket and read it to him. She was
reading the final paragraph when Stash sauntered in for another cup of
coffee.

"What's going on, Ma? Is that letter from Aunt Josephine?"

"Yes, Stash, it is. Your Uncle Stanley has disappeared. Josephine is beside
herself with fear. She and the children are being evicted from their house in
a few days."

"Of course, we will help them, Maryanna," Michał interjected. "They must
come back to the city."

"They have no means of travel and no money."

"We will provide. Tomasz has a car. Perhaps, he can drive to Ottawa and
bring them back. We will have to find an apartment for them."

"When we took Mike's nephew home, I saw an apartment for rent in the building where he lives at 83rd and Baker. It's small but nice." Stash refilled his coffee cup and sat down at the table. He reached for a prune-filled kolacky.

"Michał, I don't know how much Josephine will have to move. The children are losing much, their dad, the house, friends. They need to bring the things they hold dear, as well as their clothes. Will there be enough room for them and all of their belongings?"

"Would Mike be willing to drive that far?" Michał asked Stash.

"Mike would love it. It's Agnieska who might object."

"She watches every penny."

"Watches it, Pa? Steve says she hoards it. She'll say you're daft for spending your hard-earned money helping someone, even a relative. She thinks that if a person needs help, they brought it on themselves, so why should anyone else bother? I don't know where she heard it, but she's a firm believer in some saying like 'God helps those who help themselves'."

"I will talk to Stella tomorrow. We will figure out how we can keep Josephine and the little ones fed and clothed. She and Stanley share the same name - Stanisława and Stanisław. They were close back home. She will be shocked and distressed when she learns that Stanley is missing."

"Write to Josephine tomorrow, Maryanna," Michał said. "Express our sadness that she is having such troubles. Tell her that we are renting an apartment for her. She should gather together clothing and treasures that she and the children want to keep. We will come to Ottawa on the thirtieth of the month and will bring her and the children back to Chicago. Enclose a ten-dollar bill so they will have enough to eat until we come."

"Ma!" Sally slammed the back door in her hurry to relay some news she had heard from her girlfriend. "Lena's dad told her that Republic Steel and the other little steels have gone on strike today. If you turn the radio on, you'll get more information."

"Pa, that means Steve is stuck inside. One of the unexpected benefits of being a foreman."

Josephine's dilemma receded as she thought of Stephan being caught in all the turmoil of a strike. She understood that men were striking for better wages and reasonable hours each week. She didn't understand why the strikes became violent. What would happen? How long would it last?

JUNE 1937

Sophie

The first glimmer of dawn arose in the eastern sky over the brown brick bungalows across the street. It was time. She hurried across the kitchen to the back door. In the darkness, Julia was stealthily opening the alley gate while cradling a sleeping Julianne. Sylvia was toddling beside her holding Teddy, her big brown bear that Grandpa Frank had given her for her birthday. They stepped through, closed the gate silently, hurried up the path and slipped into the house.

"Thanks, Mom," Julia said. She noticed the worried look on her daughter's face. This was the first time that Steve was coming home since the massacre at Republic Steel.

As the depression receded and men returned to work, aided by the unions, the steelworkers had rebelled against the steel corporations. They were no longer willing to work twelve hours a day for six and seven days a week. In March, U.S. Steel had signed an agreement that guaranteed steelworkers would have an eight-hour workday and a forty-hour workweek. The little steel companies refused to sign the agreement. Republic Steel had been stockpiling cots, food, ammunition and guns. The supervisory employees would keep the mill operational, should the laborers go on strike.

On Memorial Day, a large group decided to march to the mill in a peaceful protest. As they walked across the prairie to the gate at 117th and Avenue O, hundreds of policemen held them back and told them to disperse. A brawl started. The mob said the police began clubbing them and firing on them; the police said the mob had pipes and bats and had fired a gun. The police maintained they had acted in self-defense. Ten men died and scores were injured.

She was inclined to side with the police. Twenty-four hours a day, a car with union men was parked across the street waiting for Steve. They positioned the car so that they could see his front door in the next building as well as her own front door and the sidewalk leading to the alley. They were not there to welcome him. They viewed him as a traitor, union breaker, scab. The men would watch Frank when he left in the mornings to go to work and in the evenings when he returned. They eyed Vicki when she left for her job at the laundry.

In a letter, Steve's sister, Estella, warned Julia not to open her door for anyone. The union men would come up with different gimmicks to gain entrance. They would pretend to be cops dressed in uniform and say something like "your husband is hurt" or "he is dead." Estella suggested that it would be best if Julia stayed with her mom and dad; at the very least, her father should put a deadbolt on her door. Estella's husband, Tom, said that the union guys didn't play games; they were vicious. And they were not the regular rank and file members. They were the higher ups in the union.

Three days ago, Steve had written a note to Julia saying that he would be home this day at dawn to bathe and get fresh clothes. Julia had brought a bag over last evening; it contained clean clothes, Steve's shaving equipment, and other items he didn't have with him when the strike started.

"B-r-ring! Br-ring!" Julia was upstairs and dashed for the telephone in the parlor.

"Mom," she yelled downstairs. "That was Agnieska letting us know the peddler is coming. Open the door when you see Steve."

"Okay, Julia. I will."

She and Agnieska had decided on coded messages to alert her when the car was coming that was dropping Steve off and picking him up later in the day. The driver was a fellow who knew Steve and Mike. He would drive past Agnieska and Mike's house. She would call Sophie with a message that would sound innocent to someone listening in on their party lines.

As she reached the door, she saw a shadow in the bushes along the fence between the house and Ostrowski's to the north. Deftly, Steve swung himself over the fence and dropped down into the yard. Bending low, he crept the few yards to the back door which she quickly opened. Steve slipped in. The door was locked.

"Daddy! Daddy!" little Sylvia squealed, running toward her father to kiss him. "Daddy, your cheeks are like the brush Busia uses to clean the vegetables." He disappeared into the bathroom for the longest time, coming out clean shaven and refreshed.

Julia served him with huge smiles and dancing eyes while Sylvia sat on his lap. He wolfed down sausages, bacon and eggs, toast, coffee and two fresh paczki from Michałowski's bakery. Clean, warm, satiated, his eyelids began to droop.

"Steve, go upstairs and take a nap on a soft bed. Julia and I will be fixing dinner. You will feel better." She shooed him upstairs.

"Daddy! Wake up, Daddy. Dinner's ready." Hours later, Sylvia shook him awake. They feasted on the beef roast which she had prepared along with gobs of mashed potatoes dripping with dark brown gravy, fresh peas from the garden, a fruit compote, freshly baked bread and butter and, of course, for dessert, her famous sponge and pound cakes.

While she and Julia cleared the table and packed up a bounty of leftovers for him to take to the mill, Steve sat with Sylvia tucked beside him on the rocker and Julianne in his arms, smiling and cooing in the inimitable way of a seven-month-old baby.

"Br-ring! Br-ring!" She heard the telephone upstairs ringing and Vicki running to answer it. Quickly, she ran downstairs.

"Ma. Julia. That was Agnieska apologizing for not being able to visit this evening. I didn't know she was coming over."

"Vicki, that is the signal, in case somebody is listening in on the party line. The car to take Steve back to the mill is waiting on Marquette Avenue."

Julia took Julianne from his arms. He hugged Sylvia and kissed Julia. He picked up the bag of fresh clothes and food.

As she opened the back door for Steve, who dashed through the darkening yard and across the alley to the waiting car, a distant memory invaded her thoughts. She had been opening the door for Gottlieb that morning, when four soldiers had dashed around the corner of the cottage across the road and grabbed him. She had screamed and stretched out her arms. He had turned to look back at her in desolation. A soldier tied his hands behind his back. A wagon came round the corner, slowing down just enough for the soldiers to lift him and toss him inside. It was the last time she had seen him alive.

Maryanna

Michał stepped aside so she could precede him into the school auditorium. This was her first time in the gigantic space. Everything in America was huge, especially when compared to Osiek Dolnoslakie where she grew up. She had never seen a space this large, except for the train station downtown when they had arrived from Philadelphia, thirty years earlier. Rows and rows of chairs stretched on both sides of the aisle before her. She didn't know where to go. Michał cupped her elbow in his hand and led her forward. There were two seats on the aisle. He smiled at the couple sitting next to them. He guided her into the row and held the folding chair while she sat down. She sat quietly, mesmerized as the space filled up with people and the noise level escalated as excited parents, most of them a good fifteen years younger than she, greeted each other and proudly spoke about their daughters and sons who were graduating.

She had been reluctant to agree to Sally's request to attend Bowen High School. Sally knew how to read and write and spell in English as well as in Polish. She had studied arithmetic, geography and history. What more did she need? Sally had said that in high school she would study many subjects, including science, home economics, algebra and geometry. She couldn't pronounce the last two words, let alone understand what good they would do for Sally.

Michał had been persuasive. He had been fully in agreement with Sally's desire to further her education. He had even lamented the fact that he had not encouraged Stephan to go to high school, instead of apprenticing as a painter. She recalled his exact words:

"Maryanna, do you remember why we came to America? We came to better our lives and those of any children we might have, and the lives of their children after them. If we wanted our lives and theirs to be the same as that of our parents, we should have stayed back home in Poland. We wanted something better, the opportunities that America provides. We are living in a big house. We have never wanted for food, even during this depression. Our children have always been well clothed. We have been free to worship in our church, as we please, and not as a ruler dictates. In the future, schooling will be most important in order to keep up with all the discoveries that are being made.

"It took almost two weeks to sail across the Atlantic Ocean. Now men are flying across it in hours. Not only can people heat every room in their house with hot water radiators, they can install pipes that bring heat into every room from a furnace that uses coal or oil or gas for fuel. There is a radio in our house. We can hear news from all over the world; we can listen to stories and music. I have read that ten years ago, a man invented a bigger version of the radio with a picture screen that shows the person speaking and moving, just like in the theaters. I am sure that this invention will become as popular as the radio.

"Stash and Estella are content with their lives. Like Stephen, Sally is curious and has the intelligence to grasp many things. She wants to go to high school and I will not oppose it."

She jumped as a gavel was tapped on the podium by an imposing man wearing a cap and gown similar to the one Sally was wearing. The enormous room grew quiet.

"Ladies and gentlemen," he announced, "I am honored and proud to present to you the graduating class of 1937." From the left corner of the auditorium, the high school band played a stately tune. Two by two, the graduates processed up the center aisle. They kept coming and coming and coming. There were over 250 graduates in Sally's class. Two hundred and fifty! That was half the population of Osiek Dolnoslakie. Incredible!

Michał tapped her wrist. She watched Sally walking slowly up the aisle. She was the mother of a high school graduate. Pride filled her heart and her head. God had, indeed, blessed them.

JULY 1937

Sophie

"Mom, the strangest thing happened today at Tillie's after you and Dad left the wake for her dad. Eddie introduced me to his best friend, Wally, who came to the wake with his fiancée, Berniece. Later on, Tillie and I were sitting in the basement having a slice of her mom's raspberry cake and coffee. Wally came downstairs, alone. He poured himself a cup of coffee and put a slice of the coffee cake on a plate. He sat down at the table with us and began a conversation. He was in no hurry to leave. Berniece came down; she was not happy to see him sitting with us. She wanted to know what he was doing downstairs; the wake was upstairs. Wally thanked Tillie for the cake and they left.

"The undertaker came down for coffee. He started telling stories about some of the wakes he attended. If the men of the family were playing cards in the kitchen, he would join them during the slow hours. At one wake, there was a time when no one was in the parlor with the casket. As they were playing, one of the men looked into the parlor and saw the woman start to slowly rise up in the casket. The guy screamed and all the other men ran out the door after him. The undertaker turned around to look at the casket; he knew what had happened. The woman was a hunchback. He had to strap her down in the casket under her clothing so she would lay flat. The strap snapped and her spine was slowly raising her up.

"I would have liked to have seen that," Vicki laughed, as she danced off to her bedroom. There wasn't much that scared Vicki.

NOVEMBER 1937

Sophie

"My Waltzing Mathilda," Frank said, smiling at her. Ever since he had heard the song on the radio, a few years earlier, he would call her that when he was in a jolly mood. He still cut a dashing figure, she thought, as she watched him adjust his tie. He favored the shirts with the starched collars that he took to the laundry each week. His charcoal gray Sunday suit accentuated the grey hairs at his temples. His mustache was still dark. She put on her navy suit with the white collar. She put up her hair using the tortoise combs Frank had given her one Christmas. Last of all, she plopped a navy wide-brimmed hat on her head. She wasn't much for hats; a big babushka was better. Vicki insisted that she wear the hat.

Agnieska had invited them for dinner at a restaurant. It was her treat, her stepdaughter said. She had demurred; Mike and Agnieska had insisted. It had been years since they had dinner in a restaurant.

"They're here," Frank said. He'd been watching for Mike's car.

"Enjoy dinner," Vicki said, looking up from her book.

Mike started driving down 83rd Street toward the Bush. He turned onto Commercial Avenue but drove right past all the good restaurants in the shopping area. He turned west on 95th Street. Wherever was he going? At South Chicago Avenue, he turned north to Yates Boulevard. He was making a big circle. She looked at Frank who was as puzzled as she. On 83rd Street, Mike headed east again toward their house. He stopped in front of Marquette

Gardens. Surprise! Their friends and family were waiting with Vicki and Julia to celebrate their 25th Wedding Anniversary.

There was an abundance of Polish food which she thoroughly enjoyed, since she did not cook any of it. There was an orchestra playing the Strauss waltzes that Frank loved and enough mazurkas and polkas to satisfy all the guests. Prohibition had been repealed and the 'shots and a beer' flowed freely. While the similarities in Frank and Michał were many, including being good dancers, there was one area in which they differed. Frank loved the measured step of a waltz; Michał thrilled to the freedom of a lively polka.

"My dearest Waltzing Matilda," Frank said, his eyes dancing with love undimmed by twenty-five years. He took her hand and led her to the dance floor as the orchestra played the first notes of *The Blue Danube*. She felt a bit uncomfortable as their guests watched. It had been a long time since she had danced with Frank in public. Sometimes, they danced to music being played on the radio, but that was in the privacy of their home. "Don't worry, liebchen. You will always be safe in my arms."

APRIL 1938

Sophie

She hurried to the front door as fast as her arthritic knees would allow. Eddie was standing on the porch, hat in hand.

"Wesołch Świat Wielkanocnych. *Happy Easter,* Mrs. Kravczyk. Is Vicki home?"

"Blessings of the holyday to you, Eddie. Vicki's downstairs with her father. Come in. Sit down. I will call her to come upstairs."

Vicki cast a puzzled look at her as she ran up the steps. What would Eddie want of her?

He stood up when she entered the parlor. "Vicki, do you remember my friend, Wally? You met him at dad's funeral? Wally just left my house. His mother died this morning. He came over to tell me. He wants me and Irene to come to the wake. He said to be sure to bring you."

"Eddie, whatever for?"

"I really don't know," Eddie said, as he twirled his hat in his hand, wishing that Irene was having this conversation with Vicki instead of him. "When he's over at the house, he keeps looking this way and asking if you are going out with a fellow."

"Eddie, that's crazy. He's engaged."

"I know he is. But he wants us to bring you. Irene will let you know the time." He was out the door before Vicki could reply.

She had overheard the conversation while putting away the dishes from a quiet Easter dinner. It had only been the three of them. Maryanna had invited Julia, Steve and the girls to her house for Easter.

"Mom, why in the world would this Wally want me to come to his mother's wake? It's crazy. I don't even know him, let alone his mother."

"Vicki, that's true. However, he must have a reason. Whatever it is, if he wants you to be there, go. He is hurting, losing his mother at such a young age. Pay your respects to the family and say a prayer for the repose of his mother's soul. You'll be with Irene and Eddie."

"Mom, it was very strange. When I walked into the parlor, I saw Wally's fiancée standing next to him. As soon as he saw me, he immediately left her, walked over and guided me toward the casket. He said, 'Take a good look at my mom, so you will remember her.' Why would he say a thing like that? It makes no sense. Then he introduced me to his father and his brothers and to his Uncle Jake and Aunt Marcy and his cousin, Jane. All the while, his girlfriend was standing in the corner watching me. She was not pleased."

"He has a crush on you, Vicki," Frank said.

"But he's engaged!"

"Will you go to the funeral?"

"I don't know. Irene, Eddie and his mother are going tomorrow. They said I should go with them. The Mass is at St. Michael's."

"I think you should go, Vicki."

"I would lose a day's work; my pay will be smaller at the end of the week."

"Go. Don't worry about the pay," Frank decided.

It was settled.

MAY 1938

Sophie

She was standing in the vegetable garden deciding what to plant. The lettuce and peas had been sown in March and were yielding the first fruits. Frank was sitting on one of the metal chairs fashioning little cages from chicken wire. The cages would keep the rabbits from destroying the pepper plants by eating the first two succulent leaves and leaving only the stem.

She looked at her love. Frank's heart had not been the same since he had pneumonia in the winter. He could no longer keep up with the workload at the B&O and had to leave. He tired easily.

Vicki came through the gate, half flustered, half elated. She plopped down on the chair next to her dad.

"Mom, Dad, you won't believe what happened. Lottie and I were taking her son, Donald, to Dr. Crohn's office in the South Chicago Bank building. The little guy has an infected ear. We were near Goldblatt's when I saw Wally walking with two of his friends. He walked across the street and asked me if I would take in a show with him on Sunday. I hesitated. Lottie gave me a good poke in the ribs with her elbow, my mouth flew open, and I said Yes. Wally gave me a big smile and said, 'I will be at your house at seven o'clock.' Then he walked back across the street to join his friends. I told Lottie that I didn't want to go to the show with him because he's engaged. She said, 'Vicki, don't you know? He broke off his engagement after the funeral for his mother.'"

"So, what is this Walter like?" Frank asked.

"He's not much taller than I am. He appears to be easy-going, smiles easily."

"Where does he live?"

"On 84th and Buffalo. He's the oldest of five brothers."

"What is his last name, Vicki?"

"Bilinski."

"Bilinski? Do you know his father's name?"

"Yes, Dad. His father's name is Peter."

"Where does he work?"

"Where every guy works. At the mill."

"What was his mother's name?"

"Josephine. His dad spoke her name as Jozefa at the funeral."

"Do you know how old Wally is?"

"I think he's the same age as Eddie. Twenty-one. Why all the questions, Dad?"

"Vicki, when you are dating someone, your mother and I want to know about this young man who will be escorting you."

"Okay. I'm going to wash my hands. Mom, I'll get everything ready for dinner." She bounced off the chair and headed for the house.

"Sophie," Frank said, solemnly. "Do you know who will be taking Vicki to the movies on Sunday?"

"How can I, Frank? We've never met him."

"Sophie, I know his father. Wally is the Władysław who was born to my co-worker, Piotr Bilinski, at Christmas in 1916."

"Oh, Frank!" she exclaimed, as she remembered her happiness that Christmas when Frank had told her about the birth. "Wally is the son of Piotr and Jozefa, who had been taken advantage of by Piotr's brother? She's the young woman in the story that shocked the entire neighborhood over twenty years ago?"

"Yes."

She plopped down in the chair that Vicki had vacated. How strange life was! The first astonishment was five years ago when she learned that Maryanna and Michał had been the couple for whom she had been the interpreter on the *SS Merion*. What an unexpected joy that had been! She took Frank's hand in hers. They looked deeply into each other's eyes and understood each other. Vicki and Wally would never hear the story from their lips.

Maryanna

"Ma, it's the opportunity of a lifetime. Joe Wieczorek wants me to partner with him in the tavern. Now that the steel mills are calling back the men and the depression is waning, there is a big demand for celebrations at Marquette Gardens. He is having a hard time juggling both the banquet hall and the tavern. He wants to do the banquet hall and have me take over the tavern." Stephan paused. She knew there was a "but" coming.

"Stephan, that is a wonderful opportunity," she said, filling in the silent gap. "Saloonkeepers back home were men of distinction. They always knew what was going on in the village and in the families, both good and bad. When a man fell into dire straits, he knew he could go to the saloonkeeper and he would help as best he could. Everyone looked up to him. He was the second most important man in the village after the mayor."

Stephan didn't reply. He drained his cup of coffee and set it on the table. He lit a Camel cigarette and puffed on it, deep in thought. She picked up the pot and refilled his coffee cup. Her eldest son had always been a private person, not given to sharing his difficulties. He preferred to resolve them himself. His coming to see her was a puzzlement. What was he facing that he didn't think he could handle by himself? Why had he come to her instead of to his father?

"Stephan, what is the problem? Do you need money to buy into this partnership? For that, you would need to talk to your father."

"No, Ma, it's not that."

"Then what?"

"Julia is totally against it."

"Why?"

"She thinks I'll become a drunk if I'm working in the tavern."

"That's ridiculous. She knew you drank ever since she met you at Mike's. It didn't stop her from marrying you."

"Julia says I have a steady job at the mill. What more could I want? That's the problem, Ma. I want more than the job that I have. I've gone as far as I can go up the ladder at the mill. I'm a foreman, which is a good job. But I can't go any higher because I don't have a high school diploma. Ma, I can't see myself doing the same job for the next thirty years."

"What can I do, Stephan?"

"Can you talk to her, Ma?"

"I think you should talk to her again. She may have been thinking the possibility over and is changing her mind. Sometimes, people need time to mull things over."

"Ma, I've tried talking to her several times. It's like talking to a brick wall. She cannot understand why I would want to leave a big company like Republic Steel where my job is secure. Julia's not an ambitious woman, Ma."

"Stephan, the work you do should be your business, as long as you provide for your wife and children."

"I know, Ma, but Julia is so adamant about this it will drive a wedge into our marriage if I say Yes to Joe. It's almost like I would be committing a mortal sin from which she could not forgive me. I thought that if you talked to her, she might listen..." He shook his head and puffed on the cigarette.

"I don't know what I could say that would change her mind. Julia hasn't exactly warmed up to me these past five years."

"She thinks that Joe is setting me up, will use me and then dump me. Then I will have nothing. The mill can be counted on."

"Stephan, I will see what I can do. Next Sunday after dinner, I will speak with her."

"Thanks, Ma." Stephan mashed the stub of his cigarette in the ashtray, drained his cup, and stood up. He kissed her on the top of her head as he always did.

She heard his footsteps on the back porch stairs as she picked up the cups and set them on the drainboard. His steps were leaden, like his spirit.

She wondered what her son had seen in Julia that made him decide to marry her? Personally, she always thought that Julia was too skinny; it wasn't healthy. She was, however, most grateful to her daughter-in-law for two beautiful granddaughters.

Her family's track record on picking spouses was dismal, she decided. Only she and Michał and Estella and Tomasz were happy with each other and their marriages.

Stash was still reeling after his divorce from Esther. Stella's Ludwig was stern and stifled her sister's fun-loving spirit. Her brother Stanley had left Josephine high and dry; he disappeared and no one knew where he was. Her cousin Josie's first husband had stifled her; unlike Stella, she had rebelled and left him. She had to admit that Josie was happy with Walter. Josie's light-hearted letters always lifted her spirits.

She wished she could say the same for her sister, Teo. Teo's latest letter was sitting on the parlor table. After a blink-of-an-eye marriage to that Jack whoever-he-was, she was now living in St. Louis and working as a waitress in a tavern. Things were not going well with her and Glenn.

Now, this friction between Stephan and Julia. She was not looking forward to Sunday.

DECEMBER 1938

Sophie

Two-year-old Julianne was toddling toward her dziadza, her arms high in the air, wanting to be lifted up. She watched as Frank struggled to bend down and pick up his granddaughter. She could see his chest expanding as he gasped for the air he so desperately needed. She blinked to corral the tears that threatened to fall onto her cheeks. She was losing her love. It wouldn't be long.

Steve and Julia were sitting on the sofa. She sensed the wedge between them; it wasn't Sylvia sitting in the middle while Steve read a story to her. Maryanna had spoken to her of her futile attempt to change Julia's mind. Julia had told her mother-in-law in no uncertain terms that the matter was one between her husband and herself and she had no right meddling. The job at Republic Steel was secure; this offer was too risky. Steve was provider for his two children and his wife and shouldn't take that lightly.

She sighed. If Julia had been born in the old country, that's where she'd be until the day she died. She was like so many of the women back home. They lived in abject poverty with no chance of improvement in the future. The husbands wanted to come to America hoping for a better life. Their marriages disintegrated, because thinking she could count on them, the fearful wife was content with the daily bowl of soup and crust of stale bread that barely kept her alive.

She shifted her gaze to the brilliant lights of the Christmas tree. Wally and Vicki were sitting on the floor by the tree. Wally had showed up early yesterday, Christmas Eve, with a huge tree strapped to the roof of his Nash sedan. Vicki had run out to help him drag the tree up the stairs and into the parlor. She had pushed the round table away from the window and put the tree in the place of honor. Wally had also brought strings of the colored electric light bulbs made for decorating Christmas trees. He and Vicki had spent the morning chatting and laughing while decorating the tree with the old treasured ornaments and tinsel and the new-fangled lights. The lights were beautiful and so much safer than the candles they had always used.

She treasured many memories of Christmases past and this one would take its place among them. She knew that God was calling Frank and would soon take him, but He would not abandon her or Vicki. In Frank's place would be

Wally. She was sure of it as she glanced at the Lady Bulova wristwatch with two sparkling diamonds that hugged Vicki's wrist. Wally intended to marry Vicki; it was only a matter of when.

Maryanna

She and Michał sat in the parlor listening to Sally play Cicha Noc *(Silent Night)* and other kolędy on the player piano. Finally, it was, if not a silent night, at least a calm night. The afternoon had been an explosion of laughter, chatter, eating, squealing, singing. Except for Steve and Julia and their two girls, she and Michał had entertained all the little ones in the family and their parents. Estella and Tomasz and Bud; her sister Stella and her first grandbaby, Theodora, with her parents; her sister-in-law, Josephine and her little ones. Stanley, her brother, was still missing. After more than a year, Josephine and the children were adjusting to their new life. Michał had provided the family with a decent apartment and sufficient food and clothing. Josephine took in wash to help pay the rent and had been a huge help to her in maintaining the vegetable garden last summer and canning its abundance. In return, Josephine's pantry was also full of jars of fruits and vegetables to feed the children through the winter.

The strains of Lulajże, Jezuniu *(Lullaby, Jesus)* floated from the piano keys expertly touched by Sally's fingers. This was her favorite carol. She had sung it to Stella and Stanley and Teo when they were babes back home. She had sung it to Stephan, Dora, Estella and Stash. Ironically, she did not remember singing it to Sally who was now gifting her with the melody. The music and the soft glow of the Christmas tree lights in the darkened room lulled her muscles and her mind. She nestled into Michał's chest as he put his arm around her.

CHAPTER EIGHT

JANUARY 1939

Sophie

"So--phie! So--phie!"
Did she hear her name? Was she dreaming? No. Frank was gasping for breath. She climbed out of bed and turned on the dresser lamp. Frank's eyes were closed; his face had a bluish pallor and his features were contorted. His chest was rising and falling rapidly as he struggled for air. She picked up the bottle of medicine and the spoon that was beside it on the little table next to Frank's side of the bed. She poured a spoonful of the medicinal elixir.

"Frank," she whispered softly, "open your mouth. This will help you." As Frank opened his mouth to gasp for air, she slowly poured the liquid into it. It was viscous and did not choke him as it slid down his throat. She put the spoon back on the tray. Then, she lifted him forward and put two rolled up woolen blankets behind him with the down pillows on front of them. She positioned Frank against the pillows. As the medicine took effect, his breathing became less laborious.

Gently, she rubbed his temples, a motion that always relaxed him. He drifted into sleep. She looked at the clock on the dresser. It was 5:20 in the morning. She was wide awake. She wriggled out of her nightgown and into a slip and housedress. She sat on the rocker, pulled the cotton stockings up over her knees and slid her feet into her house slippers. She undid her braid and brushed her hair, coiling it at the nape of her neck and securing it with pins and two combs. She turned out the light and crept out of the bedroom, closing the door behind her, noiselessly.

In the kitchen, she pulled the cord to light the lamp over the table. She filled the coffeepot with water, scooped fresh grounds into the basket and put the lid on it, set the basket into the pot and clamped the outer lid securely. She lit the burner with a match and set the coffeepot on top of it. The coffee would be hot for Vicki when she woke up. She set about fixing a ham sandwich for her lunch, using homemade bread slathered with mustard. She packed pickles and oatmeal cookies that Vicki had made the evening before. She filled the vacuum bottle with the steaming liquid, added a dollop of milk and closed the lid tightly. She packed the lunch in a brown paper bag.

Then she set about scrambling eggs and toasting bread. Vicki walked by on her way to the bathroom to wash her face and put on her makeup.

"Thanks, Mom. You were up early and you're all dressed up. Is everything okay?"

"Your dad was a bit restless this morning."

"Does the doctor need to come?"

"I'll call him later this morning."

"Should I stay home?"

"No, Vicki, go to work."

"Wally is picking me up after work, Mom, so I will be home earlier than if I had to take the train."

"He's a good man, Vicki, just like your father."

Vicki downed her breakfast and donned her woolen coat, hat, gloves and galoshes for the long walk to the train station on a cold January morning. She kissed her mother, grabbed her lunch bag and purse and hurried down the stairs.

Once Vicki left, she opened the door to the bedroom so she could check on Frank. He was asleep, but his breathing was erratic. She called Dr. Piczkiewicz. After describing Frank's condition to him, he said he would stop by the house in the afternoon after office hours. He suggested that she might want to call the parish. It was time for Frank to receive the sacrament of Extreme Unction.

Monsignor Kozlowski answered the telephone. He would come to the house in an hour, after celebrating Mass. Quietly, she cleared the bedside table next to Frank. She placed a spotless linen cloth on it and set up the crucifix and two candles in silver candleholders. She placed a bottle of blessed holy water on the table. Monsignor would bring all the other items necessary for the sacrament.

"Agnieska, your father is not doing well," she said when her stepdaughter answered the telephone.

"You do not need to come immediately. There is time. Come with Mike when he gets home from work. I need to call Julia."

"Julia, Dad is not doing well. I know Steve is working until three o'clock. There is time."

"Yes. I did call the doctor. He suggested that I call the Monsignor. He will be here in an hour."

Julia, her little ones and the monsignor arrived within minutes of each other. She and her daughter knelt together on the far side of the bed while the priest imparted the sacrament which prepared Frank for his final journey to his eternal home. She watched silently as the priest blessed him with holy water as a reminder of his baptism, then anointed his eyes, nose, mouth, ears and hands with the holy oil, praying, "Through this holy unction and with His most tender mercy may the Lord pardon thee whatever sins or faults thou hast committed by sight, smell, taste, hearing and touch." At the end of the sacramental prayers, the monsignor turned to her and Julia and blessed them asking God's mercy on them as they grieved the loss of husband and father.

She rose and thanked the monsignor, profusely. She asked Julia to give him a loaf of the fresh bread that she had baked the day before. It was a favorite of his.

She blew out the flames on the candles, then sat down on the bed next to Frank. He tried to speak, but his breath failed him.

"Hush, Frank," she said, tears forming on her eyelashes as she witnessed his struggle. She touched his face tenderly. "Words are not necessary. I know what is in your heart. We have always known each other's hearts. Half of mine will go with you, my love. But do not worry. You have given me so many precious memories, my time here will be up before I am halfway through remembering."

The day would always be a bit of a blur to her. Julia spent time sitting with her dad. She sat with Julia in the kitchen afterward. Julia was not given to many words and this day did not change her. Yet, she knew that this day was different for Julia, too. Her daughter was lost in remembering. She would take a sip of coffee, look toward the bedroom, then stare into space.

"Mom, you and Dad have always been good to me. And to Steve and the girls. I am grateful. I will go home and fix sandwiches and salads so that you and anyone who comes today will have something to eat. I'll wait until Agnieska arrives. I do not want to leave you alone."

"Leave Sylvia and Julianne here. They are a comfort to me."

She reached across the table and pressed her daughter's hand. As she did so, she heard the knocker on the front door. Agnieska had arrived. From then on, it was a haze of people coming in and going out. Julia left to walk the half short block to her apartment to fix sandwiches. Agnieska had run into Olga on her way over; soon Olga was at the door with a fresh streusel coffeecake. Olga had told Lottie Wasniewski who stopped by with a hot potato casserole. Julia returned with the sandwiches. Mike arrived; then Steve.

Every few minutes, she would slip into the bedroom, if no one was with Frank, to see how he was doing. His eyes were closed and his breath was increasingly shallow. He made no response to anything that was said to him. About five o'clock, Vicki arrived home with Wally. She was dismayed to see Julia and Steve, Mike and Agnieska.

"What's going on?"

"Dad is dying, Vicki. Come." Vicki peeled off her coat and hat.

She entered the bedroom with Vicki and Wally. "Vicki is here," she said to Frank. At the sound of Vicki's name, he roused and opened his eyes. Vicki hugged him and kissed him.

"Vicki," he whispered. He had waited. He knew how much his youngest daughter needed to see him one last time.

He closed his eyes and sank into the pillows. Two shallow breaths later, he was on his way to spend an eternity with the two daughters who had never had the opportunity to grow up.

Her heart convulsed as she realized her Love was no more; at least not physically for her to see and hear and touch and feel.

⊰ ⨯ ⊱

Frank got his last wish, she thought, in a comforting way. He always said that he didn't want a big falderal funeral. He wanted his immediate family. Mother Nature listened. On January 30th, the date set for the funeral, fifteen inches of snow fell on the entire Chicago area. The drifts were hip high and the streets were not plowed. The funeral Mass and burial had to be postponed for two days. Only four cars were able to make the miles-long trek to Holy Cross cemetery.

She stood in the snow-packed cemetery watching the casket being lowered into the frozen ground. As the committal prayers were intoned by the Monsignor, she raised her head toward the east, toward the Guardian Angel section where Albina and Irena were buried. For a brief moment, she envisioned them running with Frank, a young, healthy dad, in the beautiful meadows outside Piotrkow where she had run with her dad many years ago.

"Idź w spokoju. Jesteś z Bogiem, moja miłość. *Go in peace. You are with God, my love,"* she whispered, as she pressed her fingers to her lips and then touched the casket. She turned and walked resolutely away.

APRIL 1939

Maryanna

The police sergeant from the South Chicago station was sitting in the armchair by the window, hat in hand. Early in the morning, she had received a call from him. He had asked her name, her maiden name and the first names of her parents. Did she have a brother Stanley in America? Did she know where her brother was currently living? Before she could ask what this was about, the sergeant said that he had information to share with her regarding her brother. He would come to the house at two o'clock in the afternoon. She called Josephine and Stella to join her.

.   "Our station has received information originating in the sheriff's office in El Paso, Texas. It has taken time to locate you." He paused and cleared his throat.

"I am sorry to inform you that Stanley Kompanski died in Sierra Bianca, Hudspeth County, Texas, on February 12th."

Josephine gasped, trembling with emotion.

"What was the cause of death? A heart attack?"

"No ma'am."

"Then, what was it?"

"He was killed...um... trying to hop on a moving freight train."

"No!" Josephine screamed as the horror of it assailed her. She fell against her sister-in-law, sobbing hysterically.

The police officer shifted uncomfortably in his chair, casting his eyes down, unconsciously twirling his hat.

"I will take her into the bedroom," Stella said, standing up and urging Josephine to do the same. Slowly, she half walked, half carried her sister-in-law out of the parlor.

"Thank you. I know that these situations are not easy for you. I appreciate your compassion."

"You're welcome, ma'am."

"What other information can you give us?"

"The gentleman had identifying papers in his pocket giving his name and date of birth, the names of his parents and that he was a preacher. However, there was nothing that indicated that he was married or where he lived. The El Paso sheriff's department reached out to the military. Often we are able to track down a family through draft registration cards. One was found for him that was filled out in 1917 during the World War. It stated that he lived in Chicago at 8809 S. Exchange."

"That was their first apartment."

"Once that information was known, the file was sent downtown and then forwarded to our station with the directive to find his family." He relaxed now that the worst was over.

"February 12th was over two months ago."

"Ma'am, your brother was laid to rest in McGill Cemetery in El Paso. If you would wish to have him brought to Chicago, arrangements would have to be made through a mortician who would contact the authorities in El Paso."

"I think he will rest most peacefully there."

"Well, if there are any other questions that you might have in the future, please contact me at the station." He rose to leave.

"Thank you. We are most grateful."

Stanley was the first of her brothers and sisters to die. Only Teo was younger than he. "Rest in peace, Stanley," she murmured to herself, as she closed the door and hurried to the bedroom to mourn his loss with Stella and Josephine, now a widow.

SEPTEMBER 1939

Maryanna

"Maryanna!" Michał called to her from the parlor. At the strident tone of his voice, she came running. He was sitting in the armchair listening to the radio.

"What is wrong?"

"The Germans have invaded Poland! The war has started!"

"Oh, Michał!" she plopped down on the sofa, her hands falling into her lap. Poland had been a free country for only twenty years. Once again, Ignacy, Katarzyna, Franciszka and their families would suffer. Food was scarce already. It would become worse. The men would join the Polish army. Wherever the Germans advanced, the women would be at peril. Cities, towns and villages would be destroyed.

Ignacy and his family were in Mostki. Her sisters, Franciszka and Katarzyna, were still in Osiek Dolnoslaskie. It didn't matter where one lived; no one would be safe. Ignacy's sons would be going to war. If they were anything like their father, they were already signed up with the Polish army to protect the homeland.

She would write to her brother immediately before the mail service was disrupted. She had no illusions about what an invading German army would do or could do. She wondered what was going through Sophie's mind. After all, she was German by birth, even though she had grown up in Poland. Was that any different than being a Pole in America?

Sophie

The thin parchment paper felt as fragile in her hand as her heart felt in her chest. She had read and reread the letter as she sat on one of the metal chairs in the back yard near the chicken coop. The warm rays of sunshine could not penetrate the chill that enveloped her like a cloud. The mailman handed the air mail letter to her, quizzically. The strange address puzzled her, too. Her brother, Auguste, explained inside the letter.

The Germans had invaded Piotrkow on September 5th. There was fierce fighting and much destruction in the city. The Germans had declared all Poles as Untermenschen *(subhuman)*. There were mass arrests of teachers, judges, activists, bankers, parliamentarians, printers, students. He was afraid the letter would be confiscated if he addressed it to her Slavic-sounding name: Sophie Kravczyk. He had decided to use her German name: Mathilda Lenz. He was also afraid that he would be questioned about his connection to a person with a Polish name who was living in America.

He did not know if or when he would be able to write again. Life was unstable from minute to minute. He was frantic.

His sons had joined the Polish army. They urged him and Kasha to leave the city and go into the countryside where it was safer. He did not think that was a good idea. The Polish farmers might be suspect of their Germanic surname and think they were spies. He did not know what to do. Pray for him, he begged her. Pray for everyone.

Pray she would, as the poisonous tentacles of a war begun so far abroad reached a quarter way around the world to wrap around her heart.

JUNE 1940

Sophie

She rose with the sun on a glorious Saturday morning in June. Vicki was still sleeping for the last time in the bedroom that had been hers ever since her dad bought the house. Tonight, she would sleep in that tiny bedroom off the parlor while Vicki and Wally shared the larger one.

"Wally, Vicki," she had asked at Christmas when they were engaged, "are you planning to find an apartment of your own?"

"Ma," Wally said, "Vicki and I do not want to see you living alone. We know how much pain the arthritis is causing. You have spent a lifetime working hard and caring for so many others, it is time that we care for you.

"But we will not live here for free. We are both working and will give rent to you and pay for utilities and food. I do not want you to worry about anything. I am happy to share life with Vicki."

She bustled around in the downstairs kitchen setting out coffeecakes and cookies and making sure there would be plenty of coffee for the bridal party and whoever else would be in and out of the house this day. How times changed, she thought. In 1912, when she and Frank were married, people worked long hours for six and, sometimes, seven days a week. Wedding ceremonies were held during the week. Her wedding had taken place on a Tuesday, as did Julia's only seven years ago. With the five-day workweek a common practice, weddings were now being held on Saturday with large celebrations afterward. Vicki's was part of the new trend.

She glanced at the clock. It was almost eight o'clock. She heard Vicki padding around upstairs in the bathroom. She untied her apron and hung it on the hook by the sink. It was time to climb the stairs and put on the dark gray silk dress that Vicki had bought for her. She heard the knocker on the front door and hurried up the last few stairs as fast as her arthritic joints allowed. The florist had arrived with Julia and two of the bridesmaids right behind.

"Julia, you are lovely!" Wearing a white chiffon gown with a ruffled bodice and a pink sash denoting her as matron of honor, Julia had arrived to help Vicki dress. A crown of white rosebuds on her ebony hair framed her face. She noted that the bridesmaids' dresses were identical to Julia's, except for blue sashes.

It seemed like she had been dressed for hours as she sat in the parlor while Julia and the bridesmaids attended to Vicki accompanied by much chatter and giggling. Several times, one of the young women would scamper to the bathroom for a cloth dampened with water or dash into the tiny bedroom for something.

"Behold the bride!" Julia intoned as Vicki emerged from the bedroom, radiant in a simple white satin dress with pearls at the neck and long fitted sleeves with three pearl buttons at the wrists. A small crown of white roses perched on her hair; yards of white tulle cascaded from it. As Vicki pinned a huge orchid corsage on her dark gray dress, she looked deeply into her daughter's eyes. They were dancing with happiness!

Mike came round with his car and escorted her and Vicki to the church. The only sadness was that Frank was not here to walk his daughter down the aisle. Mike would do the honors.

Maryanna

Michał crooked his right arm so she could slip her hand past his elbow and rest it on his forearm. They were part of the wedding party that made its way one block up Marquette Avenue from the church to the Marquette Gardens where the bridal party would have breakfast. Their steps slowed as they walked past 8345. All the memories of the years they had lived there beckoned to them.

The cook met the newly married couple at the door of the banquet hall. In her hands she held a small plate which she gave to the bride and groom. On the plate were two one-inch square pieces of bread which were sprinkled with salt. She said, "Congratulations on this happy occasion. Wally and Vicki, take this bread and eat it. It is a symbol of a long and happy life together." The bride and groom took the pieces of bread and ate them. Everyone clapped their hands and shouted, "Stolat! *One hundred years!*"

As breakfast ended, the bridal party left the banquet hall to go to Urbanowicz's Portrait Studio on Commercial Avenue to have the formal portraits taken. As she rose from the table, Sophie invited her and Michał to come to the house until the evening reception. It was only a short block and a half to walk, instead of the five blocks to Essex Avenue. It was a warm day and she was grateful for the invitation. Stephan walked with them to Manistee, then turned the corner instead of crossing the street. He was going to the apartment to check on Sylvia and Julianne. A neighbor was looking after them.

Sophie's house was a hub of activity all day long. There was a seemingly endless supply of coffeecakes that Sophie produced. While she wasn't great at baking them, she could certainly serve the coffeecakes. She set about slicing the cakes. She refilled the coffeepot three times. This was a bottomless bunch.

At six o'clock, she and Michał joined the bridal party and any stragglers in the walk back to Marquette Gardens for the reception. She counted about two hundred people having a grand time. Her own Stephan and Agnieska's boarder, Victor, were the bartenders. Watching her son deftly serve the drinks and share a few genial comments with each man who came up to the bar, she wondered why Julia couldn't see what she did. As his mother she might be biased, but the man she saw loved what he was doing. He basked in the camaraderie of the men he served.

She rose readily as Michał extended his hand and they danced one dance. Although the chords were enticing, especially to him, when the frenzied rhythm of a mazurka wafted through the air, they yielded the floor to younger limbs. With perfect timing, they echoed to each other, "Shall we go?" They congratulated the newly married couple and thanked Sophie for a lovely evening. Then they stepped from the joyous noise of the banquet hall into the sapphire quiet of a June evening with enough light on the western horizon to see them safely home.

DECEMBER 1941

Sophie

Sunday dinner was history. She and Vicki and Wally were settling in the parlor to relax and listen to music. As soon as Wally turned the knob on the radio, a distressed voice was shouting, "The Japanese have attacked Pearl Harbor! The Japanese have attacked Pearl Harbor!" Every station, including Oskerke, the Polish radio station, was devoting its air waves to the devastating news. The Japanese had conducted an air raid on the American base at Pearl Harbor in Hawaii at eight o'clock on a sleepy Sunday morning. The stationary American fleet of ships was a perfect target.

The few reporters in Honolulu were relaying information via long distance telephone and the wire services. All afternoon, they sat in silence absorbing every new tidbit of news that was broadcast. The Japanese had used hundreds of planes in the seemingly unending wave of attack. All eight battle ships in the harbor were heavily damaged, as were destroyers, cargo ships, and aircraft carriers. Ships were sunk or were sinking. It was feared that thousands of men were lost to the waters of the Pacific Ocean.

The wintry sun sank in the west and the ominous greys of dusk descended before any of the three thought about turning on a lamp. Suppertime came and went. No one was hungry. Vicki looked fearfully at Wally. There would be war.

During the ensuing days, Japan did declare war on the United States. Thinking that a war fought on two sides of the world would undo the might of America, the Germans and Italians also declared war. Life had changed in an instant, as it always did.

She had not heard from Auguste since the war began two years ago. She did not know whether he or Ludwig and their families were alive. Was German heredity a help or a hindrance? The declarations of war lessened her chances of knowing. There had been rumors of mass incarcerations of the Jews in Piotrkow, as well as Poles. She wondered about the Jewish families for whom she had worked. Her employers had probably died before the war, but their children and grandchildren would be suffering now. Many of her Jewish customers had more angst than she would ever have. They also had close relatives living in Europe where to be a Jew was to be untermenschen.

APRIL 1942

Maryanna

For the second time in twenty-five years, Michał had to go to the draft board on Exchange Avenue to fill out a draft registration card. At sixty years of age and working in the steel industry, he was not top priority for the draft. Neither was Stephan, a steel industry foreman at thirty-five with two children. Stash was thirty and single; so far, as a crane operator at Republic Steel, he had not been drafted. The only relative she had to worry about was Valentine (Sally called him Wally), her new son-in-law. He and Sally were married on February 28th, before he reported for enlistment. Sally was living at home while he was in service.

It was a different story with her family in Poland. The letters from Ignacy and Franciszka's grandson had ceased. She didn't know where her brother and sisters were, or even if they were alive. She didn't know if Ignacy's sons were fighting with the remnants of the Polish army. She prayed for them every day when she prayed for Valentine and all the men who were wearing Army green or Navy blue.

Every day, Michał listened attentively to the radio reports of the latest battles in Europe. They were devastating. The Germans appeared to be invincible. There was much talk of the Germans incarcerating hundreds of thousands of Jews and Poles and people from many other countries in labor camps, forcing them to do all the hard work necessary to feed, clothe and arm the German troops. The arrogance galled her.

There were also reports that said the Germans were killing those who were deemed useless. Old men and women, children, those who were lame, blind or deaf, those who had mental issues and couldn't take care of themselves. There was talk of chambers that were built for the sole purpose of killing hundreds of people at one time. She doubted those reports were true. Who could be that inhumane? It was unthinkable.

JANUARY 1943

Maryanna

Who would be calling at this hour of the night?. She heard Sally pick up the telephone and start repeating: "Calm down, Estelle. Calm down. I can't understand what you are saying."

She slipped out of bed, put on her chenille robe and padded into the dining room where the telephone stood on a little round table.

"Estelle, calm down. Here's Ma. Talk to her. I will be right over." Sally handed the telephone to her. She could hear Estelle's loud sobs as she put the telephone to her ear. Sally shook her head. It was not good.

"Estelle, what happened?"

"Aun-aun-auntie Maryanna, Le-Leon was run over by a train at 82nd Street." The sentence gushed out of her mouth, together with a horrendous moan.

"Estelle, I will come now with Sally." She hung up the telephone and called to Sally who was putting on her heavy coat. "Sally, wait for me."

"Ma, it's a long walk to her house on a cold night like this."

"She needs a mother right now, Sally, this minute. She lived with us for so many years. I've been like a mother to her. Give me a few minutes to change clothes."

She walked into the bedroom, moving as quietly as she could so as not to awaken Michał. Off went the flannel nightgown; on went the woolen dress and cotton stockings. She pulled out a small cotton drawstring bag and tossed her house slippers into it. She put on her heavy black woolen coat and tied a square woolen babushka over her braided hair. She grabbed her purse, and the woolen gloves that Estelle had knitted for her last year. Her snow boots were on the mat in the entrance hall.

As she padded into the parlor in stocking feet, Sally said that she had left a note on the kitchen table letting her dad know where they had gone at such an ungodly hour.

"Good." She sat down on the armchair and slid her feet into the boots, latching them securely. She was ready.

She and Sally left the warmth of the house and turned north toward 83rd Street. The 11:00 p.m. shift at the mill had started an hour ago. The buses had stopped running. Seven blocks were quite a walk for her at her age. Sally offered her arm and she hung on to it. The frigid air was crystal clear and the cobalt night sky was ablaze with stars undimmed by the waning quarter moon. She plodded on. As they neared Saginaw Avenue, a police car pulled up alongside. The officer rolled down the window.

"What are you ladies doing out so late on a cold night?"

"My niece's husband was hit by an IC train tonight. We're going to be with her."

"Oh, that accident...You don't have an automobile?"

"No."

"Well, ladies, it's too cold for you. Hop in the back seat and I will take you to your niece. What is her address?"

"Thank you. The address is 8224 Muskegon"

Four-year-old memories surfaced of another train accident in Texas. The one that had killed her brother, Stanley. Twice now, a family member had been killed by a train. She shuddered as her mind raced to conjure up images of the horror. She would have to distract Estelle so that her thoughts did not embark on that perilous path.

Another police car was parked in front of Estelle's apartment building. Sally jumped out and helped her exit the police car. She thanked the officer, then took her mother by the elbow and guided her up the sidewalk toward the building. It was quite a climb to the second-floor apartment. She stopped counting the steps at twelve.

Another officer heard their footsteps and opened the door before they reached the landing. She thanked him for his kindness. They would be staying with Estelle and caring for her, she told him. He skipped down the stairs and was climbing into his patrol car before she closed the front door. She slid her hands out of her gloves and Sally helped her out of her coat. She embraced her inconsolable niece.

"Estelle," she said, softly, as she held her close.

"Ciocia Marisha," she sobbed, using her pet name for her aunt. Tears flowed freely as her chest heaved with violent emotion and her breath was sucked in, involuntarily.

She patted Estelle's head which was buried in her damp shoulder. Slowly, she guided her niece toward an armchair.

"Sit down, Estelle," she said, gently, leaning over so that Estelle had no choice but to incline into the chair. She untied her babushka and removed her snow boots.

She headed toward the minuscule kitchen. She lifted the coffeepot on the stove. There was brew inside that just needed reheating. She lit the burner beneath it and the other burner where the tea kettle was sitting. She freshened the water in the kettle, then set it to boil. The cups were in sight hanging from hooks attached to the shelf above the sink. She had to search a bit in the pantry until she found the whiskey and the tea. She filled a steeper with loose tea leaves and placed it in an empty cup. She poured boiling water into the cup and let the leaves steep for a full minute. She removed the steeper, then poured a jigger of whiskey into the steaming brew, stirred it and took the cup out to Estelle.

"Drink a sip of this," she said, holding the cup to Estelle's lips. "Blow on it first." The commands distracted Estelle and she ceased sobbing, at least momentarily. After a few sips, she saw that the liberal amount of whiskey in the tea was taking effect. Estelle's trembling lessened and her facial features relaxed.

"Estelle, tell us what happened," she said, tenderly, knowing full well that the telling would bring on fresh tears which would help calm her niece's emotions.

"I was waiting for Leon to come home. He was already an hour late and I was starting to worry. I heard a knock on the door. When I opened it, two policemen were standing on the porch. They asked my name. I told them. They asked if I was married; if so, what was my husband's name. They asked if they could come in. Once inside, one of the policemen asked me to sit down. I knew it was bad as soon as he said that.

"I asked them: What happened to Leon? Is he hurt? Is he in the hospital? Where is he? They told me what happened. Leon had waited for the train to leave the station; he did not try to cross in front of it. But he didn't see a train that was coming out of the yard on another track and..." She collapsed into another unstoppable torrent of tears.

She rose from the sofa, took the empty tea cup from Estelle's hand and put it on the side table. Then she took each of her niece's hands and pulled her up. She guided her toward the sofa and bade her sit down next to her. She put her arm around Estelle and let her sob her heart out.

When the sobs lessened, she asked, "Where is Leon?"

"The policeman said he would contact Mr. Dalewski at his funeral home on South Shore Drive. He'll take care of everything."

"Barney will do a fine job. Have you called anyone else?"

"I've been crying so much, I can't talk."

"I will let Leon's parents know in the morning. What time is it?"

"It's going on five o'clock, Ma," Sally informed her.

"Tomasz should be getting up soon. Since they live on the next block, run over there, Sally, and let them know what happened. Ask Estella if she could drive me to Leon's parents and then home."

"I will, Ma. Esta and Tom told me and Stash that we could use the car whenever we needed to."

She shot a look at Sally. Why did people feel a need to shorten everyone's honorable name? Tomasz and Estella are good names. It made sense when a name was too long, like Stash's. Stanisław was a mouthful to say. Or her sister, Stella, who was Stanisława. She had clenched her fists the day she heard someone say 'Mike' instead of Michał. Headstrong Sally had shortened her own name as a little girl; she hated the name 'Sabina'.

Here she was going off on a tangent when Estelle needed her. She checked her errant thoughts, focusing on what needed doing.

"If Estella can drive me home, we will give your dad the sad news, fix some food and bring it over. Many people will stop by to comfort Estelle. We need to provide for that."

She glanced over at Estelle. Bereft of tears, hands limp in her lap, eyes staring vacantly at the photo of Leon that adorned the tiny table by the sofa, she sat entombed in her unfathomable grief.

Sophie

"Good morning, Vicki, Wally." She padded into the kitchen, tying the pink chenille robe tightly around her waist. The aroma of coffee perking and bacon frying had awakened her.

"Hi, Mom," Wally and Vicki chorused, like two little magpies. "Happy February!"

She smiled. It always warmed her heart to see these two every morning. Her heart was even warmer when she realized that the longest, coldest month of winter was over, the month that brought back all the painful memories of Frank who had left her widowed four years ago. She picked up her coffee cup from the table and walked over to the stove to fill it.

Vicki was scrambling a frying pan full of eggs. The bacon was sizzling in another frying pan. Wally was popping bread in and out of the toaster. The grape jam that she and Vicki had made, was on the table with the pitchers of milk and orange juice. She loved the richness of flavor in jam made from the concord grapes that her nephew, Louie, brought up from Nokomis each September.

The juice tumblers were on the table; she lifted the pitcher of orange juice and began to fill them. Her arthritic hands objected to the weight and she had to hold the pitcher with both hands. Vicki was ladling the scrambled eggs onto the plates, adding strips of bacon and handing the plates to Wally who added slices of toast. Coffee cups brimming, they sat down to breakfast. The rising sun cast pale, anemic rays through the kitchen window and onto the toast with the grape jam which sparkled like a purple jewel.

B-ring! B-ring! B-ring! The telephone in the parlor disrupted their hearty eating and happy talk. Vicki jumped up to answer it.

"Hello? Good morning. Yes, I will have her come to the telephone."

"Mom, it's for you; it's Steve's mother."

"Good morning, Maryanna." She listened intently as Maryanna related the tragedy that had come upon Estelle, who had been Julia's maid of honor. She did not know Estelle well, seeing her only at family gatherings. She liked what she saw in the young woman whose quiet, pleasant nature endeared her to many. That nature blanketed a core of strength that would serve her well in this devastating time in her life.

"Oh, Maryanna, what can we do to help? You said that you are home fixing food for the mourners who will come to console Estelle? Well, I will make some streusel and fruit-filled coffeecakes. Wally will drop them off after work. Maryanna, my heart goes out to you and to your family. Especially to Estelle. I will pray a rosary for her this evening, so God will ease the pain in her heart. I know what it is like to lose a husband. For it to happen to one so young and in such a tragic way..."

"What happened, Mom?"

She thumped down heavily on the kitchen chair and related the conversation to her daughter and son-in-law.

"Oh, Mom! I will help you with the baking. You can't do all that work by yourself. Your hands hurt too much. I will call the laundry and tell them I am taking a vacation day."

"That would be good, Vicki. At a time like this, we must do everything we can to help. First, though, you must run over to Julia's and let her and Steve know. He may have already left for work."

"I'll drive you over," Wally said, as they rose from the table.

"It's only a half block."

"True, but it's still faster than walking. If Steve is still home, I can give him a lift to the bus stop before I head for the mill."

"I will clean up the kitchen, then go downstairs to start the baking."

"Be careful on the steps, Mom."

Two hours later, she and Vicki were elbow-deep in dough and fillings when they saw Julia walking in the back door with a canvas shopping bag. Sylvia and Julianne were in school.

"I used my ration cards for whatever ingredients I could buy for you. You both know I'm not much of a baker like you are, but I came to help. I know that my fingers can knead dough for you, Mom."

All morning and afternoon, the three women worked at making coffeecakes and sweet rolls for those who would attend the wake for Leon. She would use up all the flour and sugar allowed that month, Julia's rations included. It was worth it. They could all do without for a month until the new ration cards were distributed.

At noon, they stopped to eat ham sandwiches Julia had made.

"Julia, you are looking well and happy."

"Mom, you are going to have another grandchild in August."

"Julia, that's wonderful news, especially on a day like this."

"Good for you, Julia." Little joy echoed in Vicki's voice as she congratulated her sister. She understood. This was a great blow to Vicki. Her fertile turtle sister was pregnant again. In the two and a half years that she and Wally were married, she had not become pregnant. It was a source of great sorrow for her younger daughter.

At four o'clock, Wally had a trunkful of fresh, homemade baked goods. Vicki sat in the passenger seat beside him while Julia and Steve climbed into the back seat. She and her granddaughters stood by the front door waving goodbye until the car pulled away from the curb. Her daughters and sons-in-law were on their way to a visit that none of them was prepared to make.

APRIL 1943

Maryanna

The aromatic sent of the lilies intermingled with the varying fragrances of dozens of roses as she knelt before the casket in the parlor at Kortas Funeral Home and stared at his face in repose. A sharp intake of breath, the heart's failure to beat and he was gone from her. For the rest of her life, she would only see him in her memories. The patrician gentleman who had been born into a once noble Polish family. A righteous man who never wavered knowing what was the right thing to do and what wasn't. A family man who had loved her and his children unconditionally. A handsome man who could rest in his casket at peace with himself.

She stood up and walked around the kneeler. She touched his hair, still thick, wavy and dark with flecks of grey. The years had made a few inroads at the temples, but she had always delighted in looking at and touching that wonderful mass of hair.

"Ma," Sally said, touching her arm. "Julia's mother is here with Vicki and Wally."

Sophie was doing her best to navigate the aisle between the chairs without letting the arthritis overtake her. She walked toward her; so far, her own knees were still good. She noticed the tears in Sophie's eyes as she drew close. She knew, instinctively, that those tears were shed not only for her loss, but also for Sophie's. She was living what Sophie had experienced four years ago. They were sisters in the sorority of widows.

She embraced Sophie, whose hug was quite strong despite her infirm joints. Together they walked to the casket. Sophie knelt on the kneeler and made the sign of the cross. She stood quietly while Sophie prayed. As Sophie struggled to rise, Vicki put out her hand to give her mother leverage. Then she and Wally took her mother's place on the kneeler. Vicki dabbed at her eyes with a hankie while Wally patted her hand, like Michał used to pat hers.

Julianne came running up the aisle and grabbed her Busia's hand. She was followed by Sylvia, who at nine years old walked slowly with her mother and father. Julia was in her fifth month and blooming. Stephan kissed her and scooped up Julianne.

Young Eugene Kortas was walking toward her with the monsignor. The funeral parlor which had been started by his dad was across the street from the first house Michał had bought on 83rd and Marquette. She had watched Eugene grow up into a fine young man. He was about twenty when his father died a few years ago. He was young, but he had taken over for his dad with the same care and compassion that August had. She had heard that Eugene's wife was expecting their first baby this year.

The monsignor took her hand and guided her to a front row seat between Stephan and Sally. Julia and the girls were seated next to Stephan. Estella, Tomasz and her grandson were seated next to Julia's girls. Stash was missing his father's funeral. He was stationed somewhere in the Pacific. Only God knew where.

"W imię Ojca i Syna i Ducha Świętego. Amen. *In the name of the Father and of the Son and of the Holy Spirit. Amen.*"

Monsignor prayed the liturgy for the dead. He blessed Michał with holy water. He spoke glowing words about him and his love of the church and the Eucharist, about his devotion to his wife and children, about his generosity during the depression helping many neighbors, about his being a credit to his illustrious family which had been as honorable as he was. He concluded his eulogy.

"Niech Michał spoczywa w pokoju. *May Michał rest in peace.*"

The kneeler was removed from in front of the casket and the mourners were asked to come forward and pay their last respects to an upright man. She had been amazed during the two nights of the wake at the number of people she barely knew or didn't know at all who had come up to her extolling the kindness that Michał had extended to them. Many of these same people were walking up to the casket, touching the sleeve of Michał's suitcoat or making the sign of the cross while tears gathered in their eyes. All too soon it was her turn. Stephan helped her rise from the chair. She walked with Sally to the casket. Sally kissed her father on his forehead and stepped aside to await her mother.

The time had arrived for the last goodbye. She gazed down at Michał, remembering that distant morning when he had saved her from a fate worse than death. For thirty-six years, he had never left her side nor had she left his. As she bent to kiss his cold lips, she relinquished that part of her that would stay with him, the part she had never shared with anyone, not even her children, the part of her being that had always been his alone.

CHAPTER NINE

SEPTEMBER 1943

Sophie

No matter how many grandbabies her daughters gave her, she would never tire of holding them and loving them. The arthritis was affecting numerous joints and movement was becoming more painful. Today was one of her bad days, so she was resting in bed feeding a bottle of milk to her newborn granddaughter. She frowned at the impersonal bottle. Whatever happened to mother's milk? Breast-feeding was the most natural thing to do and so much better for the baby. When did the shape of the mother's figure come before giving her baby the best nourishment?

Julia had brought over foodstuffs for the christening which would be held at the house. She was downstairs setting everything up. On Friday, she would come and fix the salads and other dishes, putting them in the icebox until Sunday when the baby would be christened. Steve's cousin, the newly widowed Estelle, was going to be the godmother; Wally was asked to be Aniela's godfather. She was happy with Steve and Julia's choices.

The stillness in the house was broken by a voice other than Julia's. She heard two sets of footsteps coming up the stairs. One set belonged with the strident voice that grated her ears. Agnieska.

"Julia, you're a fool. You wouldn't let Steve take over the tavern when Wieczorek offered it to him."

"Agnieska, it was too risky."

"What's risky about it? Don't you see how much business Joe has with the tavern and the banquet hall?"

148

"I don't think running a tavern is a good job for Steve. At the mill, he's a foreman. He has a title. It's keeping him from being drafted."

"But that's all he'll ever be at the mill. He can't go any further without a high school diploma."

"All he'll ever be at Wieczorek's is a bartender, surrounded by a bunch of drunks."

"You don't get it, do you, Julia? In the old country, the tavern keeper was a man of distinction. He was looked up to. He had his finger on the pulse of what was going on. Men went to him with their troubles. Do you think that if Steve runs the tavern, he will succumb to temptation and become a drunk himself?

"That's it, isn't it, Julia? You don't trust your husband."

"You're wrong, Agnieska. We have another child. What we need is security, not some proposition."

"That's another thing I don't understand. Why in heaven's name did you have another child? Another girl!"

"I didn't do it alone! And no one has control over the sex."

"It was a stupid thing to do. Sylvia and Julianne are both in school and will soon be old enough to look after themselves. If you were worried about security, you could have gone to work. Instead, you saddle yourself with another mouth to feed."

That did it. She held her sleeping granddaughter tightly in her left arm as she maneuvered herself out of bed. She slid her feet into her house slippers and padded through the parlor into the kitchen.

"Enough! Agnieska, you have an opinion on everything. Not everyone sees things your way. I do not see my granddaughter as just another mouth to feed. If your father were here, he would be in total agreement. Don't ever let me hear you say that again!"

Aniela stirred in her arms and whimpered. Julia took the baby from her mother and went into the bedroom to change her diaper. Agnieska glowered at her stepmother and stomped downstairs.

For thirty years she had tolerated her stepdaughter's criticisms to keep a peaceful household for Frank for whom she would do anything. Frank was gone and, oh, it felt so liberating to be able to say what she was thinking. The euphoria of speaking her mind also seemed to liberate her from the incessant pain, at least for the moment. If she could, she'd jump in the air and twirl around.

Instead, she sat down on the rocker in the parlor. Julia placed the freshly changed Aniela into her arms. She cradled her tenderly, slowly moving the rocker back and forth, back and forth. The little imp snuggled against her, her face a kaleidoscope of expressions that charmed her. She watched the tiny chest rhythmically rising and falling with each breath. As long as she herself could breathe, never would this child be just another mouth to feed.

DECEMBER 1944

Maryanna

Sally was hanging tinsel on the Christmas tree. The scent of fresh pine filled the air together with the sound of Christmas carols being played over the radio. The melodies were familiar, but the words were not. She knew that in the evening, Sally would sit at the piano playing her favorite kolędy. Tomorrow Estella, Tomasz and Bud would come for Christmas dinner. Not only was Sally a good cook, she also had a knack for baking. Except for her son-in-law, it would be a quiet Christmas, bereft of men.

Both sons were now in the army. She didn't worry about Stephan. As the father of three children and a foreman in the steel industry, he would be kept stateside doing a clerical job, freeing a young single man for duty overseas. Stash had received a few deferments as well since he was a crane operator in the steel industry. The deferments ran out two years ago. If only she knew where he was and that he was safe. Valentine was also overseas. For these three, she was latching on to the saying that one heard everywhere during these war years. No news is good news.

For her, there was the heartbreaking absence of Michał. This was her second Christmas without him. She had thought the first might be the hardest; she wasn't so sure this year. Memories overwhelmed her of that Christmas night, when she sat on the bed in that tiny apartment on Buffalo Avenue, Michał holding her in his warm, strong arms as she cradled the most precious treasure in the world, their son, Stephan.

Sophie

All those spices in the Polish sausages and kielbasa were catching up with her. She had prided herself on her cast iron stomach. No foodstuff had ever bothered it, until now. For the last few months, she had become more selective in what she ate and how much. She noticed that she felt full much sooner than before. More signs of getting older were rearing their nasty heads. What did she expect at sixty-two years of age?

According to the insurance salesman who tried to sell a policy to her a few years ago, she had already outlived her life expectancy by at least seven years. In Poland, she would have been lucky to see age fifty.

Vicki was bringing up all the ingredients for Christmas babka. They would do the baking upstairs. Lately, Vicki was doing most of it, as her own fingers became useless. Julia and the girls were coming on Christmas day. Julia would bring her delicious coleslaw and a hot fruit compote made with the fruits from the trees. Vicki would roast the last goose in the pen.

She had sold all the poultry in the cages. She would not be restocking in the new year. She had a Christmas surprise for Wally. She wanted him to tear down the chicken coop and the cages and build a garage in their place. Like most men, he prided himself on having a shiny automobile. He worked so hard to keep his in good condition. In a garage, it would be safe from rain, snow and sleet and even the scorching sun in the summer. Happily, she anticipated his surprise at her gift.

AUGUST 1945

Maryanna

"Ete Missa est. *Go, the Mass is ended.*"
"Deo Gratias. *Thanks be to God.*"
"Today," Monsignor Kozlowski said, turning to face his parishioners, "we have great reason to sing Serdeczna Matko (*Affectionate Mother*). Today, Emperor Hirohito of Japan has surrendered to the Allied Forces in the Pacific. The war is over. I think it is providence and not coincidence that the

war in Europe ended on the 8th of May, in the month dedicated to Mary. The war in the Pacific ended today, August 15, the Feast of the Assumption of Mary, Mother of Jesus, into heaven."

The long-awaited news generated smiles, signs of the cross, hugs, kisses. The ripples spread out onto the sidewalk and street as people left the church. Too many houses had a flag in the window: a flag with a red border and stars in the white center. A blue star signified a family member who was in the service while a gold star stood for a hero who had been killed in action.

Her Stash would be coming home. She almost felt giddy at the thought. It seemed like he had been gone forever. It would be good to have a man in the house again. Sally had done amazingly well doing the chores that had been Michal's. She cut the grass in the summer and shoveled the snow in the winter. In spring and fall, she washed all the windows and swapped out the storm windows and the screens. She'd become quite adept at keeping the plumbing working as it should.

Sally, too, had a spring in her step. After three years overseas, Wally, her husband, would be coming home. They had only been married for three months before he entered the army. They would live in the house with her until Wally had reestablished himself in the mill and could make plans for their future. It would be good to have two men in the house, men who would want a hearty dinner of meat and potatoes, instead of the casseroles and salads that Sally favored and made because meat was rationed. She knew that her men were hankering to sink their teeth into a good steak. So was she.

Sophie

Slowly, she made her way from the bedroom to the rocker in the parlor. Her joints ached from the immense effort of taking off her nightgown and putting on a dress, brushing her hair and trying to braid it. She did not want Julianne to see her in bed. She turned the knob on the radio. Vicki always made sure that the dial was on the right station number for Oskerke, the Polish program.

"Busia! Busia!" She heard Julianne running in the back door which was unlocked and bounding up the stairs. "Hi, Busia!" She was beaming from ear to ear. Her black hair was clinging in damp tendrils around her face. Tiny flashes of light glinted in her dark eyes. She stood on tiptoe, reaching over to kiss her on one cheek while she patted the other. She pulled the hassock from in front of the armchair, dragging it over to the rocker. She sat down facing her.

"How is your day, Busia?"

"It is a good one, moja kochana *(my love)*." In her book, any day that Julianne came to visit was a good one.

"Good," Julianne replied, contentedly. She stroked her Busia's hand, tracing the veins that were like so many blue roadmaps of adventures taken long ago.

"How was *your* day, Julianne? What did you do?"

"It was a good day, Busia. I helped Mama preserve peaches this morning. I like canning, even though it was steamy in the basement."

"Such hard work deserves a treat. Go and get the little brown leather change purse from the bedroom."

She watched peacefully as Julianne jumped up and ran to the bedroom. She walked out slowly fingering the leather change purse worn by so many decades of use.

"Here it is, Busia." She unclasped one side of the change purse and searched for a nickel. She gave it to Julianne, saying "Go and get 5 for 6." She shook her head. She always said the numbers wrong. It was a small box of six ice cream bonbons that cost five cents at the corner grocery store.

"Be careful crossing the street," she said, automatically, as her granddaughter hurried to get the delectable treat. How she loved that girl! Sylvia had been Frank's favorite; Julianne was definitely hers. Once Julia had allowed her daughter to cross busy 83rd Street by herself, Julianne was always by her side. In her better days, they would sit in the back yard by the cages of chickens and ducks and geese. Julianne would keep her company while she stripped the feathers for goose down pillows and pierzynas.

She heard those strong, little legs bouncing up the stairs.

"Here you are, Busia."

She opened the box and let Julianne pick the first bonbon. She took two, leaving the remainder for her granddaughter. Companionably, they savored the cold sweetness that melted in their mouths as they listened to the familiar Polish melodies wafting from the radio.

FEBRUARY 1946

Sophie

Dr. Haraburda was not smiling when he entered his office where she was waiting, patiently. "You have stomach cancer. That is why you have been feeling full without eating great amounts. The tumor is obstructing a large part of your stomach. The weight you have lost is a symptom of the cancer. So is the nausea.

"The best treatment for the cancer is removal of the stomach. However, since the stomach digests the foods we eat, after removal of the stomach a person is limited to soft and bland foods. There are some new treatments that try to keep a tumor from growing; they are expensive. Because they are new, we don't know how long they can be used. If you experience unremitting pain from the tumor, there are some medications that we can use to make it tolerable. They might also be helpful in relieving the pain from the rheumatoid arthritis."

"Does removing the stomach cure the cancer?"

"It will remove the tumor that's in the stomach."

"Will it give a person a longer life?"

"It can give a longer life, not too long because there will be other digestive issues. Talk to your daughters and family. Once you have made your decision, I will visit you at home. Have Vicki call and set up a time. Whatever decisions you make, I will do everything to keep you as comfortable as is possible. You have my word." Dr. Haraburda helped her up and walked with her to the waiting room.

Wally was in the car ready to drive her home. It was only two blocks, but the arthritis had destroyed her capability to walk even that short distance. Going down the steep staircase was easier than the climb up had been. Vicki held the heavy door as she carefully stepped outside.

She looked to her left at the church across the street. How many times had she walked to that church, from the Bush, more than a mile away, when Frank was courting her and she was learning the catechism before being baptized? How quickly the years had flown by leaving their marks on her. After seven years she missed Frank and his absence in her life still hurt, but how happy she was that he was not here to see her in this pitiful state. He would have been so distressed.

She walked the few steps to the car. Vicki opened the door. She helped her sit down on the front seat and move her feet inside. Then she went into Pietrusinski's pharmacy on the first floor of the building to pick up the prescriptions that Dr. Haraburda had called down to Walter, the pharmacist. Within a few minutes, she was out the door and hopping into the back seat for the short ride home.

"A tumor, Mom?" Tears were running down Vicki's cheeks as fast as the words flew out of her mouth. "Of course, you must have the surgery. Dr. Haraburda will let us know who is the best doctor to perform it. Wally and I will take care of you, Mom. Whatever needs to be done, we will do it."

"Vicki, stop. I need time to think about this. And I will tell Julia and Agnieska. Julia, Steve and the girls are coming for dinner on Sunday; invite Mike and Agnieska. By then, I will have decided what I want to do."

"Mom, you have to have the surgery. It's the best thing to do."

"Vicki, again I say stop! I will decide what will be done or not done. I have been making decisions for myself since I was nine years old. My instincts have never failed me."

"But, Mom, you must have the surgery. If you don't, the pain will get worse."

"Do you think that there will be no pain after the surgery? There will be. Not only pain but an inability to eat anything that isn't pureed like baby food. And there will be other complications."

"But, Mom..."

"No buts, Vicki. I will decide what to do. I know this is hard on you. I did not want to lose your father seven years ago. I have missed him every day since then. But I also did not want to see him suffer. God knew what He was doing and He will guide me in making the right decision. Now, ring up Agnieska and invite her and Mike to dinner. And not a word about this. I will tell her after dinner on Sunday."

The last piece of pineapple-upside-down cake sat forlornly on the cake plate as the dregs of the coffee cups were drained. A fresh pot of coffee was percolating on the stove. Julia was clearing the dessert plates and flatware from the table. Steve, Mike and Wally were debating going to Calumet Park next weekend to see if the lake perch were biting; the winter had been warmer than usual. They were hankering to get their lines in the water and see what the prospects might be for Lenten fish fries. Sylvia, Julianne and Aniela were sitting on the sofa in the parlor. The older girls were taking turns reading to their little sister.

She motioned for Vicki to fill the coffee cups with the fresh brew and take her seat at the table with Julia.

"On Thursday, I went to see Dr. Haraburda. For a while I have been having stomach problems, in addition to the arthritis. After an examination and consideration of the symptoms that I have been having, he said that I have stomach cancer."

"Will you have surgery to remove it?" asked Julia. She and Agnieska sat up rigid in their chairs.

"Yes, she will."

"Vicki, I told you that I would decide what is to be done. I wanted all of you together today so that everyone in my family knows what my wishes are.

"Stomach cancer and diabetes are two diseases that seem to occur more frequently in eastern European people than in other nationalities. Dr. Haraburda said that doctors do not know why. There are several treatments, including surgery, for stomach cancer which may give the person a little more time. I have considered all the treatments and I have made a decision. I do not want surgery. There is a treatment that is new that Dr. Haraburda recommended. It is expensive, but not as drastic as the surgery. It is a medicine that should shrink the tumor. A specialist will come to the house to administer the treatment."

"How do you know it will work?" Agnieska asked.

"I don't. But I have decided it is the best option."

"Seems foolish to spend a lot of money on a cockamamie treatment that may not work."

"Agnieska, let Mom finish," Julia said, calmly. She saw Vicki getting ready to open her mouth; what would have come out of it, she wasn't sure. It was better to intervene. She wanted to know what her mother was thinking.

"Thank you, Julia. I don't know what will happen in the next few months, so I have decided to discuss my wishes now.

"Vicki, you have lived in this house for over twenty years. Since you married Wally, he has spent time and money keeping it up. When I am gone, the house is yours to continue to live in."

"Mom, don't talk like that!"

"Julia and Steve, you need a house for yourselves with a yard for your three daughters to play in. Find a house and I will give you $3,000 as a down payment."

"Mom, thank you," Julia said, elatedly.

"That is most generous," Steve added. "Thank you."

"Agnieska and Mike..."

"I don't need anything, Sophie. Mike and I have more than enough."

"Then it is settled. I am content. And tired. I will go and rest."

Emotionally, she was drained. She made her way out of the kitchen and through the parlor to her bedroom. She closed the door as she entered it. She could hear the muted voices of her daughters and their husbands discussing this latest change in life. She propped a pillow against the headboard and sat down on the bed leaning against the pillow. She lowered her eyelids and willed her brain to conjure up memories of Frank. She smiled. "I'm coming, Frank. It won't be long now," she whispered, jubilantly.

JULY 1946

Maryanna

"Busia, do you know those ladies?" Julianne asked. She was sitting in the same parlor where Michał had been waked at Kortas Funeral Home. She was amazed at the stream of mourners who had come to pay their respects to Sophie, who had gone to her eternal reward. Quiet Sophie had bustled around raising her poultry, cooking and baking until the rheumatoid arthritis and cancer got the better of her. Of course, she surmised, some of these people were her customers and some would know Vicki, Julia or Agnieska.

"Which ladies?"

"The two ladies who didn't kneel down. They stood by the casket and didn't make the sign of the cross, either. But they looked so sad."

"I don't know who they are."

"I do," interjected Vicki, who had walked over with Aniela. "It's Mrs. Hyman and her sister, Mrs. Freund. I used to work for Mrs. Hyman, years ago. She and her sister were taught Hebrew when they were young ladies.

When I told Mrs. Hyman that my mother knew Yiddish and had learned some Hebrew while working for families in Piotrkow, she called Mom up and they became telephone friends. Both sisters were so good in calling Mom frequently during the last months when she was housebound. Because Wally and I were both working, the days were lonely. Telephone calls like that were wonderful therapy for Mom."

"That's why I came over and sat with Busia every day that I could," piped up Julianne. "I liked sitting with Busia."

"You have been a wonderful granddaughter, Julianne. I know that my mother loved you very much." Vicki smiled at her niece. "I must go and greet some coworkers of mine who just came in."

Stephan sat down next to his mother. He lifted Aniela and sat her on his knee. She nestled into his black suit, contentedly.

"How are you doing, Ma?"

"I am good. I didn't anticipate so many people."

"She was very well liked."

"I'm surprised that the two Jewish ladies came to a Catholic wake."

"I'm pleased that they did."

"But some people are so different."

"Ma, we just got through fighting a world war because some people decided they were better than the different people."

She was pondering how to change the subject when Father Ed walked into the chapel. Once again, prayer had saved her.

⸎⸎⸎

"Sally, she's beautiful." She was holding her daughter's first child. She was a robust little one with fair hair and her father's blue eyes. As tiny as she was, she squirmed and kicked in her busia's arms, impatient to be free, as if she couldn't wait to crawl and walk and run. "She's going to be like you, a handful."

"Thanks, Ma." Sally wasn't quite sure if it was compliment or indictment.

"Minka will make you proud, Sally. I can feel it."

She looked around at her full house. Stephan, Tomasz, Stash and Wally were playing cards at the dining room table. Estella and Julia were in the kitchen putting away the food and washing the dishes. The remains of the christening cake sat on the sideboard. Bud, Sylvia and Julianne were racing up and down the spiral stairs that went from basement to attic. Aniela was sitting beside her. Her newborn cousin fascinated her. Silently, she watched every move the baby made. Michał would have loved this scene.

CHAPTER TEN

JANUARY 1947

(Sophie)

If she had only lived six more months! It wouldn't have mattered how much pain she would have had to endure. She would have been here in the flesh to comfort Vicki.

"Mom, you're going to be a grandma again!" Vicki was beaming the day she had announced her pregnancy. It was June 15th, the sixth anniversary of her marriage to Wally. How they had rejoiced together that the womb that had been barren for all those years was now full of life. She had forgotten her pain in the euphoria of that day. Three weeks later, the cancer won. In her terminal moments, she had been happy. Vicki would miss her, but now she had the birth of her child for which to look forward and prepare.

Today, the little one was stillborn. She saw Vicki in the hospital, alone, bereft. Wally had been by her side, but left to make arrangements for the burial of their son.

"I must go to her," she thought.

"Kiss her for me," Frank thought, as he cradled the soul of this tiny little grandson of his. His first grandson.

"I will." Effortlessly, she stepped through the flimsy veil that separates those who are confined to life on earth and those who have passed through it. The very first time that she had floated through it, she had been astounded at how fragile the veil really was. She floated toward Vicki's bed.

"I'm here, Vicki," she thought forcefully, willing her daughter to know her presence in her mind.

Vicki sat propped against pillows, her pink bed jacket a stark contrast to her lusterless face and mournful eyes.

"I'm here, Vicki," she repeated, voicelessly.

Vicki stirred. She turned her head slightly.

"Vicki, your son is safe with us. He is a beautiful boy," she thought. She hovered over the bed and kissed her daughter on the cheek.

Vicki touched her cheek and looked around, puzzled.

Wally walked into the room and sat at the top of the bed next to Vicki.

She flitted away, as he bent over to kiss his wife tenderly and envelop her in his arms. Vicki leaned into him as tears gathered on her cheeks.

"I'm sorry, Wally."

"Vicki! Don't ever say that!".

"I know how much you wanted a son and I can't give..."

He stopped her words with a lingering kiss. They sat silently entwined until Vicki's tears and breathlessness subsided.

"I made the arrangements. I know how much you wanted to give a grandbaby to your folks. I've arranged with Gene Kortas to bury our son between your parents at Holy Cross." He kissed her forehead and resumed their silence. Words were unnecessary.

She floated over the bed, kissing Vicki on the top of her head. Slipping through the veil, she was eager to join Frank. Not only was their grandson safe with them forever, but he would also be with them forever on earth.

JUNE 1947

Maryanna

"Stephan, it isn't my place or my right to tell you what to do. You didn't get married because you had to. You didn't rush into a marriage. You were twenty-six years old when you married Julia. Old enough to know if she would be a good wife. Old enough to know that the vows you took were forever, not until things weren't going your way."

Once again, she was sitting at the kitchen table with a hot pot of coffee, sweet rolls and a family member with marital difficulties. Stephan and Julia appeared to be as mismatched as were Josie and Joseph. Josie was open to change; Joseph abhorred it, wanting only the same old routine. Josie and Walter were happy.

Teo and Mike would have been a good pair, if they never had children at such a young age. It was a getting-married-because-they-had-to situation. Both felt saddled with three children; Mike, because he had to provide for them and Teo who had to care for them. She had no idea where brother-in-law Mike was and, personally, didn't care. Flighty Teo was already divorced from her third husband, Glenn. Teo was living in St. Louis near her namesake daughter, who had married a jeweler and now had a son.

After Stash agreed to divorce Esther so that her family was no longer torn apart because of her dictatorial father, Esther refused to return home which angered her father even more. He had gotten his wish by breaking up her marriage, but she would never live under his roof again. She threatened to call the police if she learned that he was abusing her mother because she wouldn't budge. Several years ago, she had remarried - another Stanley, no less. For a while, they were living only two blocks away with their children.

Stash was the one for whom her heart ached. He never looked at another girl. Esther had been his one and only true love.

Stephan was sitting across from her in a quandary. She watched him light up a Camel cigarette, smoke it down to a nub, then light another, as if the solution to his problem would flare up in the smoke. His ambition to make something of himself was in conflict with Julia's contentment with the status quo.

Where had that attitude come from, she wondered? The vows left unspoken in a marriage ceremony were those a married couple tacitly understood: the husband would work to support the family while the wife managed the household and cared for their children. Neither of Julia's parents nor Vicki or Agnieska were content to sit on their duffs and follow that literally. Sophie raised poultry to help Frank, Vicki was still working at the laundry even though Wally was also a foreman at US Steel. Agnieska had made a bundle bootlegging beer during prohibition. Then, there was Julia. She was following that unspoken understanding to the letter.

She and Stephan had purchased a house at 84th and Manistee last year using the money from Sophie for the down payment. Julia did keep a tidy house and did not neglect her girls the way Teo had neglected her children. She taught them good manners and insisted on sending them to St. Mary Magdalene grammar school for solid religious and academic education; the Felician sisters were excellent teachers. However, she expected Stephan not only to provide for his family, but also to do it her way.

"Stephan, if there is one thing I regret it is that your father and I did not insist that you receive a high school education. We should have because you are so intelligent, as was your father. We were both so proud of his rising to the level of foreman. He knew that that was as far as he could go. It was enough for him to think that he had achieved so much in this new homeland. We should have given more thought to your future in America."

"Ma, don't beat yourself up."

"You know, I am not much different than Julia. I like the simple routine of daily living. I loved having all my babies. I didn't care how many we would have because they were your father's children. I took in boarders in the early years because it helped to make ends meet. I have been quite content to keep a house, cook for my family and tend to the vegetable and flower gardens. I like staying in my home. Julia likes staying home, too.

"There is one difference between us. Whatever decisions your father made regarding the future, I accepted, wholeheartedly, as his wife. They were not dictatorial decisions. We discussed everything. But the final decision was always your father's; this is where Julia and I differ."

"That's the problem, Ma. She wants to make all the decisions. Mike says she wants to wear the pants in the family. Agnieska does and Julia is so much like her. I don't know why I never saw that. She expects me to provide well for her and the girls, then curtails my ability by dictating where and how." He pulled another cigarette from the pack, lit it and took a deep puff.

"Ma, I don't want to be doing the same thing at the steel mill for the next twenty-five years. The war is over, the men are back, the tavern is busy and Marquette Gardens is always booked solid. Joe really can't handle it all. I tried to explain this to Julia, but she wouldn't let me finish. She says that being in the mill is what kept me from being drafted and stateside when I was."

"Stephan, the tension between you and Julia was evident at Sylvia's graduation party last Sunday. It felt like being between those two doggie magnets you and Stash had as boys. If you turned them the wrong way, no matter how much you tried to put them together, they repelled each other.

"Julia did look good, I noticed. Her cheeks had color and she is putting on a little weight. That's good."

Stephan eyes looked down into his empty coffee cup. "That's because she's expecting, Ma. In January."

≼◌◌≽

JANUARY 1948

Maryanna

She would never tire of babies - having babies, holding babies, feeding babies. Babies were the future of a family, of a community. They were the lifeblood, the continuity.

She was especially pleased that Stephan's fourth daughter was named after her, Marysia. She was a cute little thing with dimples and huge dark brown eyes in a tiny face framed by wisps of curly amber hair. She had secretly hoped that this child might be a boy to carry on the family name. Now that she was here and bearing her name, it didn't matter. She was sitting in Julia's kitchen on the bench beneath the west window. The mid-winter sun enveloped her in warmth before scattering its light throughout the room. Marysia was nestled in her arms, sleeping soundly.

"Julia, where's the paprika?" she heard Estella ask. They were all in the kitchen - Julia, Estella, Sally, Vicki - putting the finishing touches on the dishes they had prepared for Marysia's christening.

The house was an old farmhouse like the one in which Julia had grown up. What had once been a ground level place for animals had been divided into a huge kitchen with a hallway leading to a large basement area. On one side of the hall was a bathroom; on the other, a large pantry.

The men were all upstairs in the original kitchen playing cards and drinking beer. Bud, Sylvia and Julianne were also upstairs in the parlor sprawled on the floor playing Monopoly. Minka and Aniela were eyeing the little pink plastic baskets filled with butter mints and almonds, favors of the christening for each guest to take home.

Julia's half-sister, Agnieska, plopped down beside her. As she did so, Estella let out a scream.

"Julia, the paprika is moving all over the potato salad!"

Aniela and Minka ran over to the table to see walking paprika. The paprika was infested with tiny bugs. A few were on the potato salad. Julia brought a large spoon and an empty brown paper bag to the table. Estella took the spoon and scooped up all the potato salad that had been sprinkled with the buggy paprika and tossed it into the empty bag. She took a clean spoon and removed bits and pieces of the potato salad until she was satisfied that the salad was free of bugs.

"Well, I'm surprised that Julia didn't toss the whole bowl of potato salad into the garbage," Agnieska commented.

"Julia manages well. She is not a spendthrift."

"She'd do even better if she didn't keep saddling herself with kids. Aniela will be going to school this fall and Julia would be free. Instead, she had another baby."

She clamped her teeth together and adjusted the bottle of formula so Marysia could finish the few drops that remained in it. Retorts kept bubbling up and hitting her teeth.

"Julia could have gone to work when Aniela starts school. Since she won't let Steve work with Wieczorek, she should start contributing to the security she's always talking about." Agnieska adjusted her purse on her lap.

She had noticed that Agnieska always had her purse in her possession at all times. She had heard Estella and Sally bantering with each other as to whether Agnieska had the keys to Fort Knox in her purse. More likely, she had two quarters and a dime in there, but even that was too much for her to risk losing.

"Babies are the future of the world," she said, evenly. Marysia had drained the last drops of formula from the bottle and she put her on her shoulder to burp her.

"If you can afford them."

Once again, she clamped her teeth together. She was unwilling to dampen the christening celebration by putting Agnieska in her place. Instead, she silently thanked God on behalf of all the girls and boys who never had Agnieska as a mother. Julia had confided in her a few years ago that Agnieska had taken in an orphaned girl with the possibility of adopting her. She put so many restrictions and demands on the poor girl that she ran back to the orphanage convinced she had a better life there.

"Dinner is ready," she heard Julia say. Saved by the dinner bell.

(Sophie)

What a relief to see Agnieska spouting off to someone else. Never again would she have to endure her stepdaughter's diatribes.

She and Frank were perched on the steps leading up to the second floor. Frank had never physically seen Julia's house. He had been dead seven years when Julia and Steve bought it. She had been in it once, before she was confined to her house. The similarity to their own house two blocks down the street was pleasing to Frank and to her.

She loved this new life of hers. No pain, no restrictions of aging body, no aching joints or wrinkles. She never tired of gazing at Frank who was as he had been the first time she had seen him strolling into the general store. Full head of hair, gleaming moustache, muscular, lithe. She knew that she also looked as she did then. Thick blond hair, clear blue eyes, firm skin, quick of movement. They were here to celebrate this moment.

She watched Vicki. She moved deftly in Julia's kitchen helping with this and that. Her usual exuberance was quietly contained. The other women in their busyness didn't seem to notice. If they did, they might have attributed her silence to Vicki's sorrow at losing her son last year. She knew it pleased Vicki that they did not notice. For though she was quiet, her eyes glowed and her cheeks were flushed with the secret growing inside her. God willing, in five months she would be cradling her own child. Until it was impossible to conceal, she was reluctant to share her joy.

"Dinner is ready," she heard Julia say.

She rose from the steps and floated over to her elder daughter. What she couldn't do in her life on earth, she could do freely now. She kissed her daughter on the cheek. Julia put her fingers to her face. She flitted over to Vicki and planted a good one on her. She rose up to join Frank.

JULY 1948

(Sophie)

"Sophie! Sophie!" she heard Frank thinking. "If there was a rug, you'd be wearing it out. Settle down."

"Frank, how can I?" she countered. "It's Vicki's first healthy baby," she retorted, as she flitted from one side of the hospital room to the other waiting for the nurse to bring Shirley in for her feeding. She loved eternity. The total release of earth's restraints. Instantly being able to go where she willed and see and hear everything. No time, no space constraints. She could survey the current moment or go back or forward to another moment. They were all suspended in timeless eternity. She had gone back a few times but never forward. She was quite content to be in the moment with her loved ones.

She did go back in time to a few occurrences so she could fully understand them. Some events she backed away from: seeing how the horse killed her father or, worst of all, seeing Gottlieb falling on foreign soil fighting a war for someone he didn't know for a reason he would never know. In all of it, she reveled in understanding how each past event affected the ones that succeeded it. Had she married Gottlieb, she would have stayed in Europe living a totally different life than the loving one she had with Frank.

She had gone back to see Frank's family; his parents, Christof and Catherine and his brothers and sisters. She was jubilant to see Catherine's mother, her arms folded tightly across her chest, her dark hair bound in a firmly knotted, brightly embroidered babushka that was in contrast to the scowl on her face and the anger in her black eyes. She was seething as she berated Catherine for her silly idea of marrying Christof. She, Catherine's mother, had decided that her daughter should marry the village butcher and that was that. She flitted about the scene jubilantly; she had discovered the source of the obnoxious streaks of personality and dominance that Agnieska had in spades and Julia had to a lesser degree - their great grandmother.

She hovered as the nurse brought her granddaughter into the room and nestled her in Vicki's eager arms. Shirley took after her and Vicki with flaxen hair, soft blue eyes and chubby cheeks. She kissed the little one on each chubby cheek. Shirley's eyes fluttered and she let out a squeal. Frank beckoned her to join him. Together they delighted in the charm of their latest granddaughter.

Maryanna

The house echoed emptily since Sally, Wally and Minka had moved to a tiny trailer surrounded by corn fields on Bock Road in Lansing. She missed the exuberance of Minka; it always took her back more than thirty years to the antics of Dora, Estella and Minka's mother, Sally. How she missed those days! Back then there were never enough hours in a day. She had to snatch tiny moments here and there to enjoy her children. Now the hours were endless. No boarders, no toddlers, no vegetable gardens, no mammoth pots of food to cook. No need to spend hours in a hot, steamy kitchen canning the vegetables and fruits she grew; in the basement was a marvel of invention, a freezer that kept meats and vegetables frozen for a long time with no decline in quality. No heavy, galvanized laundry tubs, wash boards and clothes lines or wringer washing machine; she had a washer and dryer that did all that.

Stash had bought the pair for her last year. He lived with her, but he was rarely home.

Bzzzt! Bzzzt! She rose from the burgundy wing chair in the parlor where she had been sitting and trotted to the door. Julia was standing on the porch with Aniela and Marysia. Julia rarely visited her without Stephan.

She opened the door. "Hi, Busia. May I come in?" Aniela asked, as a smile creased her face. She smiled at her granddaughter who wore a green seersucker sundress that complemented her hazel eyes, Michał's eyes. Her brown hair was neatly braided. She carried a picture book.

"Of course," she replied.

Julia was silent as she followed Aniela into the small hall. It was a steamy, sunny day but she looked cool as a cucumber in a floral print dress. Marysia was dressed in a pink seersucker sunsuit; her skin had been protected from the sun by the hood on the pram. Her damp brown hair curled into wispy ringlets like a frame around her huge brown eyes.

"Marysia!" she said, holding out her arms. The brown eyes sparkled and the tiny mouth spread into a toothless smile that prompted two dimples to pop up on her cheeks. The little one held out her arms and reached beyond her mother. She grasped Marysia firmly as Julia relaxed her own grip. The six-month-old squirmed in her arms until she was comfortable.

"Please, sit down," she said to Julia. She settled herself in the wing chair that she had just vacated.

Julia sat on the matching chair across the room while Aniela put her picture book on the sofa and climbed up on the plump cushion retrieving her book once she was safely seated.

"Where are Sylvia and Julianne?"

"They are at home. The grass needs cutting and Julianne is using the push mower to cut it."

"Is Stephan that busy? Has he been working overtime?"

"I thought you might know how busy Steve is."

"Julia, how would I know?" She was puzzled. Her body tensed and Marysia felt it. She began to squirm.

"I thought he might be staying here."

"Stephan is not living at home?"

"No."

"I haven't seen him since the 4th of July." A memory flashed into her brain of Stash and Stephan on the back porch, talking animatedly. She couldn't see

Stephan's face, but she did see Stash. He had appeared upset, trying to talk his brother in or out of something. At the time, she had thought it was their business, whatever it was. Now, she wondered.

"Has Steve been in touch with Stanley? Maybe he knows where Steve is staying."

"Julia, you would have to ask Stash."

"Somebody has to know where he is."

"I do not. Perhaps Mike or Victor know where he is; they're his closest friends."

"But you're his mother."

"Stephan and Stash are both grown men. I don't keep tabs on them. Besides, you were the one who told me in no uncertain terms years ago that your marriage was your business and Stephan's and I had no right meddling."

"That was when Wieczorek put that crazy idea into Steve's head of partnering with him. Joe's been doing it again. This is different."

"It is not a crazy idea, Julia. Look at how well Wieczorek is doing. He's making money hand over fist. Marquette Gardens is busy every weekend, all weekend. I'm sure..."

"Joe wants Steve to run the tavern, not the banquet hall. A proposition that is too risky."

"What is risky about it? All the men need a place to relax after the brutal work they do in the mills. Stephan himself has been a customer; that's how he and Joe became friends."

"Steve has a good job in the mill."

"But he has nothing to look forward to. Like his father, Stephan wants to better himself."

"His father always seemed content to be a foreman. Why isn't Steve as content?"

"Michal was content because he had accomplished his goal. He started out as a lowly helper, an immigrant who didn't speak English, but he rose through the ranks to become a foreman. He was much older when he became a foreman. He only had a few more years to work. Stephan is forty years old. He will be doing the same job for the next twenty-five years. I know he wants more than that."

"It's a good job. It has benefits. It's safe. It's secure."

"Julia, in one respect, you are not too different from me. You don't like change; neither do I. Without change, we go nowhere. If I did not make the biggest change in my life by leaving Poland and coming to America, where would I be? I was young; it was easier. You are only ten years older than I was when I traveled thousands of miles on a perilous journey eager for a better life. I found it with Michał and the life we have lived here.

"There is one big difference. Unlike some men who insist on being king of their castle, Michał never made a decision without talking it over with me. However, the final decision was always his. And, even if I disagreed with it, I supported him in that decision. I trusted him. You are not doing that with Stephan. You want the decision to be yours."

Julia pursed her lips and said nothing.. The room was growing warmer, both temperature and tension-wise. Marysia was squirming, feeling the warmth of her grandmother's body. She put the baby on Julia's lap.

"Aniela, would you like a glass of lemonade?"

"Oh, yes, Busia. Can I help you?"

"Yes. Come with me into the kitchen."

"Julia, do you have water for Marysia?"

"I have water for her. I fed her before we left the house."

She took Aniela's hand and went into the kitchen to get the pitcher of lemonade from the refrigerator. She took two large glasses and one small glass from the shelf. She pulled out a steel ice cube tray from the freezer and pulled at its handle to loosen the cubes. She put several ice cubes into each glass, then returned the tray to the freezer.

"Take each glass one at a time into the parlor," she said to Aniela. "Put one on the table next to your mother, one on the table next to my chair and the little one on the coffee table in front of the sofa."

Aniela traipsed back and forth doing as she had been told. She accompanied her on the last trip and poured the tart beverage into each glass. She placed the pitcher on the glass-topped coffee table. Marysia sucked water from a bottle she was holding by herself.

Julia took a sip from her glass and replaced it on the table next to her. "It's not the same," she said, eager to defend her position. "Michał always had a steady job and you were secure."

"Not in the early years," she informed Julia. "Until ten years ago, the men in the mills were at the mercy of the owners. They worked six and seven days a week, twelve hours a day. There were only two shifts, not three as there are now. It scared the daylights out of me when Michał decided to buy the house on 83rd and Marquette. We were bound to pay the mortgage every month.

But I trusted his decision. I did everything I could to help him. I saved as much as I could on household expenses and took in a boarder."

As the words flowed out of her mouth, she realized that was the big difference between her and Julia. While Julia did what was necessary for daily life, she did not go above and beyond. She did what she thought every wife was expected to do and nothing more. This conversation could become contentious if it continued; she did not want that. She wanted to keep the lines of communication open, not severed by animosity.

"Julia, I'm saddened and upset that Stephan is not living at home. If I do see him, I will remind him of his duties."

"Thank you." Julia drained her glass of lemonade and settled Marysia into her left arm. "Come, Aniela," she said, as she rose from the wing chair and hoisted the diaper bag, putting the water bottle into it as she did so.

Silently, Aniela picked up her empty glass and carried it into the kitchen. When she returned, she picked up her picture book and stood by her mother ready to leave.

"Aniela," she said to her, holding her arms out widely. Aniela put her book down on the floor and ran into them eagerly, hugging her ample Busia tightly. She kissed Aniela on the top of her head. The little girl picked up her book and contentedly followed her mother out the door.

She watched as they walked down the stairs to the baby pram. People called them buggies now. It was a weird word, she thought. She watched Aniela as Julia settled Marysia in the pram. Aniela was a solemn thing. Skinny like her mother. She watched everything the way Stephan did as a little boy, but said nothing. She wondered how much of the conversation Aniela had understood. She would be five years old in a few weeks and would be entering kindergarten in September.

She had wondered why she felt an antipathy toward her daughter-in-law. She had chalked it up to embracing the typical attitude that no other woman was good enough for her son. She knew Julia loved Stephan; whenever they were together, it flamed in her eyes when she looked at him. It was only today that she realized that as much as Julia loved Stephan, she was willing to do what she thought was expected of her as his wife and the mother of his children. Nothing more. It was a mindset she could not fathom; she had always supported Michał in whatever way she could.

She turned away from the window as Julia and the children disappeared down 84th Street. Her house may seem empty; her life never was. Once one problem was resolved, another surfaced. She picked up the large glasses from the side tables and took them into the kitchen. She would wash them with the dinner dishes.

JANUARY 1949

(Sophie)

She floated up the staircase to the second floor as Dr. Haraburda wearily climbed the steps. The lines in his forehead and by his mouth were like a timepiece announcing that his day which had begun at five o'clock in the morning was not over even though it was already seven o'clock in the evening. Reaching the landing, he straightened his shoulders and quickened his steps. He strode down the hall to the far bedroom where Julia was battling pneumonia.

Julia struggled to sit up as he entered the bedroom. The effort triggered a bout of coughing and she gasped for breath.

Dr. Haraburda opened his satchel and pulled out a thermometer, a blood pressure cuff, his stethoscope, tongue depressors, a syringe and a vial of penicillin. She watched him check Julia's blood pressure and pulse. He spent much time assessing her lungs with the stethoscope.

"Good news," he said, smiling at his patient. "The fever is abating; it should be gone by tomorrow or the next day. That means your body is fighting the pneumonia. That is a good sign. The penicillin is doing its job. There is still much congestion in both lungs; it will clear. This is your fourth injection of penicillin; you will need at least six more." As he spoke, he filled a syringe with the antibiotic and injected it into Julia's butt.

"Your throat is getting raw from the incessant coughing. It is necessary, however, to cough up whatever mucus you can to clear your lungs. When I get back to the office, I will call Walter in the pharmacy and he will mix up the cough syrup that always works. It will soothe your throat. Have Sylvia or Julianne run over to the drugstore and pick it up in about a half hour. There will be no charge.

"I will see you again tomorrow evening," he said, as he repacked his satchel. "You have turned the corner; each day you will feel better and breathing will be a little easier. I will take a quick look at Marysia on my way out; she's already a year old." He smiled and left the sickroom.

She watched as he walked over to the crib in the corner of the large room at the top of the stairs. Her granddaughter was holding on to the railing and bouncing on the balls of her feet. She was only an nth away from walking solo. He relaxed as he felt Marysia's forehead and did a cursory check of her limbs while the little imp smiled and giggled.

She watched as he turned away from the crib and trotted over to the chair near the staircase where Aniela was sitting quietly, waiting for him.

"How's my kindergartener?" he asked, as he approached.

"I'm good," she said, smiling shyly, as she swung her skinny legs to and fro.

"Have you been a good girl today?"

"Yes."

"I think you are always a good girl and deserve a treat." He reached into his coat pocket and pulled out a handful of cellophane-wrapped caramels. Aniela cupped her hands together as he gave them to her.

"See you girls tomorrow," he said, as he traipsed downstairs.

She watched him until he disappeared where the steps turned toward the kitchen. She could hear him giving instructions to Sylvia in a kindly voice. He was a good man. He had cared for her in her last months and was now fighting to keep her daughter alive.

She flitted down the hall to check on her daughter. Julia was fast asleep. In the timelessness of eternity, she watched her chest as the heaving with each breath gradually lessened; the penicillin had begun its work.

Maryanna

"Stephan, what is the matter with you! Julia almost died. Stash told me that Dr. Haraburda has been caring for her every day after his office hours are over. He has to be doing it out of the goodness of his heart." She was irate. How many more times would she be required to sit at the kitchen table with an errant relative?

"How could you just leave her high and dry? And what about your children?" She watched her elder son closely as he wrapped his hands around the hot cup of coffee and drank it heedless of its temperature. He was forty-one years old and still in good shape, physically. A few fine lines were etching his face and he needed a shave. His thick dark beard needed shaving twice a day if he were to be always clean shaven. She couldn't see any signs of gray in his unruly dark hair. Angst was written all over his face.

"Ma, I can't go back. I feel sorry that Julia's ill. I care for her, but I know that once she is better, she will go back to being the Julia that I don't want to live with." Stephan reached into his shirt pocket and pulled out the pack of Camels and lit one.

"What about the children?"

"Ma, I love my girls. If I could raise them without her interference, I would. We could be happy with each other. But you know that will never happen."

"You can't walk away from them, no matter how you feel about the situation. You are their father; it is your duty to care for them."

"I know, Ma, I know. I did go back last fall. For a little while, Julia was fine. Then, she was right back into her old ways. She has one of the most negative personalities I have ever seen. I don't understand why.

"She was great when the girls were babies. She took excellent care of them, as long as she could put them down somewhere and they stayed there. As soon as the babies start to crawl and walk and want to do things their way, she begins to stifle them. If they want to do what she likes, it's okay. Sylvia hasn't been a problem; she's like her mother, happy to sit and sew and embroider all day long. She's little yet, but Aniela might go the same route. Julianne is altogether different. She's my little dynamite. She wants to run and play and climb trees and ride bikes. Julia wants none of that. She scolds her for being a tomboy and not being ladylike. Ma, she's only doing what Sally did at her age. She is not a tomboy. She will be a knockout in five years."

She watched Stephan as he reached for a donut and dunked it in his coffee before taking a bite. "What do you mean 'knockout'? Is she that much of a tomboy that she fights? She's always charming in my company."

"Ma, it's a slang word. It means she will be very beautiful. She will never lack for guys who will want to date her."

"Slang, shmang. English is difficult enough to understand without all the crazy words."

"I'm sure there are words in Polish that have double meanings, words that we were never taught." As he drank the last dregs of coffee, the light-hearted moment vanished as quickly as it had popped up. "So, what am I going to do, Ma?"

"Stephan, you know what is the right thing to do. Your father and I raised you in the Catholic faith, teaching you right from wrong. You know your duties as father and husband. You know that all of us are given a cross to carry. For your father and me, it was the loss of four children that we would never see grow up. For Estella, it is her rheumatic heart disease. Stash gave up the love of his life so Esther could have her family in her life. For you, it is Julia's rigid personality. I will pray that God will soften her heart and her mind. I know that she loves you; I've seen it in her eyes when she is with you."

"But how do I live with that rigidity every day?" He smashed the stub of his cigarette into the ashtray.

"You have to find a way, Stephan. Go back to Julia and your daughters. Look for all the good that is in her. Hold fast to that."

She stood up when her son did. He was a head taller than she. She buried her face in his chest and held him as tightly as she could. Not even the Old Spice lingering on his face or the aroma of coffee and cigarettes on his lips could totally mask the unique scent of him that had delighted her since he was a baby. He kissed the top of her head as he always did. He stepped away from her embrace, donned his thick woolen jacket and slipped through the back door and down the stairs. She trotted as fast as she could to the living room windows and watched as he reached the front sidewalk and turned left toward 83rd Street, instead of right toward 84th and his home.

NOVEMBER 1949

Maryanna

"Ma, what are you doing up? It's three o'clock in the morning," Stash asked as he wandered into the parlor.

"How can I sleep when your brother is in jail?"

"I'll warm up the coffeepot. Or do you want a glass of warm milk? They say it helps one sleep."

"Ugh! Coffee might help my nerves."

Stash walked through the dark dining room and into the kitchen. He flicked the switch and a beam of light shot across the dining room floor, almost to where she was sitting. That's what was needed now, she thought, a beam of light to brighten the current situation.

At supper, it was Stash who told her that Stephan had been arrested on Saturday. He had returned home last February, but it was temporary. She had learned that for a few months, he would come and go, staying at his house during the week when he worked, going off on the weekends, who knew where. In late September he had gone off one weekend and never returned home. Julia had sought a garnishment of his wages for child support. Republic Steel did not take kindly to having one of its foremen in a less than desirable financial situation; he was fired. Julia was desperate. She needed money for food. She sought his arrest.

Stash had learned of the arrest from a coworker who lived down the street from Stephan and Julia. He had gone to the house after work. Sylvia told her uncle that the police had pulled up in front of the house on Saturday morning as her mother was fixing breakfast. They had located her dad and needed her mother to come down to the station to formally file charges. Sylvia had finished fixing breakfast for her sisters.

Stash returned to the parlor with two large cups of coffee. He handed one to her and sat down on one of the wing chairs with the other.

"Thank you. I'm keeping you up when you should be sleeping. You have to be up for work at 5:30 a.m.."

"It doesn't matter, Ma. I'm not tired. I'm worried about you."

"What good will it do for Stephan to be in jail? How will it help pay a mortgage or buy food for the children?"

"I don't know, Ma. Julia didn't know where Steve was and secured a warrant for his arrest. I think she was hoping that he was working elsewhere and could give her some money. Now that he's been arrested, it has to go through the system unless she drops the charges."

"Can she do that?"

"Yes. But I don't think she will. She's afraid that he will disappear again which won't solve her problems paying the bills. Ma, don't take this the wrong way, but she was tightlipped when I was there. I could be wrong but I sense that she's starting to think that we knew where Steve was but wouldn't tell her. Most of what I learned came from Sylvia. I gave her some money to give to her mother after I had left."

"You're a good man, just like your father, Stash."

"Oh, Ma, Sylvia said her mother is expecting again in February."

FEBRUARY 1950

(Sophie)

"Sophie, you spend as much time down here as you did when you were alive," Frank was thinking.

"I do not!"

"So where are we now?"

"This is exciting, Frank. You have a grandson!"

They were resting at the top of the staircase just above the steps where *Aniela* and *Marysia* sat watching *Sylvia* and *Julianne* who were sitting on the landing below using the telephone.

"Hi, Busia! It's a boy! He was born early this morning around 7 a.m....Yes, Mama is doing well...Mama says he weighs 6 lbs. 5 oz. and has brown hair and dark brown eyes...She said his name is David Francis. Uncle Wally drove her to the hospital last night. He will bring her home...Thank you, Busia. I will tell Mama."

"Hi, Aunt Vicki. Mama had a baby boy this morning...He's fine and so is Mama.....She said his name is David Francis....Yes, Auntie, after your dad...He weighs 6 lb. 5 oz. and has brown hair and dark brown eyes...Mama asked me to thank Uncle Wally for driving her to the hospital at such a late hour. She is grateful...About 7 a.m. this morning...Thank you, Auntie, I will let you know. We love you and Uncle. Give Shirley a kiss from us. Goodbye, Auntie."

"Hi, Aunt Estella. I have good news. Mama had a baby boy this morning...Yes, Mama said he is healthy. He weighs 6 lb. 5 oz. and has brown hair and brown eyes...His name is David Francis...Yes, Mama is doing well. She sounded happy on the telephone...I'm okay, Auntie. Everything is okay in the house. It's really only Marysia that needs to be watched. She's into everything...Thank you, Auntie. I will tell Mama that you want to come out and help her with whatever she needs. We love you, Auntie."

"Hi, Aunt Sally. Mama had a baby boy this morning. His name is David Francis. He weighs 6 lb. 5 oz. and he has brown eyes and hair...Yes, Auntie....Mama is fine.... Thank you, Auntie. We love you and Uncle Wally. Say 'hi' to Minka. Good bye."

"Hi Ciocia (aunt). This is Sylvia. Mama had a baby boy this morning...Yes, Ciocia, he's healthy and so is Mama....His name is David Francis....Thank you, Ciocia. Dobranoc (good night)!"

Did she really have to call Agnieska?

"Sophie!" she heard Frank think. *When she was on earth, she had heard someone say that there is a downside to everything. If there was a downside to spirit life, it was that your*

thoughts were no longer your own. As soon as you thought something, it was as if you said it out loud.

"Come, Sophie," Frank prodded. "The girls are fine. Let us go and thank God for giving Julia a healthy son."

Maryanna

It was like looking at Stephan when he was a baby. David was his son. His hair was baby fine, but as he grew it would morph into the dark, thick, wavy hair that she had loved on Michał. Like Stephan, David had inherited her deep sable eyes. She wondered what he would be like as he grew up. Would he dream of bettering his life like his father and Michał did? Would he be content with what life gave him like Estella and Stash? Would he be strident, but loving, in his ways like Sally? What marvels of science and technology would he be privy to? How long would he live?

She sat in the first church pew nearest the baptismal font trying to ignore Agnieska who was sitting next to her. Mike and Sally were David's godparents. Agnieska was quietly 'harumphing' all through the baptism; she whispered, "If Julia has any more kids, she'll be hard put to find godparents; she's used everybody she knows." Lord, put your hand over my mouth, she prayed silently, not even deigning to give a glance to Julia's stepsister.

The ceremony was over and Julia placed David in her eager arms. She cuddled him, contentedly. There would be no Christening celebration. Stephan was still in jail. She had put a sizable gift in the Christening card for David that she gave to Julia who stuffed it into her purse with a mumbled Thank You.

She would like to do more but the tension between her and Julia was like an over tightened violin string that could snap at any moment. Ever since November, she had spent sleepless nights trying to reconcile her mother's love for Stephan with his irresponsible actions and their consequences on her grandchildren. She kept trying to figure out how to help these grandchildren without slighting the others. She wished Michał were still alive. He would have the diplomatic solution that eluded her.

JUNE 1950

Maryanna

Stephan had been a son in absentia for a year and a half. She didn't know the man who was sitting across from her, who had been released from the county jail that morning. It was kitchen table time again. The pot of hot coffee was brewing on the stove. The mugs were filled and there was a plate of kolacky sitting in the middle of the table. It was two days before the official start of summer. The late morning sun was beating down on the roof and warming the interior of the house before noon. A languid breeze did nothing to bring refreshing air into the house through the open windows. She felt her skin growing sticky under her housedress.

"Ma, what can I do? The jobs are limited. A company will require a reference from Republic Steel. Once they get that, I'm done for."

"Stephan, you ruined your own good reference from Republic Steel. What did you expect Julia to do when she had no money for food? For your children! And another one on the way?! Since you did not provide voluntarily what was needed, she did the only thing she could."

"I can't see myself going back to painting and plastering. That's boring. Where will that get me?"

"You talk about the future as if there were steps for you to climb. If you were tending the bar at Wieczorek's, wouldn't you be doing the same thing for the next twenty-five years?"

"No, Ma. Yes, I would have been bartending, but Joe expected me to run the tavern. Joe isn't satisfied with the same old, same old. That's why he built the banquet hall. It was a step forward. The tavern is making money. Joe expected me to improve its profitability. To find out how and then do it. It would have been perfect, if it weren't for Julia's stubbornness."

"Don't put all the blame on Julia. You could have gone against her wishes and accepted the offer from Joe."

"Ma, she would have made life unbearable with her displeasure."

"For a while, yes. But once she realized that you were still providing for her and for your children, I think she would have lightened up."

"But she would have been so miserable to be with."

"Only for a while. Maybe you took the easy way out blaming your decision on her because you didn't want to deal with her unpleasantness."

179

She had hit a nerve. Her son lapsed into a glum silence. She stood up, let her stiff knees relax, then walked to the stove and turned off the burner under the freshly brewed coffee. She refilled their cups. Stephan pulled out a cigarette, lit it and puffed away, sending spirals of cigarette smoke up toward the ceiling. She sat quietly sipping the calming brew which was tolerable in the morning but would be replaced by lemonade as the day wore on.

"I got to go, Ma." he smashed the stub of the cigarette into the ashtray.

"Go see your son. Talk to Julia."

There was no response. He was out the door as quickly as he had come. She didn't bother to look out the living room windows to see which way he was headed. She sat motionless at the kitchen table realizing that he had left without giving her the cherished kiss on the top of her head. What was happening to her son?

(Sophie)

She was perched on a window sill in a patient's room at South Chicago Hospital. There were two iron beds in the room, each one only wide enough for one person. They were separated by a curtain hanging from a track on the ceiling. One bed was empty. The other held the body of a woman who had died within the hour. Frank had gone over to "the pearly gates" awaiting the arrival of the woman's spirit. The woman's husband had worked with Frank at the railroad yard; they were good friends of his. In the stillness of the room, she wondered where on earth people had gotten the expression "the pearly gates". It wasn't anything like that.

She heard a voice echoing in the quiet hall. Julia was coming. This was her first day working as a nurse's aide. She was on the 3 p.m. to 11 p.m. shift. Sylvia was looking after her younger sisters and brother.

"Julia," a pleasant, lilting voice addressed her daughter. "I know this is your first day as a nurse's aide. This may seem like going from the frying pan into the fire. But, if you can handle this, you will make a fine nurse's aide. The woman in Room 207 has died. There is a gurney at the far end of the hall. Bring it to the room. I will help you move the patient from the bed to the gurney. You will then take the gurney down to the morgue in the basement. Do you think you can do that?"

She heard no response from Julia. She must have nodded her head because she heard the nurse reply, "Good." She watched as the nurse entered the room. A loud rattling sound erupted in the hall. She started to float toward the door when Julia entered the room pushing the gurney. They certainly need to do something about those contraptions! If anyone on the floor had been sleeping, they weren't now. The noise was enough to wake the dead!

She watched as the nurse explained to Julia how they would move the body. The nurse released the bed sheet that had been tucked in under the mattress. The top sheet was already in place covering the woman in her entirety. The nurse directed Julia to stand on the opposite side of the bed and bring the under sheet up and over the woman's body. First, the head and foot parts, then the sides. When the body was securely wrapped, the nurse instructed Julia to join her on the same side of the bed at the foot of the bed. At the count of three, they would lift the woman by her shoulders and legs and move her onto the gurney. One, two, three. Mission accomplished.

The nurse helped Julia maneuver the gurney out of the room and walked with her to the elevator, giving instructions as to where to go when she reached the basement. She followed her daughter and the nurse, floating above them as they made their way down the corridor. The weight on the gurney silenced the rattling it had made when empty. She stayed close as the gurney was rolled onto the elevator. The basement was not dark and dank; in the hospital, it was alive with activity. There was the pharmacy, the x-ray lab, blood testing lab, the staff lunchroom. Julia wheeled the gurney down the hall toward the morgue. She was met by an orderly who thanked her and took over.

She watched her daughter's face as she reversed her walk down the corridor. The task had not bothered her. The daughter who hated to touch dead chickens was not fazed by human death. She would do well as a nurse. Good job, Julia, she thought, as she kissed her on the cheek. She smiled as Julia touched her cheek.

NOVEMBER 1950

(Sophie)

It was icy cold on the porch. She couldn't feel it, but she knew her granddaughter did. Aniela was wrapped up in a pierzyna from her neck to her toes and Julia had tied a babushka on her head. She was sitting on a chair with her feet propped up off the cold concrete floor. Sylvia and Julianne were making a snowman in the front yard. She knew Aniela longed to be outside, instead of watching through the window. But her lungs had started wheezing like an accordion last night and the frigid air would only harm them.

Bleurghhh! Bleurghhh! Aniela's aggressive cough erupted, startling her and bringing Julia running out to the porch.

"Aniela, it's cold out here. You need to be inside where it's warm."

"Please, Mama. I'm not choking. Let me stay out here. I'm okay. Syl and Julianne are almost done. I want to watch."

"You'll get pneumonia."

"Please, Mama."

Julia shrugged and walked back into the warm kitchen. She flitted in behind her daughter. Delectable aromas of Thanksgiving dinner permeated the kitchen. A turkey was roasting in the oven together with sweet potatoes; white potatoes were boiling on the stove, almost ready for mashing; dinner rolls were on the kitchen table with a bowl of coleslaw, ribs of celery and carrot sticks.

Yesterday, she and Frank had prayed in gratitude for the men from the parish who delivered a box filled with Thanksgiving fixings and other food. Julia had been beside herself wondering how she was going to provide a Thanksgiving dinner for her girls. The little income she earned as a nurse's aide had been spent paying the utility bills and for coal for the furnace. She had a bout of bronchitis and asthma in October and couldn't work.

She floated out to the porch to see how Aniela was doing. Through the intervening window into the kitchen, she could see Julia drain the potatoes and begin mashing them.

Bzzzzz. Brzzzz. The timer on the stove blurted. Julia turned it off, grabbed potholders and reached into the oven to bring out a pie. She placed it on top of the stove to close the oven door. She brought the pie to the porch and set it to cool on the lid of the metal trash can. As Julia reentered the house, the extreme cold of the trash can broke the hot pie plate. It began to slide off the lid of the can.

She swooped down and put her evanescent hands under the pie plate. It fell through them spattering pumpkin all over the trash can and the floor. If there ever was a time when she wished that she was not a spirit, it was now. She saw Julia come running out onto the porch. Her daughter's usually expressionless face crumpled as she reached for a dustpan and began picking up the shattered, splattered pieces of glass and pumpkin that littered the floor. Snow-embellished light through the porch windows caught the shards of glass from the pie plate. They glistened on the floor, but not as brightly as the tears that trickled down Julia's cheeks. If she had a physical heart, it would have been broken by those tears flowing from her daughter's eyes. She had witnessed a miracle. Julia, in a moment when she thought no one was watching, had succumbed to her feelings. She now knew how much Julia loved her children, even though she could not express it.

APRIL 1951

Maryanna

Katarzyna's letter lay on her lap, the thin onion skin air mail paper flapping in the spring breeze wafting through the open windows. Even though she had not seen him in over forty years, it still hurt to know that her older brother, Ignacy, had died. She had always looked up to him, even as an adult. When she was a little girl, he had been for her what Stephan had been for Dora and Estella. He was the older brother who was happy to play with her, talk with her and treat her as an equal, inviting her, a girl, to join him and their cousin, Ciesław, the son of their dad's brother, when they went roaming the countryside around Osiek. Memories of those golden fields and happy days flooded her mind. How she had missed him when he married and moved to Mostki with his wife. '

If it had not been for his extolling the possibilities in America after his first year of working in the mill and returning home and saving up for her passage to America on his second trip, she would not be sitting in a house to large that not even the mayor of Osiek Dolnoslakie could have afforded it. Most of all, she would have never known the love and life she had shared with Michał and the joy of having his children.

Ignacy could read and write, but he was not quick to do either. The elder son of their sister, Franciszka, was the letter writer. Once he learned cursive, Stephan was eager to keep the relatives in America informed of the happenings in Poland. Once in a while, a short note would be included from Ignacy or Katarzyna. For the most part, Stephan was the connection, even after he married Leokadia the same year that her Stephan had married Julia. She had empathized with him and Leokadia when their second son, Tadeusz, was stillborn. She understood the heartache all too well.

Last year, Katarzyna sent her a note filled with heartbreak after losing her husband. She had sent her sister a number of letters consoling her; they were now more closely bound as members of a sisterhood few women wanted to join, widowhood. She had children; Katarzyna had no one.

After the Germans invaded Poland in 1939, the letters stopped. For eight years she did not know what happened to her brother and sisters and their children. The first letter from Stephan was like the first glimmer of sunrise illuminating the darkness of night. Waves of relief, pride, and sadness had coursed through her as she read it. Her siblings had survived. Ignacy's three sons, Stephan himself, and Ciesław's two sons had all enlisted in the Polish army immediately after the invasion.

As the Polish army was decimated, all six joined the resistance movement. Both of Ciesław's sons, Ignaz and Stanisław were captured. Stanisław was sent to Dachau; Ignaz to a camp called Augs SS Arb. Pfersee, not too far from Dachau. Both concentration camps were liberated by the U. S. forces on April 26, 1945. Ignaz died four days later; two years passed before his father learned his fate. It took Stanisław a year to make his way home.

She and Michał had sent condolences to her cousin; he did not reply. Stephan wrote that Ciesław was devastated. His wife had died during the war for lack of medical care, Ignaz was dead and Stanisław was a shell of the young man he had been.

Since then, most of the letters were greetings for Christmas, Easter and one's names day, the feast day of the saint whose name you bore; each letter included an appeal for help. She and Stella did as much as they could, sending clothing, other necessities, and, most important of all, medicines. Under Communist rule, the scarcities of the war were exacerbated and the poor were even poorer. Each letter that arrived was a reminder of how blessed she was to be living where she was. Any problems that she had paled when compared to the day-to-day struggles of her relatives for the basic necessities. Nothing had changed since she left home; it was actually worse.

Ignacy, her dear brother, had witnessed much and survived through a long life; at 74 years of age, he had been felled by a massive heart attack. She was comforted to know that his death had been quick.

Spoczywaj w pokoju, Ignacy. *Rest in peace, Ignacy.*

MAY 1951

Maryanna

She sat waiting impatiently for Estella and Tomasz to arrive. She was hoping that they would be bringing her word about Stephan. It was almost a year since she had seen her elder son. She wondered if Stash knew where his brother was; if he did, he never shared such information. To prevent an uncomfortable situation, she never asked. Since the day he had walked out of her home last June, she had spent many days and sleepless nights trying to figure out what Stephan was thinking. And, most of all, why he was just giving up. She had heard that last year he had stopped to see his son, David. There had been harsh words between him and Julia and it had been a brief visit.

She couldn't blame Julia for being bitter towards him for leaving her alone to raise his four children with another on the way. Her own sister, Teo, had lived through that with Mike. But Teo had never blamed her or Stella for Mike's departure. She had heard that Julia was blaming everybody, her own sisters and her sisters-in-law and brothers-in-law for putting grandiose ideas into her husband's head. That attitude of her daughter-in-law she could not understand.

She heard a car door slam and Estella lightly ascending the cement steps. She rose to open the door. A warm lilac-scented breeze enveloped her as she did so. Estella's eyes were dancing as they usually did.

"Ma," Estella greeted her warmly as she wrapped her arms around her mother in a bear hug. She looked stylish in a navy print dress with a peplum. Scattered on the fabric were ochre baskets of blushing pink roses entwined with ivy.

"Estella, you are looking well," she praised her daughter. Sitting back down in the wing chair, she said eagerly, "Now, tell me about the graduation."

"It was lovely, Ma," Estella said, as she and Tomasz settled on the sofa in the parlor. "It was beautiful to see the grandeur of St. Michael's Cathedral again. I miss it. I love the simplicity of Annunciata, but my roots are at St. Michael's. Since the juniors escort the graduates into the church, we also saw Doris."

"Doris?"

"Your cousin Theodor's daughter. She's a junior at St. Michael's. There are so many Theodoras in this family and neighborhood, she likes the nickname 'Doris'.

"Sylvia graduated as a member of the National Honor Society. It's a shame that she isn't going on to college."

"Did you see your brother?" she asked, quietly.

"No, Ma, I did not."

So, Stephan did not attend his daughter's high school graduation. She closed her eyes, as if that would ease the pain in her heart.

"Ma, let me fix a pot of coffee. I know that Tom and I could use a cup."

Estella hurried toward the kitchen. She could hear her daughter running water into the pot, measuring out the ground coffee and putting the pot on the burner. There was a swoosh of the gas flame as Estella opened the burner. There were clinks and clanks as she rummaged around for cups and spoons, milk and sugar. The little glass knob on the lid of the coffeepot began to jiggle; the coffee was almost ready.

Estella brought the coffee pot, the three cups and the necessities out on the wooden tray together with the metal trivet that had the Polish eagle painted on it. Stash had found it somewhere and thought his mother would like it. She filled the three cups, then set the coffeepot on the trivet. Spoons rattled as milk and sugar were added to each cup, as desired.

She took a sip of the fresh coffee, then asked, "Did you give my card to Sylvia?"

"Tom had it in his coat pocket and gave it to her together with ours."

"Good."

"Vicki had a lovely celebration for Sylvia. That woman always outdoes herself with cooking and baking. But it was most gratifying to see Sylvia being honored in this way. While her classmates have been going to movies and parties the past two years, she's been playing mother to Aniela, Marysia and David."

"How is David?"

"The little guy is good. A bit solemn and way too thin for your liking, Ma." Tomasz and she had hit it off shortly after he had married Estella and he was comfortable calling her Ma. "But his legs are sturdy and he walks and runs with Marysia and Vicki's daughter, Shirley. Esta took some pictures with her Brownie camera. We'll get prints for you."

"Who else was at Vicki's?"

"Besides us, Julia and the children, Vicki and Wally, of course, and Mike and Agnieska, Sylvia's godmother."

"How is Julia?"

"She looked good after that second bout of bronchitis and asthma earlier this year. She recently started working the 3-to-11 shift part time at South Shore Hospital. She's a nurse's aide in a department that's perfect for her, the nursery."

"She has always been good with babies."

"It is a bit of a walk, but easier than South Chicago Hospital."

"What is the latest on your son?"

"The rumors that you heard about Bud are true. There's no doubt that he will be drafted soon."

"I thought that when Stash came home in '45 from the second world war, we wouldn't have to worry about our children going to war again."

"Ma," Tomasz explained, "the Chinese leaders are making China a communist country. It borders the northern part of Korea. The Chinese are trying to convince the Koreans to become communist. Many in south Korea are opposed and fighting has begun. President Truman and the military are intervening to stop the spread of communism which dictates everything a person can and cannot do. Who would want to live like that?"

"Estella's aunts and uncle and their children are living like that in Poland. Only twenty years was Poland a free nation between the two world wars. Once again, she is oppressed because the Russians claimed it after the war and have made communism mandatory." She shook her head, sadly. "It is a good thing that your father is not here to see it. He was ecstatic when Poland once again became a free nation.

"Do you know when Bud will go into the army?" she asked.

"He has not received a date," Tomasz replied. "Don't worry about it, Ma. Being drafted doesn't mean he will end up fighting in Korea. We still have a big presence in Europe, especially Germany. If he is sent to Asia, he could end up in Japan or South Korea."

"Bud won't give you any extra gray hairs, Ma. There's no place for them on your snow-white head." Estella gathered up the empty coffee cups and all the other paraphernalia and trotted into the kitchen.

"Leave everything on the drainboard. I'll wash it in the morning with the breakfast dishes."

She kissed Estella and Tomasz, who bent down to facilitate the process. Estella wrapped her arms around her tightly. "I love you, Ma."

"I love you both," she murmured in return. The setting sun cast long shadows of her house across the front yard and onto the street. She waved goodbye as the Buick pulled away from the curb. Since her daughter had moved to the East Side after the war, she didn't see her as often as when she had lived on Muskegon, only a few blocks away. More homes were being built on the East Side north of Republic Steel and extending all the way to the state line between Illinois and Indiana.

She missed Estella. If she was troubled in any way, she always grew calmer when her daughter was nearby. Estella's smile and the peace in her eyes radiated beyond her person and enveloped all who were in her presence. She closed the door, locked it and walked into the kitchen. On second thought, there was enough golden light streaming into the window above the sink. She would wash the cups and spoons and have a fresh pot of coffee ready for Stash when he came home from wherever he was.

NOVEMBER 1951

(Sophie)

She perched herself on top of the unplugged refrigerator; the electric cord was taped securely to the back. She listened to Julia giving instructions to her middle daughter.

"Remember, Aniela, do not come home at lunchtime. Go to Aunt Vicki's. She will have lunch ready for you. You know how to get to her house from the school. Go up Marquette Avenue to 83rd Street. Look both ways very carefully before crossing the street. Make sure there are no cars coming from either direction. Walk one block to Manistee.

"After school, you will do the same thing. The furniture will be moved by then and I will be there. Will you remember everything I told you?"

"Yes, Mama," Aniela answered. She picked up her little red schoolbag and looked around. She trudged out the door. Her outgrown navy spring coat was no match for the sunless, windy November day. It hurt her heart to see her granddaughter so poorly clothed. She had been in similar circumstances when she was a little older than Aniela. But that was in Poland after her father died. It was not an uncommon occurrence in the old country where food and clothing were always scarce for many people. In America, where there was an overabundance of everything, her grandchildren should not be wanting.

She watched as Julia washed the last few kitchen utensils that she had used, dried them and put them into a box with the washcloth, soap and dish towel. She heard the squealing of brakes. Marysia and David had been sitting quietly on a blanket in the corner near the refrigerator. David let out a frightened howl as the movers walked into the kitchen. Julia scooped him up, simultaneously telling Marysia to sit where she was.

Julia directed the men upstairs, telling them to take only the pieces of furniture that had an orange square of paper taped to them. The rest of the furniture would not be moved. Within a few minutes, one of the men trotted downstairs asking about the piano and the second bedroom set. She saw the hurt in her daughter's eyes as she repeated that only the furniture with orange papers taped to it was to be moved.

Had she done the right thing? she wondered. True, she had given Julia the money that had been used as a down payment on this house. But, when she had made the decision to leave the house to Vicki and Wally, had she made a mistake? At the time, they had no children; Julia already had three. Vicki and Wally were the ones who had lived with her and cared for her. It had seemed only fair at the time.

She felt Frank's presence next to her. "You did what you thought was best," she heard him think. "How were you supposed to know what Steve would do?"

So now, Julia would be moving into the ground level apartment in the house where she had grown up. Wally had remodeled it so that it was a full apartment with a bedroom, a living room, a small in-between room for the oil stove, a full bath and a large kitchen and pantry. He and Vicki had been renting it out. The most recent tenants were a medical student and his wife. He had graduated and took a residency in California.

Companionably, they sat watching the movers ply their trade. It was time for the refrigerator to be put on the truck. They left their perch. The truck was full and ready to drive the two short blocks to the house that Frank had bought thirty years ago. It was lunchtime and the driver and his crew were stopping for lunch. They would be at the new house at 1 p.m., the driver said.

That gave Julia time to walk through the house and make sure that all the necessary items were now on the truck. When she was satisfied, she pulled the buggy out from under the porch stairs. She put jackets and hats on Marysia and David. She settled David inside the buggy giving him stern instructions not to try to kneel or stand up. He could sit against the pillow she had tucked behind him. She tucked her purse into the buggy behind the pillow. She pushed the buggy out the door making sure Marysia followed behind her. She locked the door, then took Marysia by the hand using her other one to push the buggy down the sidewalk. She walked north, never looking back.

Maryanna

Sally was shaking the dust out of the pierzyna from the bed in the spare room so forcefully that she thought her daughter would dislocate her shoulders. Last week she had moved all that she had stored in the closet. Some went into the basement; some went into the trash can. Stash was now helping Sally clear out the bedroom so he could wax the hardwood floor.

After the first of the year, Sally and Wally and Minka were moving in. Wally had decided to buy one of the new houses that were being built on the East Side. It would take at least a year for the project to get under way. They would stay with her and Stash until the new house was move-in ready. The money they saved by not paying rent on the trailer could go toward the down payment or the furniture they would need for a larger house.

It would be an adjustment to have a child in the house again, after all these years. Sally wanted Minka to receive a good education. Cole School was a much better school than the one in Lansing. Minka would start kindergarten in January. Sally had taught her all a six-year-old girl could learn of manners, respect and politeness and Minka had learned well. She was a happy, pleasant child who was brimming with an inexhaustible energy that needed constant release. She was her mother's child.

Every child that Michał had given to her was a source of excitement and joy. Soon she would be living with his granddaughter. That knowledge was balm for a heart still tender from losing her husband and wounded even more by her wayward son.

CHAPTER ELEVEN

APRIL 1952

Maryanna

Who would be ringing the doorbell at eight o'clock on a Sunday morning? She slipped her feet into her house slippers, grabbed her burgundy chenille robe from the foot of the bed and wriggled into it as she started for the front door.

"I'll get it," Sally called from the kitchen.

"Who is it? Who is it?" six-year-old Minka repeated, excitedly.

As she reached the dining room, she heard Sally exclaim, "Estelle!" Rounding the corner, she saw Teo's daughter standing in the parlor with an unknown woman. Estelle ran toward her.

"Ciocia (aunt)!" she exclaimed, giving her a hug that knocked the wind out. "It's so good to see you! This is my friend, Helen," she said, introducing the woman who was with her.

"Estelle," she said, breathlessly, but happily. "It's been years. Where is Martin?"

"He couldn't come, Ciocia. He's on duty today."

Sally interrupted. "Please sit down, Estelle, Helen. The coffeepot is about ready to perk. Come, Minka, help mama." She moved toward the kitchen, shooing a curious Minka ahead of her.

She settled herself in her favorite wing chair while Estelle and Helen plopped on the sofa. It warmed her heart to see Estelle looking so hearty and happy. Her niece had met Martin two years after Leon was killed by the train.

Martin was gentle, considerate, consoling. They married in a quiet ceremony and moved to Knox, Indiana, a small town where he had a home on several acres of land and worked for the sheriff's office.

"How long a drive is it from Knox to here?"

"It's about 90 miles. Helen and I switch off driving. We work together at the Fireside restaurant in Knox."

"It was good of you to make that long trip for Aniela's First Communion." How she would have loved to be there, today. She had seen Sylvia and Julianne make their First Communions. But Julia was still smarting and bitter toward her husband's family. Neither she nor her daughters wanted to spoil Aniela's day.

"I've been somewhat remiss as a godmother. When Julia invited me, I was happy to come."

Sally bustled into the parlor with the wooden tray loaded with cups, milk, sugar, spoons, napkins, and the coffeepot. Minka followed her carefully holding a plate of jelly-filled biscuits from Michałowski's bakery across from the church. She put the plate on the coffee table, then darted back into the kitchen where a chocolate-frosted cinnamon roll and a glass of milk were waiting for her on the kitchen table.

"How is your mother doing?" Sally asked Estelle, as she settled into the other wing chair with a cup of coffee and a prune-filled biscuit.

"Mom is doing well. She's living in St. Louis, not far from my sister, Theodora and Lester and her grandson, who's already eleven years old. She has a small place. She's waitressing at a tavern. I guess waitressing is in our blood. She's almost sixty years old; it is getting harder for her. Josie has been urging her to move back to Hamtramck. Walter is ailing."

"Josie's urging doesn't surprise me. Your mother and Josie were like two peas in a pod when they were living in Chicago. Stella, would be right along with them, whenever she could. Ludwig has never been open to letting her do what she would like. He's not doing well, either."

"I haven't seen Ginny in years," Sally cut in. "Wally and I drove up to Detroit to see her when Minka was two years old. Ma, it was almost like seeing Ginny and me before Aunt Teo moved to Detroit. Gerry was to Minka what Ginny was to me as a little girl."

"So, you kept in touch with Virginia all these years?" Estelle asked.

"Yes. We started writing to each other when we were in our teens and haven't stopped." She took a sip of coffee. "Have you heard from John?"

"Heard from my brother?" Estelle said, sadly. "He's fallen off the face of the earth. They say 'The apple doesn't fall far from the tree'. That couldn't be truer of my dad and John."

"So, you don't know where Uncle Mike is, either."

"No, we don't, Sally. Our family must have inherited wanderlust from some ancestor." She finished the last few drops of coffee in her cup and glanced at Helen.

"Thank you for your hospitality. These biscuits are delicious," commented Helen, as she finished a lemon one which had succeeded one with raspberry filling.

"I hate to leave," Estelle said, wistfully, looking at her wrist watch. "It's 9:30. I don't want to be late for Aniela's First Communion Mass."

"Will you be stopping by afterward?"

"I don't think so, Ciocia. Julia is having lunch afterward. Helen and I want to be home before dark. I wouldn't want the sheriff's deputy looking for me," she laughed.

"Martin is a good man. Estelle, you have been blessed to have two good men in your life." She rose and stood on tiptoes to give her favorite niece a kiss.

"You take care, Ciocia," Estelle admonished her, as she gave her another smothering hug.

"It was a pleasure meeting you," Helen said, with a smile as she and Estelle walked toward the door.

She would have given anything to follow them.

APRIL 1953

(Sophie)

She was with Wally on this one. But Vicki wasn't one to be swayed easily.

"I'm making good money. You don't need to work, Vicki. We're comfortable." He was sitting at the kitchen table, gulping an after-dinner cup of coffee.

"This is a good opportunity, Wally. It's an evening shift. Julia has agreed to look after Shirley until you get home from work. You can pick me up at the train station when my

shift is done. Shirley will be sleeping and Julia and the girls will be downstairs if she wakes up and needs anything." Vicki picked up his plate and flatware and carried them to the sink.

" Vicki, it will be late when you will be taking the train home."

"Wally, Kodak is a great company to work for. The salary is good and there are great benefits, just like at the mill."

"What will you be doing? You could get hurt working with the chemicals used to develop film."

"I won't be anywhere near that. My job will be to take the dry prints and the negatives and put them in the correct envelopes." She grabbed the bottle of milk and the butter and stored them in the refrigerator.

"It doesn't sound hard."

"It isn't. I will not be so tired that I won't be able to keep up with all my usual chores. I will make sure that your supper is either in the oven or the refrigerator before I leave. You won't lack for anything because I'm working," she said, firmly, as she picked up the salt and pepper shakers and the sugar bowl and stored them in the cabinet.

"Try the job for a few weeks," he suggested. "If it doesn't work out, you can always quit." She grabbed the placemat from under his elbow so energetically, he almost spilled the cup of coffee.

"I'm not a quitter, Wally. You know that."

JULY 1953

Maryanna

Nothing changed in death, she thought, as she stood next to the casket where Ludwig lay. With the set of his mouth, his stern ways were engraved on his face for all eternity. Barney Dalewski had done his best to prepare him for viewing, but there's only so much a mortician can do. She sensed Stella walking up behind her. She turned and put her arm around her sister. Stella might be one of the few women for whom widowhood was not a traumatic tragedy.

Many widows moaned that now they had no one to *care* for them. She always thought that needing to be cared for by a man was a falsehood perpetuated by men to keep women subservient. Women were more than capable of caring for themselves. They had spent centuries caring for their children, their husbands, their aging relatives. There was only one real thorn and that was the male resistance to women working for money so they could care for themselves financially. It was never said aloud, but she thought that many men were domineering because they were fearful. If a woman could earn her own living, would she need a man? Or want one? Would men have to become more thoughtful of women, more caring themselves? Would they have to learn to take care of themselves? Horror of horrors, would they have to start seeing women as equals, not inferiors?

She had been blessed with Michał who always thought of her as an equal. He was cut from a different cloth, as they said. Ludwig had been one of the pack. Few tears would be shed for him.

She turned toward the rows of chairs neatly spaced in the funeral parlor. Her nephew, Vincent, and his daughter were sitting in the first row, leaving the first chair open for Stella. She walked toward them to express her condolences to her nephew. His daughter was patting the empty chair urging her grandmother to sit next to her. Gratefully, Stella did.

She was going to sit down when she saw Sally motioning to her to come where she, Wally, Stash and Minka were standing. As she walked, she changed her course. Julia was walking into the parlor with Sylvia and Julianne. She allowed them to pay their respects as she waited quietly on one side. As Julia turned away, she walked up to her and held out her arms. Julia touched her lightly on the shoulder. Julianne ran into her arms and hugged her, as Sylvia stood quietly, smiling.

"Julia, it is good to see you and your girls."

"Stella is a good aunt to my girls. I wanted to pay my respects."

"How are you doing, Julia?"

"We're doing well," Julianne informed her, readily. "Uncle Wally found a job for Sylvia at U.S. Steel. She's working on a machine that's like typing. Instead of words on paper, the keys make holes in cards that are fed into a machine."

"It's called keypunch, Busia," Sylvia explained. "The machine reads the cards and sets the type for printing from that."

"Good for you." She had no idea what they were talking about.

"And I have a job, too, " Julianne added. "I work at Cunis'. It's an ice cream and candy shop. Mr. Askounis makes all the ice cream and candy."

"Is it like Gayety's?"

"Yes, but better," Julianne stated, emphatically.

"That is good news, Julianne."

"Busia, please call me Julie. That's what everyone at work and in school calls me."

"Julie," she said it, slowly, letting the word roll off her tongue like molasses. "It is Julie, then."

"Thank you, Busia. I have to leave soon to catch the bus. I'm working this evening." She gave her a gentle bear hug and a huge smile. Julie was a younger version of her Estella.

"How are the little ones?"

"Aniela is home with Marysia and David."

"Isn't she a bit young for that responsibility?"

"My mother was nine when she took care of her younger brothers who were orphaned."

"Julia, I didn't mean to imply that you were lax."

"Vicki is upstairs if anything goes wrong," Julia added, walking away.

She sighed, deeply. She really screwed up that chance for a truce. She felt old and tired. She needed to sit down. She plopped onto the nearest chair.

Stash came running over from where he had been chatting with Tomasz, Sally and Wally. "Are you okay, Ma?" he asked.

"I'm fine, Stash. Just a little tired of tightrope walking."

"Are you sure you're alright?"

"Yes. Let me sit for a few minutes." She wanted to close her eyes. She didn't dare. If she did, all her children would be running over. She focused her gaze on the floral arrangement next to Ludwig's casket. It was a grandiose display of white carnations and lilies. Without her eyes closed, it was hard to bring Michał to mind. Lately, she had been doing more and more of that. Wishing he were beside her to calm her with his compassionate, sensible ways.

Years ago, when her children were young, she had heard a neighbor say, "Little kids, little troubles; big kids, big troubles." She had laughed it off at the time. How could that be? Little ones demanded so much of your time and energy and worry. As they grew older and learned to do for themselves, how could they be so much trouble? Now she knew.

She had a son who had left his wife and five children; a daughter whose rheumatic fever was threatening her heart; a grandson who was stationed in

Korea, a land she had never heard of until now; a son who should have been happily married, except for a rotten father-in-law; a daughter-in-law who blamed her for her husband's behavior. Sometimes, it was too much. She closed her eyes.

Sure enough, she felt Sally sitting down beside her. She opened her eyes. Instead of asking if she was okay, Sally was beaming. "Ma, living is always a matter of life and death. Uncle Ludwig has died. But, I want you to know that there is life. In me, Ma. I'm going to have a baby in January."

JANUARY 1954

Maryanna

She wished the miraculous moment could last forever. She knew this was the very last time she would be holding a newborn grandchild. There were seven years between Minka and her little sister, Donna. She was a beautiful baby with wideset blue eyes and honey hair. As little as she was, her face had an aura of gentleness that she knew the little one would carry throughout her life.

Sally, Wally and Minka had moved out of her house last year shortly after Ludwig's funeral. Today, Tomasz had driven up from the East Side to bring her and Stash to Sally's new home on Avenue C. She marveled at the modern design of the home. It was a Chicago-style bungalow built with light bricks, a sharp contrast to the dark ones used in her house. The parlor, now called a living room, had plush carpeting and blue and green floral drapes that hung on rods and could be opened and closed with the touch of a cord. She was sitting in a light blue wing chair that complemented the green and blue paisley sofa.

The kitchen had birch cabinets everywhere. There were cabinets hanging from the walls and lower cabinets with countertops. There weren't open shelves where dishes and pots and pans got dusty. Everything was put away on shelves in the cabinets or in drawers for flatware, towels and cooking utensils. The wall space between the upper and lower cabinets was covered in squares of tile that were easy to clean. The bedrooms were carpeted and had spacious closets. The bathroom had a bathtub with a shower head attached to one wall. Sally said that taking a shower instead of a bath was the latest thing.

Donna stirred and opened her eyes. She felt like her granddaughter was looking right through her, even though her eyes were unfocused. She adjusted the precious bundle in her arms, reveling in the incredible warmth of this tiny bundle of love.

"Are you tired, Ma? Do you want me to take her from you?"

"I will never tire of holding babies, Sally."

"Okay, Ma. I'll get her bottle ready."

"Hey, Ma." Estella and Tomasz were comfortably ensconced on the plush sofa. Estella's gaze was directed toward her feet. "Your ankles are swollen, Ma."

"Just a bit too much salt."

"If that keeps up, you'd better see Doctor Haraburda."

"Nothing to worry about, Estella."

Actually, she was worrying about it. It had started a few weeks before Christmas. The swelling in her feet and ankles made wearing her oxford shoes difficult. She had been padding around most days in her house slippers, only enduring the shoes when she had to go out. Like now, she thought. The shoes felt tight and conjured up scenes of the relief she would feel when she was home and could take them off. If that were her only problem, she wouldn't be so worried.

She had been bringing Christmas decorations up from the basement when she noticed that she couldn't go up and down the basement stairs without becoming breathless. She would have to sit on the old metal yard chair in the basement before ascending the stairs with whatever she went down there to fetch. When she came back up, she was even more winded and plopped on the closest kitchen chair until she felt her heart stop racing and her breathing become stable.

It's just old age, she told herself. After all, she had celebrated her 71st birthday last year. How much longer could a person expect to live?

Sally brought the warm bottle of milk to her and she settled in, totally focused on what she loved best, cuddling babies and feeding them.

JUNE 1954

(Sophie)

She and Frank settled themselves on top of the ornamental cornice that defined the niche where the statue of Mary was placed to honor her. Theirs was a bird's eye view of the graduation of Julianne in St. Michael's cathedral. Oops, Julie, not Julianne. She had heard her granddaughter asking the relatives to call her Julie. She watched as Julia, Sylvia, Aniela, Marysia and David entered the pew assigned to them. As tight as money was these past five years, and, at times, nonexistent, Julia had insisted that her girls go to a Catholic high school. She was pleased that her daughter had not waivered; it was one time when stubbornness bore good fruit.

The organist began the first few notes of the processional with such enthusiasm that she was startled back into reality with a jolt. St. Michael's was a small, all girls' school; there were only 65 graduates. She watched as Julie, (yes, she would remember to call her that) marched solemnly down the aisle toward the altar. She had grown into a beauty. Her looks were reminiscent of Steve's sister, Estella, but they were more refined. Her curly black hair framed a high forehead and a face with eyes so brown, the pupils disappeared in their liquidity. Her full lips rested comfortably against each other adding to the sheen of forthrightness that radiated from her face.

As she watched her granddaughter genuflect before the altar and take her place in the pew, she began to reminisce. In the timelessness of eternity, every moment of one's life was present. As some moments stood out more than others in one's memory on earth, in eternity, they glowed with a deeper intensity of iridescent light. So, it was with all the days when young Julianne would run over to be with her, to sit with her outside while she stripped feathers for pierzynas, before the arthritis and cancer slowed her down, and inside in comfortable companionship during those last painful months. Julianne had never wanted anything from her; she just wanted to be with her.

Today, that granddaughter who loved her unconditionally was graduating and stepping out into the world as an adult. All that she wanted for her granddaughter was a man who would love her unconditionally. A man like Frank, she thought. He heard her thought and squeezed her invisible hand. In a way that only spirits can know, she nestled into him, just as she had often done on earth, in total contentment, eternal contentment.

JULY 1954

Maryanna

She hoped that Tomasz knew what he was doing with Estella's Brownie camera. She would treasure this photo as long as she lived. She was standing in the backyard with Minka, Estella who was holding six-month-old Donna, and, God be praised, Julia and four-year-old David.

Except for a few brief moments after his Baptism, she had never had the joy of holding her grandson, David, when he was newborn. For several long years, she had missed First Communions and Graduations, not willing to go where she felt unwanted or could disrupt what should only be a happy occasion for the celebrant.

Last month, Estella and Sally had visited, unexpectedly, but most welcome in her increasingly long, dreary days. She knew without a doubt, they had something up their sleeves. As she sat down with them at the kitchen table with the coffeepot and the plate of fresh biscuits from Michałowski's, they were grinning.

"Ma, Esta came up with a great idea for celebrating Minka's eighth birthday. We want to do it here!"

Before she could say 'Of course', Estella took the floor.

"Ma, Sally and I have it all figured out. You won't have to lift a finger. We will provide everything: food, cake, plates, flatware, beer, soft drinks. Everything. I'll even bring the 30-cup coffeemaker that Tom gave me for Christmas, so we don't have to keep refilling this old pot," she gestured to the well-worn but still useful coffeepot that had been privy to the joys and griefs of so many years.

"We want to invite Julia and the children," Sally chimed in.

"Are you okay with that?"

"Of course, I'm okay with that! My grandchildren are growing up and I have missed so much, already. I know that you and Stash have been seeing Julia and the children since Ludwig's funeral last year. Stash was at Julianne's graduation."

"We have, Ma. I don't see Sylvia or Julie often; their lives are busy as young adults. I do see Aniela. Julia has allowed her to ride the bus on her own, so she will come to visit me. She's lonely; she's too young for her older sisters and too old for her younger sister and brother."

"Julia has softened. She will never be as outgoing as her sister, Vicki. The years have dimmed the rawness of the uncertain times right after Steve left her. Those days of having no money, not knowing where to turn and all the malicious neighborhood gossip are behind her. Sylvia has been advancing in the mill in this new field of computers. Julie is working downtown for First Federal bank. Julia feels more secure financially, so she is relaxing a little. "

"Is she still working at South Shore Hospital?"

"No. She keeps having bouts of bronchitis and asthma. Living on ground level like that with only a thin wooden floor on top of the ground doesn't help. It's too damp for her. And the place is only heated with that oil stove in the middle room. There can't be much heat reaching the bedroom.

"Aniela keeps getting sick, like her mother, with asthma attacks and bronchitis. She's inherited her mother's lungs."

"Do you think Julia will come?"

"Yes, Ma. We do."

Here, she was, holding still, while Tomasz fiddled with the camera.

"Pierogi!" he shouted.

"Pierogi!" they all shouted back. Click. It was done.

DECEMBER 1954

Maryanna

She glanced around the dining room table: Tomasz and Estella, Stash, Wally and Sally, cradling a sleeping Donna. Minka was sitting in one of the wing chairs in the parlor eying the packages under the tree wondering which ones were hers. The lights from the Christmas tree flickered red, blue, green, yellow over the white tablecloth. The remains of Vigilia, the traditional Polish Christmas Eve dinner, were stashed in the refrigerator. Her children and spouses were devouring the cookies which Sally and Estella had made, drowning the crumbs in large gulps of coffee.

"You have all been hounding me about seeing the doctor because I have been short of breath and my ankles swell. Earlier this month, I went to see Dr. Haraburda," she began.

Before she could continue, Stash interrupted. "Ma, how did you get there? Why didn't you tell me? I could have taken you."

"How, Stash? It is too far for me to walk. Virginia drove me there and back."

"Virginia?"

"Yes, Rybarczyk. She lives across the street. She stops by sometimes during the day when she's walking her son to school. In the bad weather, she drives him back and forth. One day, she said that if I ever needed a ride, she would be happy to take me."

"But, Ma..." Stash interrupted again.

"Stash, you work during the day. You don't have a car. It's too far for Sally and Estella to come from the East Side. And for all I knew, it could have been for nothing."

"So, what did the doctor say?" Sally inquired, anxiously.

"Well," she said, taking as deep a breath as was possible, "it is something. He called it congestive heart failure."

"Ma!" the chorus of voices startled Minka who had been sitting quietly in the parlor.

"What's wrong, Busia?"

"Nothing, Minka. Come and give Busia a big hug. We will be done soon. And then you can open your presents."

Minka ran over and smothered her with all the enthusiasm of her eight years.

"You are a good girl. Have a cinnamon cookie while you are waiting." Minka took one off the cookie plate and retreated to the parlor to continue guessing what was in each gayly wrapped package.

"I know about that, Ma," Estella said. The rheumatic fever she had as a child predestined her for the same disease.

"I know you do. Dr. Haraburda gave me medicines to take for the shortness of breath and the swelling in my legs. They might help for a time. There is no cure. I am content with that. Every day I miss your father even though it has been more than eleven years since he died. Because of his love, I have had a life more wondrous than I ever dared imagine as a young girl in Poland.

"Your father was a man of great foresight, always knowing what to do and doing it. Many years ago, he decided that we needed to make out a will, a legal document that would go into effect when the last of us dies. In that document, we stated that when we both were deceased, all our possessions - this house and whatever else may be valuable - would be divided equally among our four living children.

"Tonight, Stephan will be forty-seven years old. We should be celebrating with him. Instead, we don't even know where he is. A few blocks from here are five children who are also well aware that today is their father's birthday and they have been denied the pleasure of celebrating it with him."

She paused, remembering that first Christmas night when she had given Michał a son. She blinked rapidly to prevent the liquid forming in her eyes to fall on her cheeks. She swallowed deeply, and continued.

"I want all of you to promise that when I am no longer with you, you will find a good lawyer and appeal the part that would go to your brother. Insist that the court rules that it be given to Julia to use for her children, my grandchildren."

Her children and spouses exchanged glances. Then, with one accord, they said, "We will." Her Christmas wish had been granted.

"Come," she said, "let's go into the parlor. Minka has been waiting long enough."

APRIL 1955

Maryanne

The 15th would be twelve lonely years since Michał had died. She sat in bed, willing her weak muscles to move, her lungs to breathe. She heard Estella bustling in the kitchen. She closed her eyes.

She was walking on the deck of the *SS Merion*; the sun was warm on her face. She breathed deeply of the fresh ocean breeze. Suddenly, pain radiated from deep inside her chest. She felt as if she were suffocating, as if a hand were clasped against her mouth impairing her ability to breathe. She reached up to remove the hand, but felt nothing. The lack of oxygen made her feel lightheaded. A thin darkness began to envelop her. She tried to walk faster to escape it. Ahead of her she saw a man approaching. Instinctively, she knew he would rescue her. She relaxed.

"It's time, Maryanna," Michał said, as he extended his hand. She put her hand into his as readily as she had almost fifty years earlier. She no longer felt the wood of the deck beneath her feet as she followed him. The darkness was dispelled by a thin iridescent glow, a curtain of light. It suffused the deck of the ship as they walked toward the bow. Beyond it, she could see the glories of her new eternal homeland.

EPILOGUE

(Maryanna)
(Sophie)

We done good, Maryanna! They did high 5's.
We certainly did, Sophie!

For two little nobodies from eastern Europe, living in an immigrant blue-collar neighborhood at the edge of the world (at least that's what some north side Chicagoans amusingly dubbed South Chicago), their progeny had made an impact on that world.

Their children, grandchildren and great grandchildren had served and were serving not only as parents themselves, but also as pharmacists, nurses, accountants, teachers, lawyers, engineers, computer program designers, chief financial officers, even an Air Force general.

They rejoiced. Their sacrifice and determination created a monument to life in America that would be a testament inspiring their descendants for many generations to come.

They were the Steel Matkas.

ABOUT THE AUTHOR

Terry Robertson is a native Chicagoan. She entered the field of journalism as a manuscript editor. She has authored manuals, training guides, newsletters and themed nonfiction articles for corporations and nonprofit organizations.

She lives in the metropolitan area and delights in the cultural differences of the city's neighborhoods and suburbs. The history of the City with the Big Shoulders has always fascinated her.

She is the author of *Reasons and Seasons*.

Made in United States
Orlando, FL
23 September 2023

37207030R00129